Wandering Souls

Philip Watkins

Copyright © 2025 Philip Watkins

All rights reserved.

ISBN:
979-8-9946379-0-6:

To my wife.

CHAPTER ONE

Awake at the End of the World

Alerted by a symphony of alarms, he shot up from a deep slumber. A blanket that had been snugly wrapped around him slowly slid off the side of the bed as his heavy eyes searched for the source of the disturbance. Struck with a curious panic, he noticed the room he found himself in was no more. He was no longer surrounded by the crisp white walls that one would expect to see. Rather, they were cracked and tattered, with the entire left side of the room missing, exposing the open city down below. A soft breeze blew through the room, carrying with it the smell of melted plastic and burned rubber.

His feet landed on the dusty wooden floor. He found it strange that he had awoken fully dressed, yet he couldn't remember why. He made his way to the large hole where a wall once had been and looked out at the street below. The destroyed remains of the city lay in mounds of displaced rubble and scattered debris. Alarms rang out, and various fires flickered off the reflections of shattered glass that lay sprinkled about only a few stories below. What little wasn't on fire was now covered in a thick layer of gray dust, the residue of the devastation.

"What the hell happened last night?" He asked aloud, confused and lost in disbelief. His breath grew heavy as he slowly stepped back from the long fall. What floor remained creaked and cracked as the room swayed with the howling wind and shifted under his weight as he meandered his way back over to the nightstand to the left of the bed. His phone sat plugged in under a thin layer of dust. He unplugged the charger, noting that the battery was only at eighty-eight percent. Whatever had happened had happened only a few hours ago and had knocked out the power to his room and presumably the rest of the building and surrounding city as well. Along with the power being out, his phone had no signal. Swiping the screen open, he noted that it was a blank device, nearly set to factory settings. Outside of an odd app with a scythe-like weapon on it that didn't seem to work, the phone had no other apps, and all text messages and call histories were empty.

What was going on? He wondered to himself while looking around the rest of the room. It was a small room, made even smaller by the sizable chunk that now lay atop the streets below. More creaks and twangs echoed from the floors above and below as the building continued to hold its ground against the increasing wind outside, a concerning sign that the building might not be standing much longer. His suspicion was confirmed as the entire building swayed more aggressively as a gust of chilled air lofted through the room. The impact was sudden enough to rattle his already shaky balance and knock him to the floor. As the building leveled out, he returned to his feet and decided it was best to get out and away from the unstable building. Once safe, he could figure out what to do next and maybe piece together what had happened last night. His memories of anything from the night prior, or even his life before waking, were hazy—as if blocked by something unrelenting in his search for what should be there. He needed to find help, and with any luck, answers. Surely there had to be others out there in the same state of confusion he was.

Making his way over to the door, he glimpsed his reflection in a small mirror that lay cracked on the floor along the left wall. An average-looking college kid stared back at him. A shaggy tussle of dark brown bedhead sat atop a lightly freckled and kind-looking boyish face. Disregarding his reflection, he reached out towards the knob when he heard something scamper behind him.

Curious, he turned around. Something was now glowing from under his bed. A bright, soft blue shimmered in the dark mystery below where he had been asleep only minutes earlier. Slowly, he made his way over to the strange light. The creaking floor gave away his quiet advance as he grew closer.

"Stay away!" a voice yelled from the dark below the bed.

"Hello? Is someone there?" he asked aloud. He paused only briefly before continuing his slow advance towards the bed, where he knelt to peek at the curious light.

"Last chance!" the same voice snapped. A large flame suddenly formed. The sudden heat and flash of flame blinded him and his curiosity. Fire blasted out from under the bed, startling him as he fell backward, nearly being reduced to ash. He scuttled back in a panic to avoid the blitz of fire as it flew by. The smell of burned hair filled the room.

"What the hell!" he yelled at the strange light. "You could have killed me!"

"I warned you! Maybe you ought to learn to listen. Otherwise, you should expect to get burned." He locked his eyes on the glimmering light, his gaze led by a long black scorch mark that disappeared under the frame of the bed. Slowly leaning over to his side, he saw what looked like a house cat staring back at him.

"A cat? Here, kitty, kitty. Nice kitty," he said with his hand extended out while rubbing his fingers against his thumb.

"Don't 'kitty, kitty' me, Ren! You want to play some more with fire?" the creature said as it finally emerged from the dark of the bed. "I am no damned house cat," the creature said flatly. Though at full revelation, it seemed the creature was correct. Though much of its size and body resembled a typical house cat, three bushy, glowing tails were a distinction.

"What are you then?" he asked, uninterested in the thought of losing any more hair. A question that seemed to catch his guest off guard. "And how do you know my name?" A question that caught him equally by surprise. A name. His name. Ren.

"I… I don't know." The creature paused and hopped up onto the bed and then onto the large wooden bedpost. Looking out at the city on fire, it answered, "I have no memory of anything before waking up on the bed. Soon after, that wall disappeared below." Following the creature's gaze at the world on fire, Ren said aloud, "So, you're just as confused as me, it seems."

"Wait." The creature paused and turned its attention back to Ren. "You don't know what's going on either?" Ren let out an uncomfortable laugh as he turned to the strange cat.

"Not even the slightest. I don't even know where we are." The building shifted hard again. Still sitting on the floor, Ren slid slowly towards the gaping hole in the wall. However, before he could even react to being dumped out of the building, he stopped in place as if he were being held back by something intangible. He turned his frazzled attention from the drop below to the creature sitting atop his bed. The building settled once again, though now it sat at an uneasy slant.

"Thank you," he said to the odd creature with a sigh of relief. "That was you, right? That just saved me?"

"It was," the creature responded flatly. "We may not know where we are, but I know it's not safe. We should get out of here, since I don't think I can keep you safe with what's in store for this building." Hopping down from its perch on the bed, it made its way over to the door. Though Ren couldn't explain it, he felt a strange connection to the glowing creature. It felt right to follow him.

"Yeah, let's get out of here," Ren said, lifting himself up and following the creature out of the room. The hallway on the other side was in equal shape to theirs. All the doors along the hall were wide open, with an uncontrolled fire burning brightly to the left of where they stood. The room directly across the hall from him was also wide open.

A small glowing bird chirped from atop a small shelf, its attention focused on the motionless body of an elderly lady. A dark red circle stained the floor that surrounded her.

"That's strange," Ren said aloud.

"What? The dead old lady? What about her?"

"The blood's dry."

"And?" the creature retorted. Ren's response was cut short as a loud bang echoed from above.

"Never mind that. We don't have much time. Let's go!" Ren snapped as the building leaned again, and this time, it wasn't going to level back out. He scooped up the strange creature and dashed down the hallway at full speed.

"Hey! What do you think you're doing?" it snapped, falsely struggling as Ren cradled it tight.

"Saving both our asses. Now shut up and hold on to your tails!" Ren yelled while jumping over various pieces of debris and the occasional dead body, each with an accompanying glowing creature lingering nearby in the narrow hallway. They reached the stairs. The building was now tilted at a ninety-degree angle. The boy slid down the stairwell wall, guiding himself with the handrail to avoid losing control. Loose objects fell from above and rained down in the space between the descending square of stairs, tumbling below the remaining two flights with loud crashes.

"Almost there!" Ren yelled as he pushed himself off the rail and back to the closest thing to a solid floor left. That was the left wall of the stairwell. Only a few feet in front of them was the door to the lobby.

"Alright," the creature said. "Now it's my turn." Its tail glowed brighter than before, and out of thin air next to them, a large ball of condensed fire formed, slowly circling them before flying by and smashing into the door, blowing it off the hinges as it vanished with an explosive blast. The duo emerged on the other side, through the smoke and flames left behind. Maintaining the same speed, they rushed through the lobby. Multiple other puffs of flame appeared in the surrounding air. Each flew forward towards the glass doors that lined the front of the lobby, pelting the glass just in time as they jumped through. With a rough landing at the end of the steps, they rolled aggressively down the stairs to the road. They quickly scooted across the dusty street as the building finished its collapse, slowly overtaking two other much smaller buildings to its side. An eruption of dust and debris rained all around as they lay under a thin dome of fire that incinerated anything that encountered it. The pair were safe and sound inside.

As the smoke and dust settled, the protective barrier of fire dissipated to reveal the devastation of the collapse. Scattered flames flickered about in the dusty, rubble-ridden streets.

"I think you really saved us there," Ren said, turning to the small creature as its glow grew faint and it collapsed onto its side. "Hey! You okay?" Ren asked, scuttling on his knees over to the small creature. He leaned in and pressed his ear to its chest to confirm the small creature was still breathing. "Thank goodness," Ren said, relieved at the slight sound of its quiet, exhausted breath.

Gently picking the small creature up, Ren looked around for a safe place to take in the situation. A long line of empty cars pointed at a relatively untouched gas station just within sight. In their current situation, it was the best option they had. With the creature snug in his arms, Ren made his way down the dusty road littered with abandoned cars. Their doors were all wide open, with no drivers or passengers to be found.

"What the hell happened?" he asked aloud as he took it all in, approaching the empty gas station. "Have I been here before? Why can't I remember anything?" As he slowly pushed the door open, the sound of a bell echoed throughout the empty store. The shelves of the store had been almost completely emptied, with hardly anything remaining. Various display racks lay knocked over, with a few remaining snack bags scattered around them. He made his way over to the cooler and reached through the shattered glass of the door to grab a warm Mountain Dew, one of the few remaining options. Ren thought it was odd that what remained was warm already, not even holding a slight chill from the day prior. As he approached the counter, Ren grabbed a bag of jerky and went to pay. Peering over the counter, he noticed a middle-aged man who was sitting on the floor in the corner. Setting the sleeping creature down on the counter next to the dew and jerky, Ren rushed around the counter to check on him.

"Sir, are you okay?" Ren asked while gently poking at the man. "Sir?" he asked again as the man slowly fell over to reveal a dried, dark red smudge along the wall where he had been leaning. Ren touched the man's neck and checked for a pulse. "He's dead," Ren said uncomfortably as he turned to get back up, only to be met by the aggressive growl of a glowing red dog.

"Hey there, boy," he said shakily, with his right hand slightly extended out between himself and the new aggressor as he stood up slowly. He did his best to maintain eye contact with the unfriendly-looking dog, while also doing his best to hide his growing fear of the hound. The dog's vicious snarl leaked warm, acidic-like drool that sizzled on the floor upon contact. Its attention was not on him, though;

instead, it focused on the body of the deceased man that now lay behind him. Trapped behind the counter, Ren could see only two options: either go through the less-than-welcoming gas station host or get over the counter quickly enough to delay their inevitable clash.

"I was just leaving," Ren said with his decision made. He quickly pivoted to go over the counter when his left leg snagged a drawer and knocked him off balance onto the floor. With his day seemingly unable to get worse, he closed his eyes and braced for the dog's attack.

A loud "Yip!" then came from in front of him, accompanied by the smell of burned fur in the air. He opened his eyes to see the dog turning tail and retreating, smoke following suit.

"You really are useless, aren't you?" said a familiar voice from above where he lay. He looked up to see the creature staring down at him. "Now, if you don't mind." The creature disappeared with a loud thud coming from the other side of the counter. "I'm tired," the creature said, now looking up at Ren, who was leaning over the counter.

He made his way around to the other side and slid down next to the mysterious creature. Together, they sat in silence and listened as the world outside the small gas station continued to crumble. After some time had passed, Ren turned to the small creature and asked, "So, what now?"

"I wish I knew; I really do. But I don't know what's happening, and neither do you."

"Not a clue. It's weird, though. I have this strange feeling that I can't explain. Like, I know what happened and why, but I just can't get to it. Like it's missing."

"Same. It doesn't help that everyone we come across isn't really in the mood for chitchat. You know, on account of being dead."

"Yeah, that's strange too. Shouldn't there be more?" Ren asked as he looked around.

"More? More what?"

"People. There are at least two or three dozen cars outside in line for the gas here, but no one to be seen."

"Hiding, maybe?" the creature said, unsure and equally perplexed at the situation. Everything had gone by so fast, and with it, so had the day as the sun set from high above the equally burning world. The sky was a stunning blend of reds and yellows that was just visible from where they sat at the front of the store.

"Yeah, maybe. That thing back there, you know, the fire. How do you do that?"

"Good question. Just add it to the list of other questions I don't have answers to. Whatever it is, though, it really drains me."

"Just one more thing to figure out, I guess," Ren said as the small creature gathered what little strength it still had and crawled up onto his lap. It curled up into a small circle and closed its eyes. Ren gently pet the small creature as it drifted back to sleep. He let out a long yawn as his eyes grew heavy.

"I wonder if anyone else is still out there?" he said as the sun passed the night to the moon, and he drifted to sleep.

CHAPTER TWO

Not Alone in the End of the World

His eyes heavy, Ren opened them to the sound of crunching potato chips. A thin shadow cascaded from the sunlit shattered glass at the rear of the store. Various colors reflected off the warm glass and plastic, no longer cooled as they sat exposed to the rest of the store.

"Stay quiet," the creature said, peering up at him with only one eye open from where it lay, still curled up in his lap from the night prior. "We are not alone. They wandered in only a couple of minutes ago—a human accompanied by an enormous creature with an odd glow like mine." Another strange glowing creature? Ren thought to himself. First, there was the deceased old lady with the bird. Then there was the man behind the counter where he sat, propped now, and presumably his dog left behind. Not to mention him with his own strange companion, and now another pair. What was going on?

Then he saw them—the terrifying pair. Ren watched silently while pretending to still be asleep, or dead, as they left the store. Multiple drinks and snacks were in hand or stowed away in the bulging pockets of the long, well-worn trench coat the man wore. A grizzled-looking man, most likely in his mid-forties, and with him was a monstrous, bear-like creature. Its paws were nearly the size of the creature pretending to sleep in his lap. It walked on all fours, at the chest height of the man, most likely standing around six feet tall. Its glow emanated from its massive paws as it walked along, bumping into what few shelves were still standing. Done perusing the store, they reached the exit and stopped. The man turned his head and stared directly at the boy.

"You're lucky I have no interest in playing his sick game. I'd get your shit together, because if your plan is to play dead till the end, I've got bad news for you. You won't have to pretend all that long, kid." The stranger's words shook Ren to his core. His eyes flashed open as he jumped up, knocking the small creature to the floor as he rushed over to the door.

"Wait! Don't go! I have questions for you." However, he was too late. The man and his bear were gone—nowhere to be seen as he scanned the lot outside.

"What the hell are you doing?" the creature snapped as it made its way over to him, fully recovered from a good night's rest.

"He didn't kill us when he could have easily done so. Maybe he can help us understand what the hell is going on?" Ren paused as the man's words sank in further. "And what game was he talking about?"

"You hear that, Basher? They don't know," a scratchy voice said from behind them. Turning around, they saw a young man of similar age to the one in the reflection from the day prior. Perched on his shoulder was a glowing red creature—a ghastly blend of scavenger bird and reptile. Glistening metallic scales covered the disturbing creature, while its wings remained draped in feathers. Its face was that of a lizard: a lazy combination made of nightmares, a deformed-looking monstrosity only possible in a madman's lab. In his right hand was a black handgun that he held loosely, either unconcerned or unfamiliar with proper gun safety and how to hold it.

"Don't know what?" Ren's glowing companion asked. The boy with the bird tilted his head.

"Judging by the awkward silence, I'm guessing your dumb little soul is talking. NEWS FLASH!" he barked hoarsely. "Other people can't chit-chat with another person's soul." He rolled his eyes as if the entire interaction was a waste of his time. "Damn, you two really are clueless." He let out an unhinged laugh that bordered on a villainous cackle, while Ren and the creature swapped concerned glances.

"Doesn't matter now, though. The game ends here for you two. Gotta clear out the competition nice and early, right, Basher? Kill 'em nice and quick."

"Kill?" Ren said aloud, confused. The young man raised the handgun, now gripped in his right hand and in proper form.

"Bang!" he said, pretending to fire the gun as his hand flung dramatically up into the air. Ren dropped to the floor in pure, reactionary panic. "It's more fun if you try to run," he said, busting up with a disturbed laugh while Ren hid, scared, behind a nearby shelf. Slowly, he looked up to see a sinister grin creep across the aggressor's face, turning the gun on Ren once again. "Well? Go on then—run, bitch!" he said menacingly, with another crazed cackle.

Ren pulled the small creature into his arms and dashed to the side and out of the other boy's line of vision.

"That's more like it," he said, licking the gun. His salivating tongue caressed it with sick satisfaction. "To the sky, Basher! The game is afoot!" he said, laughing, as Ren crawled farther away before finding temporary safety a couple of shelves over.

"This guy is nuts! What the hell is going on?" Ren said, his entire body trembling.

"Like I know!" the creature said. "But we need to get out of here, and fast."

"Scurry and hide, my prey," the young man said as he kicked over a shelf and fired the gun into the air. "Come out, come out, wherever you are."

"Kid, run!" a familiar voice yelled as the wall to the right of the gun-wielding boy exploded inward with ice, glass, and wood. The force of the blast sent the boy backward through a display rack and across the store. Standing in the dusty, cold wreckage was the gigantic bear from before, with the man standing close behind.

"Let's go, kid. We don't have much time!" the man yelled, his voice quickly drowned out as another gunshot rang out from the opposite side of the store.

"You sneaky little piece of shit!" he snarled as he got to his feet and fired again, aimlessly, into the dusty cloud that hung in the air around the affected area. Then again and again, until he had no more bullets left to fire, pulling the trigger only to be met with a dissatisfying click. "Fuck it! Basher, now!" he barked as the strange bird flapped up into the air and turned toward the cold, lingering smoke. The tattered feathers on its wings separated to reveal more scales hidden below. With an uncomfortable peeling and snapping sound, dozens of the hidden scales detached and hovered in the surrounding air, each one quickly replaced with another. "Do it, now!" he commanded as the scales flew in the smoke's direction and obliterated everything hidden in and beyond the smoke while he laughed maniacally at the destruction. "That's what you get! This is my game! Slimy little shits like you are not even pawns worthy of sitting atop the board I play on."

He excitedly and aggressively marched at his victims while fumbling about with a fresh clip for his pistol. "Give up yet?" he asked as the clip clicked into its dispenser. He pointed the newly loaded gun into the dissipating smoke, only to be met with silence as the thinning smoke revealed that his prey had successfully escaped. A frustrated howl echoed through the winding alley behind them. Startled, Ren paused briefly to confirm they were not being followed.

"Keep moving," the man said from ahead with a nod to his companion. The colossal bear turned around and nudged past Ren and the creature tucked in his arms. "Gur will follow behind. Let's go," he said, continuing forward. Silently, Ren followed the man further away from the lunatic and his bird born of nightmares, down a winding, damp maze of an alleyway until they came upon a fire exit.

"Climb," the man said sternly, motioning at the ladder. With no other obvious options, the small creature made its way to Ren's shoulder as he climbed the ladder as instructed. A brief flash of light beamed from behind as the man followed, pulling each ladder up behind them to make sure no one followed. Finally reaching the roof after climbing what felt like one hundred stories, the boy plopped to the ground with a sigh of exhausted relief. The creature landed elegantly next to him after being shoulder-taxied to the top. While the man pulled up the final ladder from the rickety platform below, the boy caught his breath. The glowing bear, however, was nowhere to be seen.

"Are you looking to die, or just stupid?" the man barked as he removed his long, heavy coat that hung down to the heels of his thick, heavy-duty boots. Covering his left arm with his right hand, a deep red liquid seeped through his fingers. "Or maybe a bit of both."

"You're hurt!" the boy said, ignoring the man's hostility while quickly getting up to his feet.

"Yeah, no shit! This might come as a surprise, but when bullets fly, people often end up hurt. What exactly was your plan back there? If you made any more noise, every goddamned Reaper in the city would have shown up."

"Reaper?" Ren asked, glancing down at his equally clueless companion.

"You really don't have any idea what the hell is going on, do you?"

"We don't. Neither of us remember much of anything, really. All I know is that when I woke up yesterday, everything had gone to hell, and this little guy was under my bed." The man quickly met his explanation with a hearty laugh, chased with an agonizing grunt and the clang of a small metal object bouncing atop the rooftop. A deep red liquid pooled behind it with each bounce.

"Just woke up, did you? Typical lazy-ass teenager sleeping in during the end of the world." He pulled out a bottle of water from the deep pockets of his coat, which hung over the rooftop rail, and poured it over the wound. With a wince, he dabbed it dry and wrapped it tightly with a torn piece of white fabric from his plain white T-shirt that he still wore. Messy, bright red blood drenched his entire left side. "No wonder you seem so confused," he said as he finished tending to his wound, slipping back into his long coat with a wince before sitting down and chugging the remaining water from the bottle. "A lot has changed since it all happened about a year ago."

"So… what happened exactly?" Ren asked, intrigued. "Wait, did you say a year ago?"

"Yeah—a year ago. And what happened, you ask? The short story is some lunatic decided he wanted to play God. 'The great rapture of souls,' he called it. Everyone with half a brain cell brushed him off as some common loon with too much money. That was, until two hours after they pulled his delusional ass from the air. Soon after, the sky lit up with a deep blue and purple fire, at which point the kooky bastard hijacked the airways and showed back up on every screen in the world, spouting some drivel about how only the strongest of souls would survive to see tomorrow and then the game would start—his game. Then, it was as if the switch to the world we all knew before was just flipped off. No lights, no internet, and no phones. Everything went silent. Everything went dark."

The man paused, snapping his fingers twice. Out of nowhere, the large bear companion that had been missing appeared from thin air next to him. Pouring another bottle of water into a small dish, he slid it over to the large glowing bear. The bear appeared uninterested in the water as it stared attentively at Ren and the small creature that sat to his right.

"Once the world went dark, chaos ensued," he continued. "Everyone flocked to the streets, looking for any chance to escape, waiting for their gods to come and save them. However, if there are any gods, they abandoned us that day." He paused again and looked up at the cloudy sky above. "With no hope left to us, it happened: a flash of bright, blinding light." A tear flowed out of the man's eye, quickly wiped away by his right arm. "When the light faded, many of those around us were gone with it." He placed his hand on the head of the colossal bear, giving it a gentle pet.

"I lost my wife and daughter that day." He snapped his fingers again. A small, glowing pink-and-white bunny appeared next to the bear. Another snap revealed a larger, snow-white bunny with a soft, pure white glow. "This was all that remained of them, each crawling about under their clothes left behind." The rooftop went quiet as Ren absorbed the man's story.

"That's a lot to take in," Ren said, glancing over at the small glowing creature with uncertain confusion. Then he turned to the small glowing bunnies, and then back to the man that had saved his life. "I'm sorry for your loss," Ren said, completing his wandering gaze.

"Save your sympathy for someone who deserves it," the man shrugged. "As I said this morning, I have no interest in this lunatic's game." The bunnies disappeared with another couple of snaps. "I don't know what that bastard did, but if I ever bump into him, he will either undo it and die quickly, or be unable to and have a long, drawn-out, and torturous end. That son of a bitch will pay for what he did—he and whatever sick soul was born from the heart of a monster like him."

"Soul?" Ren asked, glancing back at the creature by his side.

"Yeah, a soul. That glowing cat next to you is called a soul."

"Not a cat," the creature mumbled while rolling its eyes.

"My soul…"

"Yeah. I don't know how or what he did, but whatever it was, he succeeded with his so-called grand rapture of souls."

"So, the two bunnies."

"My wife and daughter. Taken from me—only their souls left behind." The rooftop went silent again, the older man with nothing else to say and Ren doing his best to process everything he had just been told.

A soft vibrating hum broke the silence, coming from the boy's pants. He reached into his pocket to retrieve his phone. The source of the vibration now sat at sixty-three percent battery life. The slow drain was a benefit of being wiped clean. Curious, the man glanced over at the boy.

"That would be your invitation to play, I assume," the man said ominously as he made his way over to Ren, circling behind to better see the phone's display.

"My invitation to play? To play what?" Ren asked as they both looked at the only app on the screen as it pulsed with a peculiar glow. "Should I tap it?" Ren asked, looking up at the man for any guidance.

"How would I know?" he replied coldly with another shrug, this time accompanied by a wince as the bullet wound reminded him of its presence. "They will get the message to you, one way or another, I suppose. Via a cell phone is a lot less creepy than mine was." He chuckled. "Bastard may be nuts, but he is just as clever."

"Sure," Ren said, unsure what he meant by that, but with no further elaboration. Ren returned his attention to the screen and gave the glowing app a gentle tap. The screen went black for a second before a glowing reaper with a white scythe faded out from the black and illuminated the center of the screen. "Stay Tuned" ran across the top of the screen, with the number ten sitting idle at the bottom.

"What the hell is going on?" Ren asked aloud, no longer expecting an answer from the man.

"I already told you, it's your formal invitation. I haven't seen one since mine way back then." A loud beep rang out from the phone, startling the boy enough that the phone slipped from his hands. Leaning over, he picked it up and dusted off the screen. A slight crack formed in the top right. Where the number ten was only seconds ago was now a sequence of numbers running down, presumably to zero.

CHAPTER THREE
Welcome to the Game

After a long nine and a half minutes of awkward silence, Ren sat, leaning up against a no-longer-functioning air ventilation system for the vacant building below, watching as the timer ran down for the last thirty seconds, while the man sat perched along the rail of the rooftop, gently petting the colossal bear as he stared out at the motionless streets below.

"Maybe this will shed some light on what the hell is going on?" the creature said as it let out a long, impatient stretch before scaling Ren's back to get a better view from atop his shoulder.

"I really hope so," Ren said as the timer hit zero. Curious, the man let out a painful stretch and meandered his way over to Ren, who stood up to better share the small view. The screen went black for a second before a bright flicker cut to what looked like an empty stage. A large podium stood in the middle of the empty room, with bright red curtains hung along the background wall. An uncomfortable audience of human silhouettes scattered about the moon-shaped seating that curved around the stage.

"Is this a joke?" Ren asked, confused, as he glanced up at the man watching from behind him.

"Just watch," he said, giving a nod towards the screen.

"Ahem, this thing on?" a slightly raspy voice said, accompanied by two loud thumps that caused popping from the phone's speakers. "What do you mean we are already live?" the voice said aggressively as it turned away from the audio source. "Goddammit, man, why do I even pay you?" The speakers cracked with a sudden loud bang before a tall elderly man with a long white beard stepped through the curtain, casually tossing a still-smoking gun off the stage to the right and buttoning his fancy suit as he approached the podium.

"Apologies for the delay. We seem to have resolved some technical difficulties we were having. However, the show must go on," he said with a kooky grin at the camera before letting out an equally kooky laugh.

"Video is just the same as it was back then," the man said from behind Ren as he leaned up against his bear companion, as if standing by himself was too much to ask. The strange character on the screen cleared his throat before then staring directly into the camera.

"Allow me to welcome you to my little game. Welcome to Wonderland." He took a slight bow and tipped his overly glamorous, enormous top hat dramatically as he reached the end of his stance. "A lot has taken place, and I am sure that you watching out there right now at this very moment are curious." A chalkboard rolled across the stage from the right, the man easily stopping it as it passed. Quickly scooping up a piece of chalk, he drew as he continued.

"Once upon a time there was a boy. A normal boy, not special in any desirable way. Raised by cartoons and a simple collection of various board games left out for the poor latchkey child." On the chalkboard was a short stick figure that sat in front of a square box, with a couple of smaller boxes scattered about. Around him were small squares and rectangles, presumably dice and cards.

"The boy loved playing games. Though a childhood alone would leave him always wanting someone to play with. School was hard for the young boy. Far ahead of his fellow students mentally, and as a loner by nature, he thirsted for the company of others. The joy of playing a game with another. One day, the boy met a girl. A darling young lady that stole his heart at first sight."

The previous picture on the board was now gone. A much taller, more grown-up-looking stick figure stood in its place. Where the large TV resembling a box had been, now stood another stick figure with long flowing white hair. They held a large white heart in their hands. He only had one color of chalk, it seemed.

"Is this guy really telling us a love story…" Ren asked aloud in disbelief before being interrupted by the creature atop his shoulder.

"Love is the true destroyer of man," it chuckled.

"Ah, adolescent love," the man on the screen continued. "So immature and so naively pure in its innocence and curiosity. However, unlike the games he was so familiar with, the games of the heart had no rulebook—no foundation to begin with—and were far from an evenly balanced game. Only the attraction to another, two pieces on the board of life, each blindly wandering their way through." His voice grew sad; the picture on the board remained the same as before. He erased the heart from the opposing figure's hand and redrew it on the ground at her feet. A large knife protruded from where it now lay. The scene on the board said it all. His tone quickly pivoted back to happiness, almost sporadically, as he continued.

"Called it," the creature snarked.

"Returning to what he understood, the boy played his games alone from that day after. Never again did he seek the affection of another, for one loss was one too many. It was on that day everything you see around you was born. A simple vision from a love-lost teenager turned into reality. Wonderland." The man paused, taking one last look at the chalkboard. With a sigh, he meandered to the side of it and, with an aggressive kick, sent it back off camera to where it came from. A series of thuds and crashes echoed from off the stage. "So how do you play?" he said aloud, pretending to hear someone from out in the cardboard cutout audience.

"What a delightful question from our totally real and not fake audience. My game is one that you may choose to opt out of anytime you like. No strings attached. Though, with the current state of things, I can't say there is much else to do. Maybe a delightful walk along the glass-riddled beach, or a relaxing nap out in the wasteland… but I digress. The rules are simple. You watching this have now woken up. In doing so, you have joined the board alongside the thousands of others playing their way through Wonderland. A devastated post-apocalyptic east coast setting. A world ravished, like the heart of a young boy once was." The man paused, turning away from the camera. A slight sigh broke through the silence of the stage.

"Back to the point. Players, referred to as Reapers, will travel across the board, a board that you may have noticed is a tad bit less crowded these days. This is due to what I like to call the rapture of souls. Pretty neat, right?" Another grin. "I may have ripped off the good book a little, but I get the credit for the whole soul-splitting thing. You watching right now may have already figured this out, but for the less intelligent of the bunch out there, or even those still waking up, I will elaborate. Through a series of overly complicated events, I turned most of the world's population to nothing more than the physical embodiment of their soul. Their body, well, who needed that, right? The rest of you, however, were separated from your soul and now have an adorable little pet to call your own. As a Reaper, you will journey across the board to find me. From there, you will play through a series of mini games for the chance to win."

"Win what? Why should I play your stupid ass game?" he mouthed, mimicking another audience member.

"Well, you rude little shit sitting in the front row, allow me to enlighten your ignorance."

"This guy seems a bit off," Ren said, his eyes still glued to the screen.

"So glad you picked up on that," the man said sarcastically from behind him. Meanwhile, the man on the screen paused and fidgeted with something at the podium before continuing.

"Yes, yes. The prize. The prize is just as simple as the rules. Well, you get to choose what happens next. Vague, right? Yeah, I know. But who doesn't like a surprise ending?" He laughed. "A hint?" he said playfully. "Okay, fine. The souls that no longer wander are only those lost forever. Through redemption, you can have back what was lost." He stared up ominously before his gaze locked back on the camera. "What was that?" he said, pretending to hear a question from the audience. "Where am I? You ask. My oh my, just want all the answers now, don't you?" He took another dramatic pause before then continuing as if he was being pressured to answer. "Okay, okay. Damn, you are so persistent, and that's why I like you. You can find me in the whitest house in America. That's a hint so easy that even the president could have figured it out." He smiled and winked at the camera. "Till next time, happy reaping!" He bowed dramatically again as the screen went black.

"Crazy bastard. He actually wants people to come and kick his ass," ranted the man, pacing away from his perch alongside the bear.

"I don't think so," interjected Ren. "Well, not entirely. I think there is more to it than that."

"Oh, and what makes you so damn smart?"

"The prize…"

"Yeah, what about it?"

"To choose what happens next. Doesn't that mean anything is on the table as a prize? Then there is the hint, which would imply what he did can be undone, at least to some extent. 'The souls that no longer wander are only those lost forever.' Then there is the whole redemption thing. 'Through redemption, you can have back what was lost.'" This caught the man off guard, and he fell silent. His aggressive pacing came to a complete stop.

"It's just a theory, but…"

"Your little theory is all I needed," interrupted the man. "Even the slightest chance I could see my wife and daughter again." He paused as a couple of tears dripped from his deeply saddened eyes. "Well, in that case." The man turned to the boy. "It's been fun, kid, but as far as I can tell, there's only one winner in this game." The enormous bear now loomed over the boy and the small creature. Fire swirled passionately around them as the bear came closer.

"Hey, wait a second, you two," Ren yelled, startled. "I don't want to fight you. You just saved my life."

"Well, kid, it seems we are at a crossroads then. I have no intention of leaving you behind to bite me in the ass later." He let out a laugh. "As if you would even make it out of the city." The bear took a powerful swing at the pair. Ren scooped the small creature up and just barely dodged the massive paw now encased in ice.

"Would you just…" Another aggressive swing from the bear, this time followed up with an enormous paw of ice crashing down out of nowhere. "Ice?"

"Seems our souls are at a similar crossroads, opposites destined to clash. Fire versus Ice." Ren whispered to the creature, "Can you beat him?"

"I think so, but I would rather not have to. There is still that crazy bird guy below to worry about as well."

"Yeah, an actual fight would draw too much unwanted attention. Okay, follow my lead."

"Your lead?" the creature said curiously as Ren stood up, setting the creature down next to him.

"How about a deal?" Ren asked. The bear paused its

aggressive attack.

"I'm listening," yelled the man from the other side of the rooftop. The flames that encased Ren and his soul slowed their swirl. He gave a sigh of relief before continuing with his proposal.

"We go together," he said before being interrupted.

"I don't think you quite get it, kid." The bear raised its paw again and readied another strike. The small creature prepared to jump in front of the aggressor. Its surrounding flames swirled rapidly again as Ren threw his left hand out to block the creature's advance.

"Let me finish!" he snapped. The bear paused once again. "We go together, and if it comes down to it, I will end my life. No matter what, you will still win." The rooftop fell silent, almost cold.

"And why exactly would you do that?" the man asked harshly in disbelief. "And if you lie to me, it will be the last lie ever you tell."

"Because." Ren paused. Tears were now rushing down his face. "This is the only way we both get what we want." It was a vague, yet emotional response. It was clear to the man that there was no lie hidden within his tears. Almost with relief, the man lowered his aggressive stance and asked.

"What's your name, kid?" the man asked as his bear companion lowered its arm and fell back to its passive stance on all fours.

"It's Ren. My name is Ren."

"Well, Ren, you have yourself a deal."

"Really?" Ren said with a tremendous sigh of relief as he dropped to the ground in tears. The creature, his soul, gave him a comforting nudge as he broke down. A loud bang rang out from the sky as it opened. The emotion of the day washed away with the rain.

"Let's head inside, kid," the man said, extending his hand out to Ren. "The name is Elio," he said with a kind, fatherly smile as he lifted Ren up—a smile Ren felt he had never known.

"Yeah, let's," he said with shaky confidence as they made their way inside. Giving his body a little shake, Ren followed Elio inside and down a flight of stairs to the building's top floor.

"The suite on this level is pretty impressive. I won't lie. Gur and I have been hiding out here since the world went to hell. I had been staying across the street when it all went down, a routine business trip that the family and I thought would make a nice vacation. When it happened, I figured we might as well upgrade while the world burns around us, right?" he said as he pushed open a pair of doors.

"Welcome to paradise lost, kid," he said as the two massive doors swung open to reveal an incredible room. Directly opposite the door was a wall of windows that had the largest sectional couch, maybe in the world, spanning the entire length of the wall. On the right of the room was a singular door, and opposite it, on the other side of the room, was the same door.

"Your room will be on the left. I have already settled in on the right."

"Uh, thanks."

"Hopefully, by morning, that psycho and his deformed death bird will be gone. Then we can stock up on supplies before we depart for D.C." The man kicked off his boots and proceeded over to the large open kitchen space to the right of the entrance. "You hungry?" he asked, making his way behind the massive kitchen sidebar. "This place came with a well-stocked fridge and freezer; the place even still has power."

"But how?" Ren said as he stepped inside and sat down across the counter.

"Wealth has its perks, but all the money in the world can't save you from death. It's the only floor in the building connected to a generator. Though, it's only enough power to keep a couple lights on, a little heat circulating, and some food chilled or frozen. Lucky for me, there is a conveniently located gas station only a block away. Fancy-ass tenants even had filet mignon tucked away in the freezer. A damned shame to freeze such a prime cut. All the better for us, I suppose. How does that sound? Maybe with some creamy mashed potatoes?"

"That sounds amazing," he said, surprised. "Were you a chef or something?"

"I was…" He paused before leaning over and pulling out three perfect-looking russet potatoes from a small wooden bin. The question of where they came from popped into Ren's head before being quickly lost as Elio continued. "The world we find ourselves in now has no place for a chef. No, now I am just a man with nothing to lose. Only the slight hope I may see their faces again keeps me going. A hope I had lost touch with until recently." Elio took out a bottle of water and poured it into a medium bowl, dropping the potatoes in and giving them a proper scrub. Pivoting the conversation away from himself, he looked at Ren.

"So, what's your story, kid? Ren, was it?"

"Yeah, Ren." He paused, unsure how much to share, and

concluded that it didn't really matter all that much now. Not that there was even much to share. "Well, to be honest, I don't have a lot to share. I don't remember very much outside of a few little things from when I was young. I was your typical child of divorce. A divorce that consumed one side with a freedom they could not handle, and the other an anger equally unmanaged. Coincidentally, both led to the same outcome." Ren took another brief pause as he became entranced by the rapid cubing of the well-washed potatoes.

"When I was twelve, my mother was in a car accident. Drunk at the wheel, she swerved into an oncoming car. She ended up killing a family of four and herself in the collision." Elio paused his knife and glanced over at Ren. "A year later, I woke up to a gunshot in the middle of the night. The next day, my grandparents from my mom's side of the family picked me up, and from then on, I lived with them. I kept a low profile my entire life, only a couple of close friends and a single shot at love lost because of my immaturity. Then I woke up one morning, and the world had ended, and yet even with all that, I can't figure out why I survived it." Ren started to tear up, slipping out of his seat and making his way over to the expansive window, gazing out as he continued.

"Why don't I remember anything good? Was there ever anything good in my life to even remember? And after everything I have lost, meandering through the joke of a life I remember, I convinced myself I had to finish it at some point. Why then, when a simple exit to it appears, am I still forced to press on?" Silence overcame the room. Ren watched the fires outside flicker on the glass of the windows as the moon clocked in for the night. Elio finished up dinner over the still-functional propane stove, successfully lit with a single strike of a match.

"Food is done," Elio said as four plates clanged gently down atop the table opposite the kitchen. Ren wiped his tears away and made his way over to the table as Elio turned his attention to him. "Look, kid, life sucks. That's just the simple fact of it." Ren looked down at the masterpiece of food that sat in front of his chair. He slid into his seat as the warm smell of melted butter and garlic stimulated his senses. An exact mirror of his plate sat in front of his soul, who sat next to him.

"However, that's not the point of it. Each of us has a choice to make in how we carry ourselves—who we want to be. Each of us makes this choice every single day from the point of self-awareness." They each cut into their steak while their souls sat idle and watched. It was perfect medium rare; its juices oozed as they blended with the fluffy white mashed potatoes that accompanied it on the plate.

"I won't lie. You seem to have been dealt a shittier hand than some. But that singular choice you made, the one to press on through it all, even if you can't remember why, displays a strength that not everyone in your situation has. Your father included." Elio paused and took a bite before continuing. "If I had to take a gamble, that strength to push forward no matter what life has thrown at you is why you are sitting here now." The table fell silent as the two ate. The meal was unlike anything Ren had ever eaten, or at least remembered eating. A perfect blend of salty and savory as the two textures blended seamlessly together in his mouth. When Elio had cleared his plate, he swapped the empty plate with Gur and started on that portion as well.

Ren looked down at his empty plate and realized how hungry he still was.

"Well, are you gonna finish your meal?" Elio commented, motioning his form to the plate next to him. Confused, Ren followed suit and swapped the plates, quickly devouring the entire second plate.

"Thank you," Ren said. Elio's gaze met his from the other side of the table. "For the food and saving me and… what you said. For everything, thank you."

"Don't mention it, kid," he said with a satisfied smile before taking his last bite.

CHAPTER FOUR
Breakfast with a Side of Battle

Ren lay sprawled out atop a massive king-size mattress, exhausted from the end of the world and the events that had all transpired since he woke up only two days ago. Yawning as he sat up with a long stretch, he glanced around the large, sunlit room. The scent of something salty filled the room, flowing in from under the small gap in the closed door. Still sleeping comfortably on the large, fluffy pillow next to him was the peculiar glowing creature he had met soon after waking up to the world's end.

Letting out another long stretch, Ren stood up and meandered around the room to see what secrets it held. Much to his surprise, he found an incredibly well-stocked closet filled to the brim with a wide variety of fashions. Slipping into a dark blue designer shirt, paired with a high-end pair of denim jeans, he stared at his peaceful soul asleep on the bed.

"Time to get up, little guy," he said with a smile as he slipped on his well-worn shoes he had found himself in since waking up in Wonderland. Watching as the creature slowly uncurled and extended its front paws out, he added, "I think Elio is cooking up something tasty for breakfast." It blinked its eyes and looked Ren up and down.

"Look at you, fancy pants. You rob a men's warehouse while I was asleep?" He glanced down. "No sale on shoes?" Tama chuckled.

"Why are you such a dick to me all the time? It's getting old," Ren snapped as he tousled his bedhead back to the casual mess he preferred. Wandering across the bed, the creature responded.

"I mean, I am your soul, so I assume some part of my personality is based on your insecurities and opinion of yourself. Though this entire situation didn't exactly come with a handbook for us to use, so that's just a guess." He landed gracefully on the floor of the room and opened the door with a quick flick of his mind. "You're hungry; go eat. It sure smells good."

"You're not hungry?" Ren asked, pausing. "Wait, how can you tell I am hungry?"

"I'm sure that's in our missing handbook as well. Let's eat," he said, disappearing out of the room. Ren followed his sassy soul to the kitchen to see what Elio had cooked up.

"About time you dragged your lazy ass out of bed. I was beginning to wonder if we would get to leave today, or if you planned on sleeping through the next end of the world," Elio said while tending to the delicious sizzle coming from the stovetop. His passive, bear-like soul was still peacefully asleep atop the couch in front of the large window. Ren's soul gracefully hopped onto a chair and silently awaited Ren to join him for breakfast.

"I didn't realize it was so late." Ren paused and looked

around for a clock. The digital readout on the stovetop blinked in error. "What time is it exactly?"

Elio glanced at his wrist. "Just after nine. Damned kids, always wasting away the most valuable time of the day." He let out a shrug. "Not that time really matters anymore, what with the world outside on fire. No need to confine our lives to some societal metric anymore, I suppose." He turned around with a plate in each hand. Each had one sunny-side-up egg, two strips of bacon, and some diced potatoes.

"Food is done," Elio said, setting the plates down in front of him and his furry creature.

"Looks delicious," Ren said as his stomach let out an aggressive growl.

"Your stomach knows what's up, but have you noticed?" Elio asked, to which Ren tilted his head. Elio stood across from the duo, two plates prepared the same way in front of him.

"Noticed what?" Elio glanced over at Ren's soul as it sat at attention at the table, paying no mind to the dish in front of him.

"This little guy knows what's up. What's its name, anyway?" Elio asked, reaching in to pet the curious-looking creature, only to be met with a sassy bat of its paw and a less-than-approachable glare. "Certainly not a friendly little bastard, are you?" he said, pulling his hand away and returning his attention to Ren, who was already halfway through his meal.

"I don't know his name. Should I?" Ren asked before taking another bite. "This is really spectacular, by the way," Ren said with his mouth full.

"Damned kids, can't even keep their mouths shut while they eat. Am I right?" he said, playfully winking at Ren's soul, only to be met with an unimpressed glare. "You need to name him. Doesn't matter what or how, but you two need to figure that out. As for my first question, have you noticed being any hungrier since all of this went down?" Sliding his now-empty plate slightly back from where he sat, Ren looked up.

"I guess, maybe. Hard to know for sure, since I didn't even remember what hungry was until I ate yesterday." His stomach echoed with an unsatisfied grumble.

"Here," Elio said, sliding his untouched plate across the table toward Ren. "I am still pretty stuffed from last night."

"Oh, you sure?" Ren responded with curious guilt in his tone.

"Yeah, something tells me you will need it more than I will. You should finish your meal as well." Returning his attention to the glowing, cat-like creature still sitting next to him.

"The second plate?" Ren asked curiously.

"Yeah. We eat for our souls. Our stamina is their power, so even though they can't eat, we can still share a meal. The extra plate, or split portion, includes them in the meal. Curious about how powerful this little guy is. Seems he drains you fast, even sitting idle." Elio smiled as Ren swapped out his plate for the creature's portion. "Any thoughts on that name yet? Or maybe I should ask you." The creature turned and met Elio's gaze with similar interest. Finally satisfied after clearing three plates of food, Ren answered the question while Elio started on Gur's plate.

"I kind of like the name Tamashii, or Tama for short."

"Oh?" said Elio.

"I think it fits. The translation would be a soul in its entirety, or jewel when shortened. I like both, personally." Ren turned to the creature to get its opinion on the matter. "Thoughts?"

"Got ourselves a little nerd," Elio laughed, also turning to the creature, but this time remembering not to touch it with his antics.

"I like it," the creature responded with a nod, satisfied with the suggestion.

"Then it's settled. From this day forward, we will call you Tamashii," Ren said with a smile.

"Lil' bugger liked it. Well, I will be damned. The soul doesn't fall far from the nerd tree. Nearly no memory from before two days ago, but that—that he remembers?" He let out another boisterous laugh before turning his attention to the sleeping bear. "Gur, get up. It's time to roll out." The massive bear let out a long, dissatisfied stretch before giving the air a prompt sniff. Gur's eyes went wide as he dashed from where he lay over to Elio's side, pushing him over and covering him with his large body.

"What the hell, Gur!" Elio snapped as the glass window along the wall shattered and exploded inward. Bullet-like feathers tore through the room as if being fired from a machine gun. Ren ducked down under the table, joined by Tama, who quickly separated the room with a powerful wall of flame, stopping the onslaught of glass and silver feathers.

"Nice trick. Did you two really think you could just wait for me to leave? That I would get bored and just move on?" a familiar voice said from the other side of the flame. Tama cleared a small circle in the wall of flickering flame to peek through to the other side. There at the window, standing atop the feathered abomination of a bird, was the same kid from the gas station the day before. The bird was nearly three times its original size now, its wingspan the length of Gur when fully sprawled. With a light step, he landed atop the glass-littered floor with a cocky bow, rolling his arm under his chest as he pretended to tip a hat.

"Don't you know? If you play with fire, expect to get burned." Elio motioned to Ren and pointed over to the exit behind them. Elio gave Gur a brief pet. "Thanks, Gur." As the massive bear faded to a small yellow light that mirrored its previous glow, he added, "We will take it from here." He placed the small floating orb of yellow light into a small, egg-shaped container that resembled one of those cheap eggs kids hunt for on Easter. Elio placed it into a small leather bag that now hung on his back. Elio then made his way over to the door, motioning to Ren and Tama. The pair swiftly followed suit as Elio shut the door tight behind them.

"Crazy bastard must have spent all night looking for us. Does he really have nothing better to do?" A gunshot rang out from the other side of the door.

"We won't have much time after I drop the flame," Tama said, turning his head up to Ren. "We need a plan."

"What should we do?" Ren said to Elio. As the wall to their left blasted open and knocked the three of them down the stairs, they banged into each other and the walls until they landed roughly on the floor below.

"That is gonna hurt in the morning," Elio grumbled. He held

his wounded arm tight with a wince as he slowly got back to his feet. Elio reached over to Ren and helped him up to standing. "He is going to take the entire building down at this rate."

"I don't think he cares about the building," Tama snarked at Ren.

"Can't Gur take him out?" Ren said to Elio, ignoring Tama. "Why are you hiding him?" Ren asked as they began their dash to the bottom floor, one flight at a time.

"Gur is more of the gentle giant sort. Don't get me wrong, he can hold his own in a pinch. But his size makes fighting in such an enclosed space very one-sided."

"Makes sense, I guess."

"I have no plans to sacrifice my soul in a fight with the odds stacked against me. Saving your lazy ass was enough of a risk for me, and to be honest, if Gur hadn't been so determined, I would have left you behind yesterday without a second thought."

"I see," Ren said, realizing that their pairing was strictly one of opportunity and that Elio had no intention of growing attached.

"This is a fight best avoided. A fight with crazy never ends well." A statement drenched in irony, considering their collaborative goal. They dashed out of the stairwell and rushed through the lobby and out to the sidewalk. Standing on the opposite side of the empty street was the kid. Perched on his shoulder was the warped-looking bird, back to its original size.

"Funny bumping into you here!" he yelled from the other side of the street, aggressively waving at them from where he stood.

"Bastard knew we would be here."

"Where the hell else would we go? He kind of destroyed the rest of the building," Tama said with sassy disapproval as rubble landed behind them.

"Yeah, suppose you're right," responded Ren.

"You and fur ball gonna let me in on the conversation there?" snapped Elio. Ren still wasn't used to the fact that only he could hear Tama.

"Sorry. He just made a comment about us having no other option than ending up here, since his soul destroyed everything." Elio turned his attention back to the ominous kid across the street.

"Well, what should we do? Can't imagine at this point we can keep running from bird boy over there." Ren and Tama adjusted their gazes across the street. He was petting his disfigured soul, the blending of both lizard and bird so eerily combined that it would make anyone feel odd.

"TIME'S UP, BITCHES!" he yelled as he finished petting his soul and pulled out a pistol before pointing it in their direction. "BANG, BANG!" he yelled as two bullets fired back-to-back in their direction. Elio and Ren ducked in separate directions, both finding temporary safety behind two evenly spaced concrete slabs, perfect for blocking bullets and cars all the same.

"Guess we run!" yelled Tama as the kid started across the road and fired off two more bullets.

"We need to get out of here!" Ren echoed to Elio.

"I'm not as bulletproof as you would think," Elio said in a dry tone from behind his slab, with a wince at his still-healing arm. Suddenly, Tama's glow shifted its color to light brown.

"Carry me!" Tama said to Ren. "You two escape while I provide cover." Ren locked eyes with Elio.

"Follow us!" Ren yelled while scooping up Tama. "Our lives are in your hands… I mean, paws."

"Just don't stop running," Tama said.

"You got it!" said Ren with a confident smile, to which Tama met him with the same response as his glow grew brighter. Suddenly, the sidewalk on their side of the street shook and cracked. The thin layer of concrete that separated the pavement of the street and the parking lot rose into the air, carried via the dirt below.

"Now!" Tama yelled as a massive wall of dirt rose fifteen feet into the air. The thick brown wall separated them from their unwanted aggressor while muffling the sound of two more gunshots on the other side. Elio and Ren ran as fast as they could from the lot and around the right side of the building they had descended from. Dirt curled along the sidewalk and formed a tunnel of concrete and debris, protecting them from the deformed eye in the sky that was undoubtedly pursuing them.

The ground continued to curl alongside them as they fled down the barren streets. Glowing lights of various shapes and sizes lit the way ahead as the tunnel enclosed them in darkness. Lost souls, hiding from the cold reality of the world they now found themselves in.

"There are so many," Ren said, surprised.

"Well, yeah—one per every human," Elio said. "Poor bastards probably don't even know what's going on. Don't let your guard down, though. Remember that each soul belonged to a stranger, and the world before had more pretenders than not."

"Pretenders?" Ren said, confused.

"Another time. Maybe once we aren't running for our lives."

"Yeah," Ren said with a nod as he jumped over an enormous chunk of random debris before noting a flickering light up ahead. "What's that?" he said, pointing as they maintained their pace.

"Probably a trap. Ignore it," Elio said as a human-like figure stepped out and waved at them.

"Quick! Over here!" a young girl's voice yelled from the direction of the light.

"It's a girl."

"Who cares? Even higher odds it's a trap, if you ask me."

"What if she needs help?"

"What if she kills us without even blinking?"

"Over here!" the voice yelled again, motioning them in her direction. Ren looked down at Tama in his arms, his glow dimming.

"He can't keep this up. We need an out, and if there is even a chance that she has one, we can't pass it up." Elio rolled his eyes.

"Fine! But as soon as anything feels off, we leave. Deal?" Elio said defiantly. However, Ren had already pivoted his path and was already well on his way toward the female stranger.

"This way," she said as they reached her. The girl was much shorter than either of them had expected. The pair followed close behind as she led them down a narrow zigzag of various alleys. Tama's glow shifted to a light red as his eyes closed and his breathing slowed in Ren's arms. A loud crash came from behind them, most likely the massive wall of dirt returning to the ground.

After a couple more minutes of silent scurrying through the alley, they entered a much larger space, fully surrounded by various shades of red brick, another alley on the opposite side of where they stood. Various levels of steps and balconies above blocked out the sun looming in the sky above. Their savior slowly turned around and removed her deep, dark purple hood to reveal a young girl no older than twelve. With a quirky smile, she waved while tilting her head slightly to the side.

"Hi, I'm Lilly!"

CHAPTER FIVE
Inevitable Conclusions

"My name is Elio, and that's Ren." Without any acknowledgment, Lilly let out a squeal of glee.

"Who is that adorable little guy?" she said, looking at Tama, who lay snug in Ren's arms, asleep.

"This is Tama, my soul."

"He is so cute!" she said, smiling from ear to ear. "Can I pet him?" Ren was pretty sure Tama would hate that, but quickly pushed the thought aside.

"Yeah. He loves pets," Ren said with an unconvincing grin as Lilly reached over and gently pet Tama on the head.

"So soft. It's like petting a cloud," she said excitedly while Elio sighed.

"Look, thanks for helping us out back there and all, but—"

"No thanks needed!" she interrupted. "It was all Haku's idea."

"Haku?" Ren said curiously.

"Your soul, I presume," Elio said, looking around for it.

"Yeah! Haku is my best friend. Well, my only friend since my mom and dad never came back."

"Have you been surviving alone all this time?" Elio asked, concerned.

"No, I haven't been alone the entire time. Though everyone I meet leaves me… or ends up dead," she said with no sadness in her tone. Ren and Elio shared concerned glances.

"But Haku never leaves me. Haku is the best."

"Could we meet Haku?" Elio asked, feeling more and more uneasy about their situation.

"He's sleeping right now. Maybe later. Is that okay?"

"Sure…" Elio said. Ren could tell that he felt off about the situation. After all, she had just said that helping them was Haku's idea and not hers.

"Why is Luka so mad at you, anyway? Everyone knows not to mess with Luka."

"Luka?" Ren asked.

"Yeah, Luka. The boy with the scary bird that's chasing you."

"You know that nutcase?" Elio asked, surprised. Lilly wandered over to a small pink couch that sat along the eastern brick wall. Sitting in front of it was a small fire pit carved out of loose bricks from the surrounding buildings.

"Yeah, we have bumped into each other a few times. He doesn't play fair—uses guns to cheat. Haku and I hate guns. Luka has a dangerous tendency to shoot first."

"And then what?" Ren asked, waiting for the rest of the expression.

"What do you mean? Most don't get away from Luka. Shoot first, win. A simple way to survive."

"So, you just avoid him?" Ren asked.

"Yeah, pretty much," she said with a bitter smile. "But if I ever get a chance..." she followed up coldly before switching the conversation. "Hungry?" Elio and Ren shared another uneasy glance when they heard another gunshot echo down the alley behind them.

"Now, now, girly. I thought we had an agreement of sorts," a voice said from the direction they had come from.

"Shit! He already found us," Elio said, turning to Lilly. "We need to go, now!"

"Going already?" Luka said, stepping out of the alley. "But I just got here." His freakish bird sat perched atop his shoulder. Ren could make out a deep reddish-brown underneath where it sat—dried blood from the deformed creature's aggressive perch.

"Go away, Luka! These are my friends now—hands off."

"Shut up, you little bitch!" he snapped at her. "I was playing with them first. You can have your turn when I am done."

"Luka, was it?" Elio said, hoping to speak reason to him. "Why not play the game? Why not hunt down the man that did this to us?"

"Hunt him?" Luka let out a disturbed laugh. "Maybe only to thank him. He freed me—freed all of us. What's left now is far more civilized than the warped dystopia of before. A world where the majority, those like me..." He paused, growing more aggressive in his mannerisms. Luka raised his right hand and pointed his still-warm pistol at Elio. "A society run by community, likes and dislikes. Farming hate or sex for the perversion of fame. He tore it all down. Kill him? He is a goddamn hero, if you ask me. Only the strong survive here, not the pretty, the famous, or the rich. Now it's all about who has the bigger gun and who will pull the trigger." With a sickly grin, Luka fired the gun at Elio, who stood his ground, unflinching, as the bullet flew by his head and shattered the brick behind him.

"That's enough, Luka! Go away!" Lilly yelled, unfazed by the gunshot.

"Oh? And what if I don't?" he said, walking slowly toward Lilly. "Huh? What is a stupid little girl going to do to stop me?" he said while the bird atop his shoulder let out an aggressive screech.

"I will show you what strength really is," she replied coldly, locking eyes with him. Luka burst out laughing so hard he bent over.

"You? The cowardly little brat that sat by crying while she watched me kill her friends one by one. What's your plan this time? Scurry away like every other time and leave these two idiots to die in your place? The trail of bodies that follows you is far bloodier than anything I could dream of."

Elio and Ren watched in silence. Together, they slowly inched toward the dark tunnel behind them in the hope of an escape. Ren looked down at Tama, who was still out cold in his arms. Without him, they had little chance of winning any fight. Both froze, however, when Luka raised his right hand and pointed the gun at Lilly.

"Not so tough now, are you, you little bitch?" Luka said, with another sick grin creasing across his face. "Nowhere to run now, little rat." Suddenly, a thick black smoke swirled around Lilly, hiding her from sight. The gun went off, then again and again. "DIE, DIE, DIE!" Luka yelled with each shot as spit flung from his mouth like venom. Then, in the blink of an eye, a massive claw of smoke formed out from where Lilly had just stood and ripped through Luka and his perched soul. Blood splattered across the back of the room, painting the walls a deep, thick red. In three slanted pieces, Luka's body tumbled to the ground.

The smoke dissipated as Lilly turned around to a more than shocked Elio and Ren, both equally confused by what they had just witnessed. Ren broke the silence as the stench of fresh, warm blood flipped his stomach over; he turned around to hurl.

"What the fuck was that?" Elio gasped at Lilly. Luka's head slowly slid down the warm red liquid of the detached torso.

"You said a bad word," Lilly said, turning her gaze to Ren. "Is he okay?"

"A bad word? You just went full slasher flick on that kid, and you want to talk about bad words?"

"I warned him. Haku doesn't like it when people threaten me."

"So that was Haku?" Elio said, doing his best to regain his composure. "And where exactly is Haku now?" he asked, looking around again. It had all happened so fast that Elio had not seen where the smoke originated. His best guess was that Haku lay hidden somewhere amongst her baggy hoodie.

"Sleeping," she said flatly, as if that would relieve the pair of all their concerns. Ren turned around, wiping his lips, and said,

"Guess that solves that." He turned to Lilly and asked, "Are you okay?" A question that seemed to surprise her.

"Yeah, why wouldn't I be?"

"I mean, I can think of three excellent reasons," Elio said, glancing at the mess of limbs and blood behind her.

"Oh, that? That's nothing. Haku is just a little protective." Elio and Ren glanced at each other, the same concerning thought on their minds.

"We should get going," Elio said.

"Already? But you just got here," Lilly said with disappointment.

"Thank you… and Haku for the save. But we have a long trip ahead of us."

"Trip?" Lilly asked, perking up at the thought. "Trip to where?"

"To D.C. We are playing the madman's game."

"Shut up, Ren!" Elio snapped.

"The man on the screen?" she asked. Both returned their focus to her. "Can I play?"

"I am not so sure that's a good idea," Elio said, obviously trying to distance himself from the strange girl and her murder smoke.

"Oh, okay," she said as tears welled up in her eyes. Ren looked at Elio with a silent reconsideration, to which he shook his head in disagreement.

"That was a much-needed nap," said Tama as he stretched out in Ren's arms. "What did I miss?" he asked as he recoiled at the smell in the air. His eyes flashed open to see Lilly standing in front of Luka's dismembered body.

"Holy hell! What did you two do?"

"Kitty!" yelled Lilly with glee, rushing over and petting Tama excitedly on the head.

"What the hell is happening right now?" Tama said begrudgingly as a ball of fire appeared in the surrounding air.

"Tama, NO!" Elio and Ren both yelled as black smoke fumed from Lilly's baggy hoodie. Ren spun quickly around from Lilly, hiding Tama from her curious pats.

"You wanna get burned too?" Tama snapped at Ren while tearing himself free from Ren's grip and plopping onto the dusty alley floor. Surveying his new surroundings, Tama glanced from the young girl to the pile of human goo behind her and then back to her. "Are you going to explain what's going on here?"

"Tama, this is Lilly, and that is…" Ren pointed to the warm pool of human behind her. "Well, it was Luka. The kid from the gas station that attacked us this morning."

"She did that?" Tama said in disbelief.

"Yeah. Let's just say we don't wanna piss her off, okay?" Tama glanced back over at the human remains.

"Damn."

"Can I pet him now?" Lilly asked, confused about what was going on. Tama looked at Ren and shook his head vehemently.

"Sure can!" Elio said shakily. "Tama loves his pets."

"Like hell I do!" Tama snapped as Lilly ran over and knelt,

gently petting the soft top of his head.

"Yeah, Tama loves pets," Ren said with a smile.

"You two better sleep with one eye open tonight," Tama mumbled begrudgingly under his breath while surrendering to Lilly and her pats.

Ignoring Tama and his plight of snuggles and unwanted attention, Elio turned to Ren.

"So, what now?"

"I mean, I guess we take her with us," Ren said, turning back to her and Tama.

"That's not exactly what I meant…" Elio responded, following Ren's gaze over to the pair. "But I guess you're right. It doesn't seem right to just leave her here."

"If she is coming, I am staying here with Luka," Tama said, slipping away from Lilly and back over to Ren while Lilly gave a playful chase.

"So, Lilly, what do you say? Care to join us?" Ren asked, kneeling to match her height, blocking Tama from her chase. Thick black smoke formed what looked like a wing out the right side of her back. "Haku can come as well," Ren followed with an uneasy smile.

Lilly went quiet for a minute, most likely discussing it with Haku, before turning her eyes up to match Ren.

"Haku approves! Onwards to…" she said excitedly before realizing she wasn't fully sure where she had just agreed to go.

"To D.C.," Elio said, glancing at his pocket—the same pocket that contained the souls of his lost wife and daughter.

Ren nodded and looked up at the sky as a loud crack rang out and the sky opened with the tears of those lost since it all started one year ago.

"To D.C., to undo what's been done."

CHAPTER SIX

Larry's World

"So, I have a question," Lilly said as they made their way away from the wretched remains of Luka to search for a dry place to wait out the rain.

"Oh? What's that?" Ren asked curiously while Tama and Elio listened in.

"Where are we? And how far away is this place you call D.C.?"

"The answer to your first question: South Carolina. As for the distance, I can't say I ever asked Google how long it would take to walk from a random place in South Carolina to D.C.," Elio said, letting out a soft, reminiscent chuckle.

"Damn Google—you never really know how much you rely on something till it's no longer around."

"It's a walk. How long it is doesn't really matter," chimed Ren.

"I suppose you're right, and since there is no other plan, I guess we should just aim for the interstate and follow the signs," Elio said. Tama and Ren nodded in agreement while Lilly listened silently.

"Better plan than I have right now," Ren said.

"That being said, we should find a store and stock up before heading out. You never know who's out there, or what," Elio said, turning to Lilly. "You seem to know your way around here. Any suggestions?"

"Yeah!" she said, excited to be a part of the conversation. "There is a massive store nearby next to the wall. We could try there."

"The wall?" Elio asked, confused. She nodded her head.

"Yup. Soon after we woke up, Haku and I wandered around a lot. One thing we always seemed to find, no matter where we ended up, was a massive wall. It runs forever that way." She pointed toward the setting sun.

"Along the west? Interesting. Like fish in a barrel, I guess," Elio said, wondering what the wall kept out, or in. Tama turned to Ren.

"Or pawns on a board of chess," Tama said ominously.

"Wall, shmall. It makes no difference to me. Last I checked, D.C. is north and not west," Elio exclaimed. "Let the damn wall follow us. Who cares?"

"I suppose," Ren said, less convinced. He turned to the others. "North is north. We will deal with the wall if it gets in the way."

"Sounds good to me. Lead the way, Lilly," Elio said as her face lit up with glee and she skipped to the only other opening in the small brick area.

"This way!" she exclaimed before disappearing into the

darkness.

"Ren," Elio said, grabbing hold of his arm. "Our deal still stands, correct? No matter what happens, I plan to be the last one standing in this mess."

"Yes. I will hold to my word," Ren replied, to Tama's displeasure. "Though, I wish you the best of luck dealing with Haku," Ren said with a sassy grin.

"I will deal with that when the time comes. I just wanted to confirm you weren't having any second thoughts," Elio said, brushing his way past Ren and disappearing into the alley behind Lilly.

"Why do we have to die for this asshole?" Tama asked as they followed. "I can take him and his cowardly little bear with my eyes closed."

"We may win the fight, but those with something to fight for always win the war," Ren said as he stepped into the darkness of the alley.

"Some of us just need the time to find what's worth fighting for," Tama said quietly as they caught up with the others.

They followed Lilly as she dashed along the winding alleyways until they could see a gloomy-looking gray light from the wet sky above.

"Almost there!" Lilly echoed as she escaped out into the open, throwing her arms up into the air with childlike freedom. "Over there!" she pointed as the others stepped out behind her. Off in the distance, just across from the large parking lot, was a Walmart. Elio chuckled.

"Even at the end of the world, Walmart is still standing."

"The generators were still running the other day—dim lights, but the freezer sections were still nice and cold," Lilly said. It was obvious to Elio and Ren that she was thrilled to be a help, happy to no longer be alone at the end of the world.

"Well, let's go shopping and be on our way," Elio said as he stepped forward toward the towering blue-and-white building.

"We need to be careful, though. Larry lives here," Lilly said as they wandered across the desolate parking lot. Rows and rows of empty cars lined the lot to the brim, as if it were just another weekend and not the end of the world.

"Larry?" Ren asked, confused.

"Yeah, Scary Larry. It's best if we avoid him and his soul, Bozo."

"That's good to know," Elio said. "In and out, then. After that, we can find a place to sleep for the night and head out tomorrow bright and early."

"Sounds good to me," Ren said, matched with nods of agreement from Tama and Lilly.

As they approached the entrance, Ren's stomach dropped. The sliding glass doors had the words "Keep Out!" smeared across them in what resembled dried blood.

"Scary Larry," Lilly whispered, putting her pointer finger up to her lips as she slipped through the gap between the doors. Tama hopped close behind, followed by Elio and Ren. Once inside, sitting between the two sliding glass doors was a headless body sitting in a neon pink lawn chair.

"Okay, I am seriously reconsidering this," Ren said, choking back what little of his breakfast remained from earlier. The stench of death riddled the air as they saw another headless body propped up at the self-checkout, its lifeless hand pinned up to simulate a wave.

"So, Lilly, are there any other options nearby?" Elio asked.

"Nopes!" she said, shaking her head. "Everything else in the area is picked clean."

"Alright then, let's make this extra quick. Lilly, you are on food. Grab a cart and load up with things that will last—jerky and the sort. Ren, grab water and such, along with anything else you find that may prove beneficial. I will grab flashlights, batteries, and take a quick detour. A Walmart this size oughta have some home defense stocked up. Sound good?" They met him with three uncomfortable, unconvinced faces staring back.

"Fifteen minutes—in and out. Go," Elio said, grabbing a cart and disappearing down a nearby aisle. Lilly skipped behind him and grabbed a cart as well before dashing off toward the grocery side of the store.

"Let's go, Ren!" Tama said, hopping up into a grocery cart. "Clock's ticking, and I sure as hell don't wanna bump into Bozo and Scary Larry," he said, glancing over to their headless greeter.

"Yeah, let's get out of here," Ren said, grabbing the blue handle of the cart and heading deeper into the store. An unfamiliar shadow secretly followed suit.

"I don't like it here," Ren said as he rounded the corner to the opposite end of the grocery portion of the massive Walmart. It was almost as if it were just after hours; the store contained inside a bubble in which the world outside had not ended.

"Something is off here," Tama said as the cart came to a stop at a large shelf containing bottled water. "Elio didn't explain how he plans to shuttle all this shit to D.C. Surely he doesn't expect us to lug it."

"Now that you mention it, I guess you're right. I just assumed he had a plan."

"Maybe. I don't know—the guy seems nice enough, all things considered, but just like this Walmart, something feels super off."

"I agree, but a trip to D.C. alone doesn't seem like a great option, either. If Luka is anything like what else is out there, I doubt many would survive a trip like that alone."

"Yeah, I suppose so. Considering how it's all set to end, though…"

"What are you getting at?" Ren said, almost offended.

"Why even bother taking the trip when you already know the destination?" Ren paused, loading the cart up with another case of water, surprised by the directness of the question.

"I guess what is in between. When you boil life down, how is it really any different? We all go through life knowing how it all ends, knowing the destination." Tama went quiet, Ren's answer much darker than he had expected.

"That's valid. Though I don't think many live their lives dwelling on that. It's less an inevitability of life rather than whatever this agreement between you and Elio is. You promised yours to another, forcing an earlier-than-intended exit."

"It was that or die on that rooftop. Or worse, put the blood of a stranger in my hands—a stranger that had just saved my life to begin with. Something I don't think I am ready to do, something I would do anything right now to avoid."

"I could have taken him and never looked back," Tama said proudly. Ren rolled his eyes.

"I find it hard to believe sometimes that you are part of me. Well, we're part of me."

"The best part, I would say," Tama said with a sassy grin.

"Something tells me I may be better off," Ren replied with an equally snarky smile. "We have the water. Let's find the others."

"Hehehe," a menacing voice laughed from behind. "Seems you two missed the sign at the entrance." Ren and Tama slowly turned around. Standing in front of them was a middle-aged man dressed in full Walmart-branded camo. His face was painted up like a clown, his hair long and unkempt, with a demented grin peeled across his face. Yet compared to whatever stood next to him, the camo-dressed circus was barely even notable: a massive gorilla with its face also painted to resemble that of a clown. Sitting atop its head was a pink pair of cat ears, and in each hand was a monstrous chainsaw. The one in the right hand was spray-painted neon green; the other in the left hand was neon pink. The most disturbing thing was the creature's face. Its eyes were hollowed out—deep black voids of nothingness—while its mouth was stitched shut with a bright neon pink thread, adding to its disgusting appearance.

"Seems our guests either can't read or are just rude. Thoughts, Bozo?" There was an awkward silence. "You're right—they must also be deaf to ignore our kind greeter and delightful customer service assistant at the self-checkout. I am thinking we have a couple of rudey-patooties." He finished with a deep, dry laugh.

"Larry and Bozo, I presume?" Tama said aloud to Ren.

"Sorry, the greeter told us to make it quick and that it was okay to grab some water and be on our way. Again, so sorry. We will be going now," Ren said.

"You hear that, Bozo? Kid can talk to the decapitated, and he's not deaf or blind to boot." The camo clown wandered over to the green chainsaw and gave it a long rip as it fired up. Yelling over the aggressive hum as the chain bounced atop the painted concrete floor, he continued. "You know what's worse than little assholes that don't listen to the kind warnings of others—even ones written in blood?" He let the pink chainsaw rip. "Liars!" he shouted before breaking into a disturbed laugh. He pulled from his back a five-foot-long branch trimmer, brandished like a sword. With one swift yank of the cord, it fell into sync with the chainsaws rattling in the giant gorilla's hands.

"RUN!" Elio yelled from behind the crazy pair before firing a rifle at the camo-dressed man and dashing away. The bullet flew by and blasted through a nearby case of water.

"You heard the man—RUN!" snapped Tama. The disturbing cackle came to an abrupt stop.

"You can run, but you can't hide. You're in Larry's world now!"

CHAPTER SEVEN

Just Another Day at Walmart

Ren dashed over to a nearby Mountain Dew display and scooped up Tama before getting back on two feet and bolting down the aisle. Cans popped and hissed as the mountainous gorilla tore through the display with a furious swing of his chainsaws.

As Tama and Ren fled, four small balls of condensed electricity formed in the surrounding air. Each one launched backward at the advancing threat. Ren glanced down to see Tama's tails glowing a bright yellow.

"New trick?"

"Another time!" Tama snapped as he hurled two more at the massive gorilla. Ren turned to the right, down a long freezer section, to see Lilly casually perusing the aisle.

"Lilly, RUN!" Ren yelled as he grabbed hold of her hand and pulled her behind him. The ominous smoke that lurked below her baggy outfit quickly dispatched his clutch with a smack on the hand.

"We can't leave behind the food. Elio said we needed it," Lilly said as the smoke retreated under the clothes, and Lilly skipped back to the cart just as the end of the freezer section shattered to pieces. The two massive chainsaws tore through it like butter as the freezer unit went dark, and glass flew everywhere.

"Bozo," Lilly said flatly as the gorilla approached slowly while dragging the running chainsaws across the concrete floor. "Where is Scary Larry?" she asked aloud to no one in particular.

"He went after Elio. Look, Lilly, the food doesn't matter. We need to go, NOW!"

"Elio is in danger. You need to go back for him."

"He's in danger!? Do you not see that thing in front of you? We're in danger!"

Lilly turned toward Ren. "Please, Ren, Tama. Go save Elio. I don't want to lose anyone else. I can't," she said as the gorilla raised the right saw up above its head.

"Lilly! Look out!" they yelled together as the saw came rushing down and a massive, smoke-scaled claw caught it midway.

"I said go!" Lilly yelled. "Haku and I can handle Bozo. GO!" she said as Haku pushed away the chainsaw, forcing it to crash onto the concrete floor. Tama and Ren glanced at one another before turning around. With one last pause, they turned the corner and rushed back toward Elio as another gunshot rang through the store.

"She will be fine… right?" Ren asked Tama as they dashed down another aisle, aiming in the gunshot's direction.

"Her? What about us? If she would rather stay back there with Bozo, just what kind of crazy are we rushing toward?"

"I hadn't even thought of that," Ren said as they once again set eyes on Scary Larry. Elio was on his back, propped slightly up by his wrists. A medium-sized rifle was lying on the ground to his left. Larry was standing over him with his long buzzing sword pointed directly at Elio's neck.

"Shoot at me once and miss—shame on you. Miss me twice… well, you're just a bad shot. What? You didn't practice for the end of the world?" He let out a gruesome laugh. "You think you can just waltz into Larry's world and take whatever you damn well please?" He licked his lips slowly, smearing the cheap Walmart face paint as his tongue made its lap. "WRONG!" Larry barked, as if the devil itself was trying to escape his throat. His right eye did a spastic twitch. "This is Larry's world, and you're just living in it. Well, you were, anyway." He let out another laugh as the swirling blade slowly moved toward Elio's neck.

Tama quickly summoned a ball of fire and launched it at Larry, clipping him on the right side of his face in a dusty puff of paint powder and flame. Tama hopped from the safety of Ren's hold as he formed another ball of flame and fired it at Larry. Ren rushed to Elio and took his hand. Elio winced.

"We got you," he said, pulling him up to his feet, the pair beginning their retreat.

"The hell you think you're going?" Larry snapped, wiping the fire from his face—skin and blood with it. "We are only getting started here," he said as he licked the sizzling flesh off his face and let out an unhinged cry of pleasure. "Now it's getting fun!" He turned his attention to the fleeing pair. Ren stumbled, and Elio's hand fell loose. Ren fell hard on top of the rifle, his head ringing and vision hazy. Larry closed the distance between them and slapped Elio hard in the face with the back of his left hand, knocking him to the ground. Then he turned his aggressive blade back to Ren, who was struggling to get back to his feet.

"Game over!" Larry said, thrusting the chained blade toward Ren's back, only to be clipped again in the head with another projectile—this time, a ball of electricity. The pulse caught him off guard, and he dropped the trimmer next to Ren as Ren grabbed the rifle, rolled over, and pulled the trigger on Larry. The bullet flew clear through his chest, chased by another shot, then another. Each one exited cleanly through to the other side, lodging in the ceiling above. Ren kicked himself out from under Larry's stance as Larry dropped to his knees, still laughing uncontrollably as blood poured from his burned face before, finally, his head hit the floor and his body went quiet.

Lilly rounded the corner as Ren swung the gun at her and pulled the trigger, and everything went dark.

Opening his eyes, Ren no longer found himself in the Walmart he had been in only a few seconds ago. Instead, he was in the drinks aisle of a small gas station. In his right hand was an energy drink, and in the left was a bag of cheese-flavored Chex Mix. A little bell above the front door rang out through the small store. He could hear a loud commotion at the register. Curious, Ren turned toward the noise and bumped into a man dressed in full black, only his eyes visible, before the collision sent them both to the ground.

"Watch it!" the man in black barked as something dropped from his hand. A loud bang rang out through the store as the man yelled out in pain. His head ringing, Ren turned to the source of the loud noise to see thin smoke floating slowly from the hole at the end of a small pistol only an arm's reach away.

Without even thinking, Ren grabbed the smoking gun and pointed it at the stranger, scooting backward across the floor until being stopped by a shelving unit behind him.

"St… stay away. I will shoot," he said to the man in black as he gripped his bleeding leg and turned his attention to the scared kid in front of him.

"You little shit!" he yelled, reaching with his other hand behind him as Ren closed his eyes and pulled the trigger. The man dropped to the floor with a thud. The freezer behind him cracked, painted red with the man's blood.

Ren's eyes were now hazy from the growing anxiety, his head still ringing as a shadow rounded the corner to the left. Ren, overwhelmed, pointed the gun at the incoming shadow and, as the figure followed, Ren pulled the trigger, and everything returned to black.

The gun was out of ammo. Nothing happened; however, not before Haku had encased Lilly in a thick veil of deep black smoke. A massive smoke-scaled tail extended out and smacked the rifle out of Ren's hands, disappearing as it flew across the store.

"What the fuck, Ren!" Elio snapped. "You could have killed her. What the hell were you thinking?"

"I, uh… I don't know what happened," he said, looking around. He was back at the Walmart. Larry lay dead at his feet in a pool of warm blood. "Oh my God! Lilly, I didn't mean to." Ren panicked as he realized what had just happened. The surrounding smoke faded back into her large hoodie.

"No worries. Haku said it was an accident. Otherwise, you would be next to Scary Larry." Blood seeped through her baggy sleeve.

"You're hurt!" Ren said, concerned. "Oh my God, I am so sorry."

"Oh?" she said, lifting her arm up to peek. "This wasn't you. Bozo got in a couple good shots in before you took out Larry." She rolled her sleeve up to reveal dozens of cuts and scars running to the recent addition. Smoke flowed down from the top of the sleeve and plucked a thick piece of glass from the wound before wrapping it in a thin layer of smoke. Once wrapped, Lilly rolled her sleeve back down. "All good. Haku took care of it," she said with a smile. The smoky bandage was visible through the small tear from the glass.

Lilly looked over at Larry, his body slowly being encased in pooling blood. Three large holes swelled with charred blood on his back.

"Back to shopping?" she asked innocently as she turned her attention back to Elio. "I don't think we will have any more trouble." Ren, Elio, and Tama all passed glances around before turning back to her, and Elio responded.

"I suppose so. Let's wrap this up and get the hell out of this place." Ren still felt confused about what had happened. Where was he when his eyes closed? Was it a dream? And if so, why did it all feel so real? Elio gave him a soft nudge. "You okay, kid? You seem like you just saw a ghost."

"Yeah, I am. It's just a lot to take in so fast. That's all." He glanced down at the lifeless camo clown that had just tried to cut his head off. "I don't think I will ever get used to this."

"That seems like a normal reaction. Not sure what kind of person would," Elio said, noting the young girl impatiently waiting to get back to shopping. "Well, I guess we might have some idea."

"Screw him, I say," said Tama. "Let's get back to our shopping and grab a snack while you're at it. All those fireballs and sparks of electricity tired me out," he said as he started back toward their abandoned cart where they had first bumped into Scary Larry.

"Well, I guess that's that," Elio said, noting Tama walking away. "I didn't even get shot this time," he joked, rubbing his bullet wound from the other day. "Let's meet back up at the front of the store in fifteen minutes, tops. I am going to go grab a couple more guns and some ammo and then circle back through for some other items," he said as he wandered off in the opposite direction of Tama. Lilly rushed off after Tama before being greeted by a ball of flame surrounding him. Disappointed, she pivoted back toward the freezer section where she had fought Bozo.

Ren sighed and glanced down again at the limp body slowly draining of blood. Out of nowhere, the body jolted, shocking Ren backward to the floor. Coughing violently, Larry's head twitched and quivered in the blood before his gaze locked with Ren.

"You saw it, didn't you?" he said, his voice bubbling with the blood trapped in his throat. "The truth of the lie that surrounds us. REALITY!" he barked as the weight of his head became too much and plunged back down into the bloody concrete floor. His voice faded as his words joined his body in death. "Lies… it's all a lie…"

Each word was weaker as they gurgled in the blood, his last words. Scary Larry, the Walmart camo clown, was finally dead.

Shaken to his core, Ren sat there in silence, waiting for the body to twitch back to life once again. One minute, then two minutes, then five minutes passed when Tama returned in search of his missing shopping buddy. He glanced over at the lifeless corpse on the ground and then at Ren. Tama broke the silence.

"You okay?" he asked before turning back to Larry. "Wait… did he move?"

"Yeah," Ren responded dryly.

"Yeah, you are okay, or yeah, he moved?" Tama said, slowly backing up from the blood-riddled, camo-dressed corpse.

"He moved," Ren said flatly as he stood up slowly.

"You wanna elaborate at all on either part?"

"Not really," he said, walking back toward their cart.

"Okay," Tama said, taking one last look at what remained of Larry before scampering after Ren. "You know… you can talk to me. I am the best at keeping secrets. Well, your secrets anyway, since no one else can understand me."

"Not now, Tama. I don't feel like talking."

"I understand that," he said, lying through his teeth, before continuing. "Screw that Larry guy, right? You really messed him up."

"Shut up, Tama," Ren snapped. "I didn't mean to kill him. I don't even know what I am doing or why I am here. It was an accident… a reaction. It was me or him. I had no choice." He started to tear up. "I could have killed Lilly, too." Everything that had taken place over the past couple of days was catching up with him. "Why did I have to be woken up? Why couldn't I have just stayed blissfully asleep, dead to the world? Dead, the way I should be after what I did."

"Huh?" Tama said, confused.

"And you. Why is it that after all the bullshit, I ended up with a pissy-ass, cynical cat? Elio gets a badass bear, and Lilly, a dragon of all things." Tama stopped walking alongside him.

"It's amazing, you know," Tama said as a tear dripped from his eye. "How could I be the worst part of your personality, and you still be such an asshole comparatively?"

"Tama, I… I didn't mean to."

"No, you're right… it is time for Tama to just shut up. Let's get our shit and get out of here. The faster we reach D.C., the sooner Elio can put a bullet in our brains, and this will all be over." Another tear dripped out as he walked past Ren.

"I…" Realizing there was no point right now, Ren held his tongue and went about gathering up their task items of food and such silently. For the first time since he had woken up, Ren felt alone.

CHAPTER EIGHT

Lost Memories and Found Nightmares

The following fifteen minutes crawled by in awkward silence. Ren slowly pushed the well-stocked cart down various aisles while Tama rode along quietly at the front, perched atop their collection of canned items such as green beans, baked beans, tuna, and chicken, along with some applesauce and various canned fruits and fruit cocktails. All of it was piled up on a few cases of water that sat below, with three more cases tucked tightly on the under-rack.

"We should head back to the others," Tama said under his breath.

"I said I was sorry, Tama."

"Save it," he said, turning his nose back to the front of the cart.

Ren sighed, disappointed, and turned the cart around as they started their way back to the front of the store.

Rounding the corner, Elio was standing alone with a cart loaded to the brim with boxes of ammo and what looked like two rifles pointing out at the front.

"How did the shopping go?" Elio asked as they approached, taking in the well-stocked cart of canned goods. "Looks to have been pretty productive," he said with a satisfied grin.

"Yeah, guess so," Ren said flatly. "Just curious—how exactly are you planning to take all this with us?" He glanced at his cart. "Pushing this all the way can't be the plan."

Elio let out a hearty laugh.

"We are going to drive."

An answer so obvious, yet so unexpected. Ren had never even considered just hopping into a car and driving.

"I never even thought about that."

"Yeah, I mean, why not? In an entire world full of abandoned cars, it should be easy enough to find one or two with some gas still inside of them. We'll just load one up and drive till we can't anymore."

Elio's eyes shifted from Ren to Lilly, who was now within sight. In front of her was an overflowing cart of jerky, chips, and boxes of various granola bars.

"Well, if this world doesn't kill us, that cart might," Elio said with a chuckle.

"They are out of jerky," Lilly said, disappointed. Nearly a hundred bags piled high in the cart next to her.

"That's a bummer. I wonder why?" Elio said with a smile—a smile that felt unfamiliar to Ren. The smile of a father.

"Well, let's load up a car and get out of this cursed place," Ren said, pushing his cart toward the door of the store.

The gap they had slipped through earlier that day was now sealed tight.

"Do you have a death wish?" Lilly said curiously as Ren stopped his advance toward the door, seeing a strange glow on the other side. The day had gone by in a blur, and the sun had clocked out for the night.

"Death wish?" he replied, confused, as the glowing light smashed violently into the other side of the door. A green liquid oozed down the glass where it made contact. Staring back at him through the smeared glass was a ravenous soul, not unlike those they had passed by earlier in the day—the same ones that cowered in the shadows.

The creature looked almost like a raccoon. Its eyes were a deep, bright red, while its fur was encased with a glowing hue of black and white that made it look almost ghostlike in the glass's reflection. Locking eyes again with Ren, the creature snarled. The green substance on the door leaked from its mouth as it lunged again at the glass, to the same result. Elio stepped behind Ren and placed his hand on his left shoulder.

"That is why we won't be traveling at night."

"Why is it doing that?" Ren asked as the creature once again smashed into the glass. Its face was now completely covered with its own green blood. Its nose now tilted sideways, and its right eye was so swollen the creature could no longer see out of it.

"When the sun sets, the unbound lose all rational thought—almost like a house pet or wild animal infected with rabies." Another thud from the creature, though it seemed to be slowing down.

"Hundreds of thousands of the unbound wander the streets and alleys during the day, innocent enough as the sun lights the day." Another thud. This time, the glass gave in slightly with a small crack. "However, when the sun goes down, they turn into what you see now. It's very important that, no matter what happens, we are in a well-lit and secure place when the sun goes down."

"It's not just at night," Lilly said, walking over slowly. "Unbound souls left in the dark for too long will also turn."

"One or two is easy enough to deal with, since with the loss of logic also comes the loss of whatever magic or ability the soul may have had when bound to a master."

"They're like zombies!" Lilly said with uncomfortable excitement. "Really dumb and easy to deal with in small numbers. However, in large numbers, the threat becomes all too real."

"Not a fan of that comparison, but it works. The point is, avoid the dark and never go out after the sun sets. It will be very important to remember if we ever get separated."

Elio looked back at the carts. Tama sat quietly and uninterested between them.

"Did something happen between you and Tama? Usually, he is right up your ass."

Ren glanced over to the closest thing he had to an actual friend, then back to Elio. Tama, curious and close enough to hear the response, perked his ears up to listen.

"Yeah. I said something I really shouldn't have—things I didn't even mean. Everything that's happened overwhelmed me a bit, and I took it out on him. He didn't deserve that."

Tama smiled. Tama knew that Ren didn't mean it, but the reality was that even if he didn't mean what he said, it was true, and that was why it hurt so much. Compared to Gur or Haku, his size and current ability paled compared to either of them.

Tama stood up and made his way over to Ren and Elio. Ren locked eyes with him, knowing he had heard his words and that they were good now. He was forgiven.

"I'm hungry, and we are going to need another Walmart if you two don't do something about her." Tama motioned toward Lilly, already three bags deep into the jerky in her cart. "That soul of hers is always active. It can't be easy on her to maintain that. The amount of energy needed would kill most after only an hour, much less all the time."

"We may need a truck to keep her fed," Ren said to Elio. "Tama says her appetite is most likely because of her soul."

"I figured. It can't be easy for someone of her size to have all that power constantly active."

"Tama said she should probably be dead."

"I wonder how she does it. Or maybe it's Haku, throttling their power. Maybe that's why we never see their full form—only smoky bits and limbs from time to time."

"That, or Haku is so powerful, that's all they need," Tama chimed.

"Well, let's join her for some last-minute shopping and food. Then get some much-needed rest for the night. It's been a long day and, frankly, I am over it."

Ren glanced back at the glass door before turning to follow

Elio. The creature on the other side, no longer able to stand, aimlessly scratched at the door with one paw before finally succumbing to its end.

"Stupid bastard!" Tama said, sickly satisfied with the creature's end. "Come on, Ren. You're hungry, so feed me."

"Yeah," Ren said as he joined the others.

"Last chance to grab anything else you think you may need," Elio said. "Though don't get too attached to anything, since space will be an issue, and food and water will take priority." Elio grabbed another cart. "Fifteen minutes, no longer. Never know what may still lurk out there, even if we are inside of a crazy clown's Walmart."

Elio picked up one of the two rifles, a small single-shot weapon used for hunting small to medium-sized game or amateur home defense.

"Be right back," he said as he disappeared once again into the depths of the deals that once were.

Lilly hopped up, tossing aside her fifth or sixth empty bag of jerky.

"I'ma go look for more snacks. Do you want anything?" she asked, looking at Tama.

"What about me?" Ren asked, insulted.

"What about you?" she said, getting closer to Tama, who quickly took note and dashed behind Ren.

Tama shook his head from left to right.

"No, he is all set."

"Okay!" she yelled before dashing off to a cart and hopping in with a gentle lift from Haku. She rode away as a small fan of smoke propelled the cart, and they disappeared into the depths of the store and its maze of discount-filled aisles.

"Well, guess it's just us now," Ren said, opening and taking a rip into a chocolate chip granola bar. His mouth was still full while he continued. "What you wanna do?"

Disgusted with the chewing speech, Tama turned away.

"Might as well look around as well. Time's ticking, though, so we better get going."

Ren took another bite as he meandered over to an empty nearby cart. Tama hopped, and they wandered back into the cursed store.

Rolling along through the desolate Walmart, Ren was still working through the events that took place earlier with Larry. What happened? And was it real?

"I should have asked this earlier, but are you alright?" Tama asked from the basket of the cart, shaking Ren from his own thoughts.

"Yeah, I think so…" He paused. "I can trust you, right?" Ren asked ominously, unconcerned with how the question may come off in his search for honesty.

"I mean, obviously. I am your soul, after all. Even if you couldn't trust me, it's not like anyone can understand me anyway."

Ren paused.

"Earlier, with Larry… something happened. Something that I can't explain." Ren threw some gummies into the cart—not one or two, but ten boxes.

"Oh?"

"Yeah, I was in a small gas station. Not unlike the same one we spent our first night in."

"Lucky we didn't bump into one of those psycho unbound souls," Tama interrupted as he watched Ren toss a couple of bags of Chex Mix into the cart.

Ren paused again as he stared at the familiar bags.

"The store was getting robbed, I think, and I unexpectedly shot one of the armed men after bumping into him. His gun went off and took out the man's knee. Almost compulsorily, I grabbed the lone gun and finished the job."

"Sounds pretty cut-and-dry self-defense."

"Yeah, but soon after, another person rounded the corner, and I unflinchingly pulled the trigger out of panic."

"Was it another robber?" Tama asked curiously.

"I don't know. When I opened my eyes, I was back—the gun pointed at Lilly. The trigger pulled."

Ren stopped, letting go of the cart as it slid only a couple of inches on its own. Tama glanced back to see Ren's eyes well up with tears.

"Tama, I almost killed her. I killed Larry, but I can't shake the feeling that what I saw, what I did in that gas station, was just as real." He wiped the soggy emotions from his face, one salty drop after another. "Why can't I remember anything?"

"I mean, you told Elio about your childhood. That's real, right? A memory."

"Yeah, maybe you're right. But what if it's not? And even if it is real, there's nothing else. Just a traumatic childhood and then nothing. Nothing until I woke up in that bed only a few days ago. Nothing until I met you."

"Hey, don't forget I can't remember anything either. Perhaps we should ask the others. Maybe they have some insight."

"Maybe…"

"I would keep the whole gas station thing between us, though—at least for now. They might start thinking you are as crazy as Larry." Tama paused. "Come on, let's head back to the others."

"Yeah… Tama," Ren said, grabbing hold of the cart's handle with his salty hands.

"What's up?"

"Thanks."

"Yeah, yeah. Don't be getting all mushy on me now."

Ren turned the cart around, and they started back toward the store entrance.

"Hey, Ren."

"Yeah, Tama."

"Maybe rethink the whole 'sacrifice yourself for Elio' plan you have. I know, all things considered, it's hard to think of a reason to keep going, but… there is more to life than just its end. Just give it some thought, okay?"

Ren didn't respond right away. Tama's words hit deep and unexpectedly. What was this emotion? As if he had never known what it was to be cared about or missed. It filled him with an unfamiliar joy.

"I will, Tama," he said with a smile as Elio and Lilly came into sight once again. They were sitting down around a small fire, bringing a new depth of light to the poorly lit Walmart.

"Welcome back, you two," Elio said as he gently set another piece of cheap starter wood atop the small pit of flame.

Lilly quickly perked up and rushed over to see and pet Tama, an effort wasted as Tama had already vacated the cart in preparation and was making his way over to the fire. A curious Lilly peeked up and over the side of the cart, only to be disappointed.

"I was about to come search for you two. Saved me a trip." Elio opened his pocket and pulled out the small container that held his soul, Gur, within. "Come on out, big guy. Time to stretch your legs," he said as a bright light flashed and dissipated to reveal Gur sitting in its place. "Atta boy," Elio said as he took a large bag of jerky from Lilly's collection.

Ren sat down across from Elio, Tama to his left next to Gur, who sat quietly next to Elio. Lilly, still disappointed at losing the jump on her prey, sat across from Tama, her eyes locked onto him with determination.

Snacking on grilled jerky and granola bars, it went quiet, almost eerily so. Only the flicker of the flames filled the empty department store when Ren finally broke the silence.

"What do you two remember, you know, from before everything happened?"

Elio raised his right eyebrow.

"Interesting question. Why do you ask?"

"Well, outside of bits and pieces of my childhood—the shitty ones at that—I can't seem to remember anything from before I woke up. I was just curious if it was just me?"

Elio slouched over into Gur, who now fully supported him upright as he sat.

"Hadn't really thought about it, to be honest. The world burns down around you, and the mind seems to forget the little thing that made us who we are today." He paused. "I will be damned. Outside of the day it happened, I can't remember much of anything either—outside of the fact that I really enjoy cooking and am good at it, to boot."

"Isn't that weird?"

"I mean, what about the way the world is now isn't a bit weird? Did you already forget about Scary Larry a few aisles over?"

"I mean, yeah, but…"

Lilly raised her head from her cold lock on Tama and interrupted Ren.

"I don't remember anything either." She paused. "But I have this recurring dream nearly every night, and when it's over, after I scare myself awake, it feels so real. Almost like I was there."

Tama and Ren shared a glance, each having the same thought.

"You want to share?" Ren asked, almost overwhelmed with curiosity. Catching himself, he added, "I mean, if you want to. You don't have to, though."

Lilly looked down at the floor; her voice grew shaky.

"I am standing in a room, a dark room. There is something in my right hand. Curiously, I look to see what it is, but I know what it is. I know every time I look. A long-bladed kitchen knife, covered in warm red blood. Glancing back, I see that drops have followed me from wherever it was I came from, from wherever the knife got its fresh coating of blood. I look forward, over at the bed, its lone occupant silently sleeping to the left side. Their companion is missing. I lose control of myself, as if someone else is driving my body while I watch aimlessly. Slowly, I approach the side of the bed, the knife still dripping as I step quietly across the carpeted floor."

Elio and Ren listened in silence as she continued.

"I watch as my right hand rises into the air, the blade glistening red off the moonlight from the nearby window. My vision is blurry with tears, I think, as I drive the blade down into the sleeping body."

Her tone shifted immediately after the story ended.

"And then I am back here, or rather, wherever I was asleep. Haku's warm embrace there to comfort me back to sleep."

Tama stood up and slowly made his way around the fire and over to Lilly. He crawled up and into her lap, where he lay down and closed his eyes. A tear formed in Lilly's right eye as she gently pet him in silence.

Elio and Ren, unsure of what to say after everything, remained silent. All eyes watched as the flames softly danced atop the wood and ash. One by one, they succumbed to the long day and drifted to sleep.

CHAPTER NINE
The Collector

Ren awoke to the sound of a cart squeaking as it rolled. Slowly sitting up, he wiped the sleep away to see Elio making his way out of the store with the cart loaded with ammo, guns, and other survival supplies. To his left, Lilly was still sound asleep on her side. Tama lay atop her like a human mattress. However, Tama was awake and quietly watching as Elio shuffled about while preparing to head out.

Ren stood up, wandered over to another cart, and followed Elio outside of the store. Stepping outside, Ren noticed the deceased soul to the left of the door. Its head was so damaged from the consistent contact with the glass window, it was almost unrecognizable as the same creature he saw the night prior.

"Still sleeping the day away, I see," Elio said, placing his cart on the sidewalk. Grabbing two large gas cans from the cart, he turned and stepped out into the parking lot. Ren parked his cart next to Elio's and followed him.

"Yeah, sorry about that," he said, finally catching up.

"Yeah, yeah." Elio tossed one of the two gas cans over to him. "Anything fancy your taste?" Elio asked as he gazed out into the sea of abandoned cars lined up side by side.

"I guess a truck would be good, or maybe an SUV. Anything with a lot of space would be ideal." They wandered along for a couple of minutes when Ren broke the silence and asked, "So, you also don't remember anything, right? But have you had any weird…" He paused. He wanted to word it correctly to avoid drawing any follow-up questions. Elio interrupted his train of thought.

"Any messed-up dreams like the girl? Nah. Can't say that I have. Poor girl must have seen some shit before the world went upside down. In her case, not remembering anything might even be a twisted blessing."

"Yeah, that was a lot. I still don't even know what to say to her."

"Nothing. Mind your own business. If she wants to talk about it, then let her. But from the way she sounded, that wasn't easy for her." This side of Elio caught Ren a little by surprise. It was almost as if he were protecting her.

"I guess you're right."

"Damn straight, I am," he said as his voice drifted away from the current topic. "What about that one?" he said, raising his right hand and pointing over at a yellow—though slightly dimmed from constant exposure to the sun—school bus. Six of them were parked side by side. "One of those bad boys ought to be able to haul us and all our shit, and it comes with extra gas from the others to boot."

"Not a terrible option. Plenty of space too; even Gur can fit,"

Ren said with a playful smile and set the empty can down. Elio rolled his eyes, unmoved at all by the comment. "Head back and get the girl up. Then push the rest of the supplies out. I will top the best bus off and fill the two tanks. Shouldn't take long, so I will be along shortly. Have her and everything ready."

"Sure." Ren nodded. Elio set down his can and quickly got to work inspecting the buses. Ren followed Elio's instructions and made his way back to Walmart to get ready. As he meandered back alone, he looked toward the Walmart and the massive wall that stood only a few miles behind it—a remarkable, massive structure that, if it were true, ran along at least half the East Coast. But why? And how did it get there to begin with? Was it keeping something out? Or perhaps something in? But if so, then what? It slowly disappeared as he grew closer to the store. Wandering past the two carts already outside, he made his way inside the store.

"Alright, time to get up. Elio will be along shortly with our new wheels," he announced as he reached their campsite, only to realize that Lilly and Tama were nowhere to be seen. "Tama? Lilly?" he said aloud, to no response. Ren looked around and yelled out again, this time louder. "TAMA! Lilly! Where did you go?"

"Would you keep it down?" Tama said, rounding the corner. "Some of us don't wake up as chipper as others." Lilly was behind him, pushing along another well-stocked cart of goodies, this time loaded up with dozens upon dozens of various nuts. A few dozen more bags of jerky mixed in.

"Everyone was gone when we woke up, so we went to grab more snacks," Lilly said as she opened a small plastic sleeve of peanuts and began tossing them into her mouth by the handful.

"Figured we should take one more lap before heading out," Tama said. "And this one here was already tearing into our jerky reserves, so it can't hurt to have extra food." Ren let out a massive sigh of relief.

"You scared the shit out of me," he said as Tama hopped down from the cart and waltzed back over to his side. "I thought something bad might have happened to you."

"Nope. All good here," Lilly said, unfazed by Ren's concern, as she tore open another sleeve of nuts.

"As you can see, we are fine. Besides, what's going to happen to us with Haku around? Pretty sure if we keep the girl all gassed up with food, we will be unstoppable," Tama laughed.

"Not funny, Tama. I was legit worried."

"Save the concern for when it's needed," Elio said, stepping inside. "Those two wandering off will probably be the least of our concerns as we venture out to D.C." He looked around. "I see they're awake, but why the hell isn't everything outside?" He shrugged while assuming control of the newly added cart of nuts to the collection and giving it a shove toward the door. "Everyone, grab a cart and come check out our new home on wheels."

"I wanna see!" Lilly yelled with excitement, quickly dashing over to the jerky-and-granola-filled cart and rushing after Elio. Tama hopped up into the remaining cart as Ren took control and followed the others.

"A school bus!" Lilly yelled with glee as she abandoned the cart and ran aboard. The top of her head was visible as she ran up and down the narrow aisle.

"I placed the two cans of gas in the very back. Capped tight, so the smell shouldn't be all that bad."

"Plenty of windows to air it out if needed, anyway," Ren said in support.

"I love it!" Lilly said, dashing out of the front, hopping over the three steps that led up into the bus.

"Let's load it up and get the hell out of here before we attract any more crazy."

"Do you think anyone else is even bothering to play the game?" Ren asked as he handed Elio the contents of the nut cart, who then passed the items to Lilly, who energetically ran them to their proper place in one of the four seats at the back of the bus, as directed by Elio.

With a proper system in place, thirty minutes passed, and the bus was nearly all loaded up—the last cart being that of the water and canned goods Ren and Tama had collected. While handing a case of water to Elio, something caught Ren's attention off in the distance.

"What's that?" Ren asked, pointing off into the distance. Elio turned to look, setting the water down inside the bus. Lilly hopped up into a seat and popped her head out an open window. Standing atop the ridge they had come from the day prior was a tall human silhouette. Gathered around and illuminating the surrounding ridge was a flurry of glowing colors.

"The Collector," Lilly said, almost impressed.

"The Collector? Who is that?" Ren asked.

"We need to go, NOW!" snapped Elio. He picked up the last

case of water and quickly set it down on the nearest seat before getting in the driver's seat.

"But what about the rest of the water?" Ren asked, only to be interrupted by an increasingly agitated Elio.

"Fuck the water. Get on the goddamn BUS!"

"The dead don't need water," Lilly said as she slipped back into her seat, pushing the window closed. Ren glanced at Tama with concern and followed Elio's instructions, hopping on the bus as the engine turned and the door slammed shut.

"Lilly, get all the windows up and locked. Ren, grab me a rifle from the back and pick your own weapon."

"Sure. Is anyone going to explain what's going on?"

"I will explain later… if there is a later, that is. Now go!" Elio snapped as the engine revved up as much as a well-used school bus could as it launched out of the parking lot exit.

Ren made his way to the back and grabbed Elio's rifle. Next to it was a black case that he picked up by the handle. Ren looked out the back window of the bus to see a flurry of color cascading over the ridge like a rainbow as it descended into the parking lot. The mob of color tore through the sea of idle cars in the lot. Various explosions lit the view behind the bus with hues of orange and yellow. The glowing rainbow split into two trails. One plowed into the Walmart with brute force, while the other turned in pursuit of them—the silhouette flying atop a large flaming bird close behind the flurry of colors chasing the bus.

"Hurry up back there!" barked Elio from the driver's seat. Ren spun around and dashed past Lilly, who was closing the last window. Ren handed the rifle to Elio and then sat down in the seat diagonally from him. Opening the case, he pulled out an already assembled handgun.

"Should be in working order. I loaded it last night in preparation. Just toggle the safety if shit hits the fan," Elio said as the bus rattled, knocking the supplies in the back all over the place. Lilly let out a shocked scream as she tumbled to the aisle. Ren grabbed hold of the gun as he hit the floor. Returning to his feet, he saw a massive ball of fire hurling toward the bus.

"GET DOWN!" Ren yelled, diving to Lilly and cradling her as the ball of fire collided into a parked car to the right of the bus and exploded into a heap of fire and metal. The rear door of the bus flung open as various supplies flew out the back.

"You okay?" Ren said to Lilly, gently guiding her into a nearby seat, watching as her hidden protector faded back into the hoodie.

"Yeah," Lilly said with a confused nod. Ren's attention was now focused on the sea of color clearly visible through the open door. Dozens upon dozens of various souls rushed after them at full speed. Ren raised the handgun and pointed it not at the sea of souls, but at the human silhouette atop the fiery phoenix, and pulled the trigger.

Nothing happened. The trigger was firm and unresponsive. Ren then remembered what Elio had said and clicked the safety with his thumb. Aiming the gun again, he pulled the trigger. The unexpected kick of the gun startled his grip, and the handgun fell to the seat on the right. The silhouette twisted to the right as the bullet ripped through its shoulder, and it dropped from the fiery bird. A dozen souls quickly halted their advance on the bus to brace for its landing.

The remaining amassed army of glowing colors increased their determination, their speed overtaking the bus. Dozens of colors hurled themselves at the bus, smashing simultaneously into the side as it sped down the center of the road.

"We need to get these bastards off of us!" yelled Elio as he braced for another impact.

"What exactly does he want us to do?" Tama asked sarcastically. A feral-looking squirrel with blood-red eyes jumped through the open rear door of the bus. It landed aggressively in the amassed stash of nuts on the left rear seat of the bus, popping its head out before quickly dashing violently at Ren, as Tama pummeled it with a fireball while midair and returned it to the street behind in a fiery tumble.

"Whatever we are going to do, we need to do it fast! These little bastards are overwhelming us." The two large gas cans tucked off to the side caught Ren's attention. Tama flung another ball of fire at what resembled a rabid rabbit.

"I have an idea, but I need some of your fire," Ren said ominously to Tama.

"I like where this is going," Tama said as Ren reached over and pulled out both tanks of gas, unscrewing the caps on each.

"Why do I smell gas back there?" Elio echoed from the front of the bus.

"Hold on and hit the gas!" Ren yelled back down the aisle.

"Hit the gas, my ass. You think if this damn thing could go faster, I wouldn't be?" Ren threw one of the two jugs out the rear of the bus.

"Now, Tama!" Ren said as the gas can flew into the army of souls.

"Oi!" Tama said as three fireballs appeared in the surrounding air before launching toward the gas can. Ren then threw the second can out the rear, three fresh fireballs chasing it down as well. In the blink of an eye, two massive explosions rang out from the sea of glows.

The screams of one hundred souls rang out in the blast before coming to an abrupt stop as the bus sped away from the carnage. Lilly hung halfway out a shattered window while a smoky claw slapped off various lingering souls clung to the side of the bus. Tama followed suit, though in a much safer fashion, poking his head out the window before sending a small puff of fire trailing along to its target. Once the bus was visibly clear of threats, the three of them all sat in silence in the narrow aisle. Tama was in Ren's lap, who was across from Lilly.

"That was a lot," Ren said with a sigh.

"That was awesome!" Lilly said, her feet skidding back and forth with excitement. "Can we do that again?"

"She's crazy," Tama said, glancing at her with discomfort. The three of them stared out the rear of the bus as the blaze of souls faded away in the distance.

CHAPTER TEN
Upping the Stakes

After a couple of hours, the bus slowed down until finally coming to a complete stop. Elio turned, glanced down the aisle, and broke the silence.

"Not my ideal way to start the morning." He turned his attention to the open rear door and the various missing items from their stock of supplies, from the food to the gas. "Let's survey the damage and figure out what's next." Ren stood up, picking up Tama, followed by Lilly. Each of them hopped off the battle-ridden bus.

"Holy shit," Ren said in shock, taking in the damage, which grew worse the farther back they walked.

"Well, that was short-lived," Elio said as he surveyed the damage. "I am not sure how much farther she will make it." The metal of the rims etched into the pavement as the tires that previously coated them lay tattered about in the distance. The rear bumper was missing altogether, with various bite marks and chunks of missing metal scattered all about the outside of the bus.

"Guess it doesn't really matter now that all our gas went up in flames back there. We will need to find another vehicle. I think it's a major risk, but we need to travel straight through the night. I don't think anything that lurks in the night is as much of a threat as our new friend back there."

"About that," Ren said curiously. "Is anyone going to explain what the hell that was?"

"That was the Collector," Lilly said while eating a bag of jerky. She had returned to the bus and was now hanging out the window, suspended by Haku, who braced her from the inside. "Everyone knows the Collector." Ren glanced over at an equally confused Tama.

"Everyone except us, I guess," Ren said, turning to Elio for a more helpful explanation. Elio let out a sigh while looking around to see if there were any promising replacement vehicles close by.

"The Collector is the biggest threat in the game. Though no one knows who he is or what really drives him. He is the maddest man in a world of madmen. Possibly even more so than the very one that landed us all here in the first place." With another unhelpful response, Ren poked at his growing curiosity about the walls that surrounded them.

"Are we sure the world outside of the walls is the same? Like, I understand that some devastating event has affected everything contained inside. But what if, outside these gates, the world goes on just like before?"

"Are you questioning my recollection of what happened that day?" Elio snapped back, offended. "Need I remind you I was there? That I witnessed it happen with my own eyes. The event that took my wife and daughter from me."

"No, that's not what I am saying. Not at all. I just don't understand how the walls play into the event you describe. If it really was a random plot of some lunatic, then where did the walls come from? Not to mention the quote-unquote game referenced by the man on the phone. Why has everyone we bumped into not seemed to care about playing it?" Lilly went quiet, unable to answer any of Ren's questions. Equally unable to answer, Elio pivoted the topic back to more pressing concerns.

"Look, we can talk about all that tinfoil-hat shit later. Right now, we need to find new wheels before the Collector catches up to us."

"What about that?" Lilly said excitedly, pointing from the bus window. Unable to see what she was pointing at from her higher vantage point on the bus, Ren and Elio wandered over in her prompted direction. Tucked off the main road was an RV, sitting snug in a narrow driveway between two large duplexes.

"Well, color me impressed," said Elio as he walked closer. "Damned thing looks almost brand new. Let's get her backed out, and with any luck, we can get back on the road in no time. Best part, we don't need to haul gas with this bad boy. Unleaded all the way." Elio stepped inside, and soon after, the RV started up and slowly began backing up and out of its narrow parking space.

Walking slowly next to the crawling RV, they all arrived back at the highly damaged school bus. Ren turned to the bus to see an excited Lilly still hanging out the window in anticipation of the massive RV's arrival.

"Great find, kiddo," Elio said, impressed, as he stepped out of the RV. "This thing is fully kitted out with all the bells and whistles you would want for a trip along an apocalypse-ridden East Coast. It's even topped off on gas." Lilly quickly disappeared from the window and scampered out and around the bus before excitedly getting aboard their fancy new house on wheels.

"It even has beds!" Lilly echoed from inside. Elio smiled and turned to Ren.

"Let's get everything that survived transferred over and get out of here."

"Sounds good," Ren said, making his way back over to the rear of the bus to unload what remained. Only ten minutes later, everything had made its way from the battered bus over to the RV.

"Alright, let's get rolling," Elio said as he buckled into the driver's seat. "You know how to drive?" he asked Ren, who was sitting in the passenger seat next to him.

"Yeah, I think so." He scratched his head. "Another thing I don't fully remember, if I am being honest."

"Eh, not like you will hit anyone." Elio laughed. "We can rotate every six hours. That should get us far enough away from here and the Collector."

"What does he want with us, anyway?"

"Our souls!" Lilly said from behind them dramatically. "He comes for our souls." She made spooky noises while wiggling her fingers in the air while Haku fabricated little clouds of smoke ghosts.

"She is not wrong," Elio said, rolling his eyes. "As the name implies, he collects things. That being the souls of other Reapers." Ren glanced over at Tama.

"Wait, he can do that?"

"Technically, we all can. Though I never had any interest in trying it."

"I did once," echoed Lilly. "It felt wrong once I started, so I gave up."

"How does something like that even work?"

"Basically, there is about a minute after the owner of the soul dies that it's still alive, though less in the physical form. It is during this brief window of time that a new bond can be formed, or forced, with the soul, placing it under the control of a new wielder."

"So, the Collector and all those souls under his control…"

"At one point belonged to other Reapers just like us," Elio said, adjusting the mirrors on the RV.

"That's kind of messed up," Ren said in disbelief. "Why? What does he gain?"

"No idea."

"I overheard from Luka once that he was building an army. An army to take on whatever is on the other side of the walls," Lilly said, ripping into another packet of jerky.

"Well, something tells me his vendetta for us is a bit more personal now that Ren melted a portion of his collection."

"I may have shot him, too," Ren said, unsure.

"YOU DID WHAT!" Elio said, in shock.

"Was that bad?"

"No…" Elio started.

"He is just surprised," Lilly interjected. "There are a lot of rumors and stories of the Collector, but none of them ever end well for those in the stories."

"I assumed he was hunting us for Haku originally, but between you incinerating part of his collection and shooting him, Haku will just be the cherry on top once he catches up to us."

"Guess we should get going, then. The farther away from him we can get, the better."

"You seem to be a magnet for crazies. Before your lazy ass showed up, I was doing just fine in my high-class apartment living out the apocalypse. Now, two dead madmen later, I am on the run from the Collector. What's next? Not to mention, it doesn't help that we just spent most of the day now being chased in the wrong damn direction. Pretty sure I saw a sign that said we entered Georgia. Goddamn Georgia. The opposite side of where we started." He kicked the RV into drive, and they set off once again toward D.C.

"Don't be so negative," Lilly said, hanging upside down from the top bunk behind Elio's seat, right above the small couch and social area. "At least you're not alone," she said, with a pinch of raw emotion cracking through her otherwise childish demeanor.

"She is right," added Ren. "This would be far worse alone. After all, we have only made it this far together."

"Yeah, yeah. You want some positivity?" Elio said, rolling his eyes as they followed a sign. "I-ninety-five is the next right. Straight shot to D.C. from there." The look of lucky coincidence quickly swapped to confusion. "You hear that?" Elio said, looking around, his eyes locking in on Ren's pant pocket as Ren pulled out his phone. On the screen was the same ominous background as before and a timer that was running down from ten minutes. At the top right, the battery sat at thirty-three percent.

"That's unusual."

"What do you mean?" Ren asked as Lilly hit the floor with a thud, quickly picking herself up and rushing to the front cabin to join them.

"I wanna see!" she yelled as she entered. Ren turned the face of the phone so she could see.

"Since it all happened, I have only ever heard the usual first-time call, the same one we watched soon after we met."

"Wait, the same one? That wasn't live?"

"God no! As far as I know, it's a pre-recorded call that each person gets soon after they awaken. It was the same video that played for me only a day after it all went down." They all turned to the timer on the phone. "But that's new."

"What do you think it means?"

"No idea. We will just have to wait and see once the clock runs its course." Once the timer had one minute left, Elio slowed down a bit before coming to a complete stop, placing the RV in park. The sun slowly set off in the distance as the three of them gathered in the small social cabin area of the RV, all three close together, with Ren in the middle accompanied by Tama, who sat on his lap. All eyes locked on the timer as it ran down the last seconds. Three, two, one. The screen went black.

The sound of fireworks suddenly rang out from the phone's speakers, followed by an overly dramatic voice.

"Ladies and Gentlemen, I present to you…" A loud gunshot rang out, followed by a thud and a high-pitched screech.

"Every goddamn time," said a familiar voice, growing louder by the word. "Is it really so hard to get a simple 'we're going live' warning or countdown? I mean, even the local news can get this right." The cameraman trembled as the camera shakily followed the Madman as he bent over and picked the microphone up from next to the announcer as he lay dead in a warm pool of spreading blood. A massive hole, clean through his head.

"Hey, hey, hey. Tut, tut, tut—over here. No need for those watching at home to see that," he said, motioning toward the camera. "Let's keep the eyes over here, bucko. That is, unless you want to join our recently deceased friend." The camera shook from left to right before centering back on the strange man.

"I'm sure that many of you are wondering what exactly is going on. Well, no matter where you are watching from, or how."

"What does that mean? Is this live to everyone right now?" Ren asked, intrigued. Lilly spun around and looked out the window before excitedly pointing and saying.

"Look! He is everywhere." Ren and Elio turned to see at least a dozen screens, all playing the same stream. Somehow, the broadcast was on every screen within sight.

"How is that possible?" Ren asked. "The power is out nearly everywhere."

"How would I know? The guy obviously has power where he is, so maybe he can turn everything else on," Elio said.

"Makes as much sense as anything else going on, I suppose,"

Ren said as they returned their attention to the small display on Ren's phone propped up on the small table. The man continued.

"To be honest, I am just a bit bored. It's been so long since anyone bothered to play my game. Everyone has just grown so content these days, living their miserable lives in this hellhole we call home now. It's no different from before…" he paused, his words trailing as if he was in some sort of existential crisis. "So, I have decided to make things more interesting for the time being. Throwing a bit of gas on the fire. You could say a bit of transparency." The screen suddenly went black, the stream ending abruptly.

"What the hell just happened?" Elio snapped. Lilly spun up and around to look out the window.

"All black out there as well."

"Transparency? What does he mean by that?" Elio barked, frustrated at being left hanging on a cliffhanger. The screen flashed back on out of nowhere, the man visibly laughing uncontrollably with no audio. His mic was then unmuted.

"Well, they didn't like that." He continued laughing while they sat huddled together, awkwardly waiting. "Guess that's a hard pass on the whole transparency thing." He winked at the screen. "So, we will keep it simple, I guess. Everything you want for the rest of your miserable lives—no matter the request—you make it here first, and it's all yours." Then he mumbled something quietly under his breath before continuing. "A simple game with a simple reward. Fight your way through my Wonderland, find me, and win. Make your dreams a reality!" he said with a dramatic bow. Tilting his head up, he raised one eyebrow and looked directly into the camera. "I hope to see you soon," he said as a sinister grin crawled up his face before the camera cut back to black. The stream ended, and all of Wonderland returned to silence.

CHAPTER ELEVEN
More Questions

"Wait, wasn't that already the prize?" questioned a confused Ren.

"I mean, that's less vague, I suppose. I guess no one's interested in playing his warped little game, so he must up the ante a bit."

"Are we still going to play the game?" interjected a confused Lilly while everyone stood up from the small couch. "I like playing games," she said prematurely, disappointed. Elio sighed.

"That's still the plan," he said, noting that something was on Ren's mind. "What's up, Ren?"

"Oh," he said, coming back to the conversation. "It's weird."

"Obviously. Can you be a bit more specific about that?"

"Well, why did the stream get cut halfway through? And by who, exactly? Isn't he the one running Wonderland and facilitating the so-called game? And what was all that about transparency? Why was that the word that caused the broadcast to go down?"

"That's a lot of questions…" Lilly said, unsure of any helpful answer.

"It is. And then there is Ren's point. Why adjust the prize? Or rather, demystify the prize. What can he really offer as a prize when the world he blasted away is over? What does everything even mean?"

"A way to the other side of the wall?" Ren said, following along, though not fully sure to what end. "What if the prize really has nothing to do with what's inside the walls, but outside?" Elio's eyes went cold as the potential of Ren's words set in.

"NO!" he snapped, interrupting Ren's train of thought. "That can't be right. It can't be. That would mean…"

"Yeah…" Ren said shakily, unsure of how Elio would react once it fully set in. Elio had already started back towards the driver's seat of the RV, frozen in his last step. He leaned forward before turning back to Ren with a pistol in his right hand.

"Elio, let's talk this through," Ren said, raising his right hand in a calming manner, slowly backing up to block Lilly's view with the other hand.

"What's the point, then?" Elio said as his emotions cracked, overflowing like a dam no longer able to contain the force behind it. "This is your fucking fault!" he barked hoarsely, turning the gun on Ren. "Everything was fine till you showed up."

"Let's calm down a bit. No need to point that thing around."

"Shut your goddamn mouth, or I will shut it for you! You and your damn hope—hope for what?"

"We don't know for sure, Elio," Lilly said, popping her head out around Ren's side. Tama watched silently from where he still sat on the couch. "Do something, Tama. Help me out." Tama let out a long, fake yawn.

"Why? This was how it was all going to end anyway, right? At least this saves us the rest of the trip." The reality of his words hit Ren upside the head with a cold realization. He wasn't ready to die; he wanted to live.

"NO!" he snapped back at Tama. "I want to live. I want to see tomorrow, to see this hell through to the end. No matter what!" Lilly watched, confused, as Elio raised the handgun slowly to his own head, the barrel pressed firmly against his temple.

"I don't," Elio said as he pulled the trigger.

"NO!" yelled Lilly and Ren in synchrony. But nothing happened. The safety was still locked safely in place. Elio dropped to his knees and sobbed.

"They were all I had, all that mattered… What's the point of anything now? Life without them, without the hope I may see them again." The pistol was still gripped tightly in his hand. "Maybe it's for the better. But why—why am I forced to keep going without them?" Lilly went to pass by Ren, who held her back with his right arm. Their eyes met for a second, and Ren lowered his guard as Lilly proceeded over to Elio.

"It's okay," she said as she embraced him like a daughter embraces a father after a long day away at school.

"Lilly… I…" His speech was broken, nearly as much as his heart.

"It's going to be okay, Elio. They would have wanted you to live on, to carry their memory. To live through you. Though they are not here in the physical anymore, they are still here with you—in your heart, in who you are today." Ren glanced over at Tama, who motioned for him to join Lilly in her support. Unsure, Ren slowly stepped forward as well and placed his right hand on Elio's shoulder in silence, no words needed in the moment.

After a few minutes of silence, Lilly leaned over and took the gun from Elio's loosened grip. She fed it into the ominous void of smoke living in her hoodie.

"Thank you," Elio said as he slowly got back to his feet. "I feel much better now, as if I had been holding that back for a very long time—longer than I even remember losing them." He reached into his pocket and pulled out the small cases that held what he believed to be the souls of his wife and daughter.

"Real or not, they still mean something to you," Ren said as Elio looked down at the blank case. "I know it's a lot." Ren paused.

"Save it, Ren. Tomorrow I am done. I only signed up for the slim chance I could get them back—a chance I have clung to for far too long." Elio slipped the two encased souls back into his pocket with Gur. "I have no interest in playing the game anymore. I never did. Once the sun rises in the morning, I concede, and we will go our separate ways."

"But!" Lilly interjected.

"I don't wanna hear it, Lilly." Elio sat down in the driver's seat of the RV and started the engine. "My mind is made up, and I won't be swayed." Lilly and Ren shared a look before Ren sighed and made his way to the passenger seat.

"I will respect your choice," Ren said, his tone filled with defeat. The RV went silent as Elio put it into drive, and they set off into the night—the last night they would all be together.

After an hour of eerie quiet, Ren turned to see Lilly sound asleep on the small RV couch, Tama snuggled up close, when Elio broke the silence.

"Why do you do it, Ren?" A loaded question. Ren turned to him.

"Do what?"

"Keep going? I know I talk a big game and all, but Ren, I'm scared."

"Scared of what? You're the toughest person I have ever met—at least that I can remember." Elio chuckled.

"Thanks." He paused. "I meant what I said earlier. Everything was fine before you showed up."

"I'm sorry," Ren said, looking down at the floor.

"Don't be. It was fine." He paused. "Fine, but it was also cold and lonely. If I am being completely honest with myself, the past couple of days have been the best I have had in a long, long time. Demented bird brains, crazy clowns, and the Collector be damned." Ren turned to him. "I am scared to care again—to become attached to anything or anyone in what's left of this world." The RV went quiet again, minutes passing when Ren finally spoke.

"Someone recently told me a simple fact of life." Elio glanced at him before turning his attention back to the darkening road ahead. "Life sucks." Ren paused. "But it's not all about that. It's so much more. It's about how we carry ourselves through it that makes us who we are—the marks we leave behind with those we meet on the highway to the end. Our hands are similar, the dealer of life now a madman with a rigged deck." Ren turned to see a groggy Lilly, letting out a stretch as she woke up from her light sleep and snuggles with Tama. "The question is now: do you fold and let the house win, or go all in and see what happens next?" Elio let out a soft chuckle, with a kind smile on his face.

"Solid advice from a wise man."

"Yeah, a hell of a cook, too," Ren smiled.

"I guess it's time I stop chasing what was and give what could be a shot."

"You mean?" Ren said, perking up.

"Yeah, it's time to go all in. Time to gamble on a madman's wager." Lilly shuffled up to the front of the cabin, with a less-than-pleased Tama following suit.

"Well, Ren, I turn the role of leader over to you. What's next?"

"You're staying!" Lilly said, confused but excited.

"I am. Sorry about earlier, you two. It all kind of just hit me at once. I didn't know what to do anymore. Ending it was all that made sense." He paused. "But it seems that Wonderland has a different plan for me."

"We're here for you," Lilly said with a kind smile, reaching up and placing her hand on his shoulder, elevated by a smoky step stool to reach.

"Yeah, we are all in this together," Ren paused. "To answer your question, I guess we see it through to the end. I mean, we don't even know for sure that there is anything on the other side of the wall.

This really could be it, and the prize could just be a promise of dreams come true in a world where dreams are all but dead."

"Sounds good to me. I am all in. After all, what's the worst thing that could happen? We get all the way there and they put a bullet in our heads," Elio said with a grin. "I already died once—why not again?"

"If we even make it there," Ren said with less assurance.

"So, we are still playing the game?" Lilly said excitedly. "All of us, together?"

"I suppose we are," Ren said with a smile. "It seems we are unified to see it through to the end."

"Yeah, I won't have to put a bullet in your brain once we reach the end now," Elio said with another grin, this one more playful than the last.

"Wait, what? Why would you do that to Ren?" Lilly asked, confused by his joke.

"That doesn't matter now," Elio said, tussling the top of her head.

"You sure you're okay?" Ren asked, surprised at the fatherly affection.

"I am. Actually, it's strange. I feel the best I have in well over a year. Since it all went down. It's as if I am back to my old self, though… I don't really know who my old self was. It feels right. But enough about that—we need to get this rig moving. I doubt the Collector will give a rat's ass about my feelings if he catches up with us."

"He's got a point," Tama said finally, waltzing past them to the passenger seat of the RV, hopping up on his personal pillow, that being Ren's lap.

"Yay! Game time!" Lilly said happily, heading back over to the couch.

"Next stop, DC," Elio said with a smile. Ren slouched back into his seat while Tama shifted begrudgingly with the odd, relaxed angle of his body as he slowly drifted to sleep. Elio glanced in the rearview to see a sleeping Lilly curled up on the small couch, then over at Ren, mumbling under his breath.

"Lazy-ass kids," with a proud, almost soft smile as he returned his attention to the road ahead.

Ren woke up to a loud thud. Startled, he jolted in his seat, nearly throwing an equally sleepy Tama into the windshield.

"Nice of you two to join us," Elio said with a hearty chuckle. "I assume you heard that?" Rubbing his eyes and looking around, Ren let out a long yawn before responding.

"Yeah, you could say that." He glanced out the window to see his own reflection staring back at him, darkness being the only thing on the other side. "What time is it?" he asked, turning towards Elio. Lilly was sitting between them atop a smoke-formed chair that imitated the one he sat in.

"Nighttime. That's what time. As for the thud that woke you up, that would be an unbound looking to hitch a free ride to DC. Get used to that, though, because the ravenous little bastards are just going to keep on trying until morning."

"Will the RV be okay, you think?" Ren said, with a glare from Tama atop the dash, before he plopped into Lilly's lap and curled back up. Ren slipped off to the back to find a snack and some water.

"Should be fine. Worst case, we have to find another set of wheels once the sun comes up. Hey, while you're back there, grab the girl and I some jerky."

"Yeah! Jerky! Two bags for me."

"Two?" Elio said playfully. "Where do you plan on putting it all?"

"Don't be silly, Elio." She let out a sassy giggle while pulling down on her right eye. "One for me, and one for Haku."

"Ha! Silly me, how could I forget about Haku?" He glanced down at her smoky seat. "That really is a neat trick."

"Yeah, Haku is the best. He can turn into all kinds of cool things."

"I don't doubt that," he said as Ren came back and sat down with four bags of jerky in hand. The four quickly devoured the bags, the last bites disappearing when Elio broke the silence.

"Alright, Ren, you good to take over for a while? Should only have to drive through the night tonight. That should put plenty of space between us and the Collector, at least for now."

"Yeah, I should be good. Just follow this road?"

"Yeah, just wake me up if anything funky happens." The RV slowed down before coming to a complete stop. "All yours, Ren," Elio said, getting out of the seat as another loud thud echoed out from the rear of the bus. Ren hopped in the driver's seat and quickly got the RV moving again. "You'll get used to that quickly," he said with a grin before disappearing to the far back cabin and closing the door.

Tama hopped over to the warm passenger seat, now unoccupied, leaving behind a disappointed Lilly alone atop her smoky seat.

"It's going to be a long night. You two ought to get some more rest as well," Ren said to Lilly and Tama with a smile. His eyes locked on the dark road ahead.

"I'm not tired," she said with an unconvincing yawn.

"Sure, she's not." Tama winked at Ren. "Well, I am going to take up the offer to get more sleep. Just do me a favor and don't do anything stupid, at least until I wake up." He finished with a sassy grin as he tucked his head into a perfect curl. Ren glanced over at Lilly.

"Guess it's just us then," he said to Lilly, who was asleep as well. Haku set her gently down atop the small couch behind and wrapped her tight in his warm, smoky embrace. The RV went quiet as Ren pushed through the dark and closer to their shared destination: to D.C., specifically the White House. The home of the Madman.

CHAPTER TWELVE
Between a Cliff and an Ambush

A few uneventful hours passed as Ren drove through the silent night, the occasional bump in the dark from the random unbound determined to board the unrelenting RV. Then there was Lilly, who would randomly jolt awake with her eyes wide open and glazed over with panic. It happened twice, and with each instance, Haku quickly formed a thin, motherlike hand and stroked her head calmly back to sleep. Around four hours in, the door at the rear of the RV opened with surprising force. The thud from it hit the wall behind, startling both Ren and the other sleeping passengers—except Tama, who didn't even budge a bit.

"How did you sleep?" Ren asked as Elio made his way up to the passenger seat, slipping past a still-groggy Lilly and nudging a stubborn Tama out of both his dreams and his bed.

"That was a lot," Elio said as he sat down, wiping the sweat from his face. "If that is what you go through every night, then words cannot express just how sorry I am," he said while looking at a very confused Lilly as she wiped the sleepies from her eyes.

"What happened?" Ren asked curiously, his eyes still glued to the road.

"It finally happened. My little breakdown seems to have unlocked some buried memories, and man, oh man, do I wish they would have stayed buried."

"That bad?"

"She was right. That shit was so disturbingly real that it rattled me unlike anything I have ever felt."

"You wanna talk about it?" Lilly asked as she came out of a long yawn. "You don't have to if you don't wanna." The sun was rising; a flurry of various yellows, reds, and oranges lit up the sky ahead. Elio went quiet as a grumpy, rudely awakened Tama hopped up onto the dash to soak up the incoming rays and go back to sleep.

"I'm sitting alone on a wooden bench, people from all walks of life going about their day all around me. I am wearing a baggy hoodie, not unlike hers." He motioned to Lilly, who was tearing into a packet of jerky. "My hands loosely touch in the shared pocket, the feeling of cold metal resting under them. Curious, I pull the unknown item out of my pocket before quickly shoving it back inside. I look around to make sure no one else saw the small silver handgun hidden inside."

"'The verdict is in,' a kind female voice said to me. I look up at her, overwhelmed with confused emotions and holding back my tears as they fight their way to freedom. I stood up and followed her down a hall to a pair of wooden doors. She opened the one on the left. 'I wish you the best,' she said to me as I stepped into the room. The door closed behind me as I walked forward to the second row.

At the front of the room was a blurry figure in a long black robe. Standing opposite her in the room was another hazy human silhouette in a fancy suit. Next to him stood a man—the only person who was clearly visible in the room. He was dressed more casually; however, something bound his hands behind him."

"My heart raced as if it might explode. A flurry of raw emotions battled it out as my blood pumped faster—sadness, hatred, and anger. The latter two tugged on the handgun in my pocket. My grip tightened as I took my seat in the aisle behind the man. The robed figure's voice silenced the commotion of the room and addressed the man. I sat quietly and listened."

"Their words are as muddied as their appearance. My heart skips a beat; my body grows tense. My eyes feel wet, my cheeks warm. I watch as the casually dressed man turns to hug the blur in the fancy suit. Then, in the blink of an eye, before I even realized what I was doing, I stood up and unloaded the gun on the man, pulling the trigger until no more bullets were available to fly. Each one tore through the body of the casually dressed man. All I could hear were the screams of those around me and a ring in my right ear. I drop the gun and fall to my knees while placing my hands against the back of my head. My vision is blurry from the water pouring from my eyes as they go black. The image of my wife and daughter flashed briefly before I awoke."

"That's a lot for one dream," Ren said.

"That's the thing, though," Elio said, turning his gaze out the windshield. "I don't think it was a dream. It felt too visceral. Rather, I think it was a memory that I can't recall." He paused. "There are few things like a sunrise. Each one is unique, never to be replicated again—like the first time you felt love, the memory of your first kiss, or your child's first steps. Though we see these things over and over, the first one is never like the others. It's special." His attention was suddenly elsewhere as he looked out over a massive body of water. "You see that sign? Potomac River. I'll be damned—we are almost there," Elio said, impressed.

"REN! Stop!" Tama snapped from his sunny perch on the dashboard. His glowing fur was standing on end.

"What's up, Tama?" Ren replied, confused, as Elio looked forward and echoed the same panic, unaware of what Tama had said only a second ago.

"Ren, stop the RV. NOW!" He reached over and pulled the emergency brake as Ren slammed his foot down on the brake. The RV slid across the pavement as the smell of burning rubber filled the air. The cause of the panic was now in clear sight. They were about to run out of bridge. "We're not gonna make it! Everyone bail!" Elio yelled as he scooped up Lilly. Haku vanished inside her hoodie as Elio opened the door to the RV. "Ren, let's GO!" he barked, jumping from the RV as it screeched toward the bridge's cliff.

"I don't like that," Tama said, watching as they disappeared out the door, before being scooped up by Ren, who took one last look out the front of the RV. Nothing but crisp blue water glistening under the sunrise.

"I like that less," Ren said before he took a deep breath and leaped from the RV, tumbling along the rocky bridge as the RV vanished over the edge. It disappeared with a massive splash soon after. Everyone rushed over to watch as the water slowly absorbed it below.

"That was a bit too close for comfort," Elio said, dusting off his clothes. "Everyone alright?" he asked with a wince. His arm still hadn't fully healed from being shot only a few days earlier, and the tumble had not helped with the healing.

"Yeah. Haku wrapped me up in a cloud before impact," Lilly said, with her clothes in mint condition.

"Would have been nice of him to wrap me up, too. I did save both your asses, after all."

"Haku is wondering if you died, though."

"What? No, I didn't die," he responded as Lilly burst out laughing.

"It was a joke," Lilly said, tears streaking from her eyes from her persistent laughter.

"Sure…" Elio said, unamused. "Well, now what?" he said, glancing back one last time to see the RV fade forever into the deep blue water. Ren turned his attention to the other side and stared out over the blue to see what remained of the bridge on the other side.

"I guess our destination is the same—just need a new plan to get there."

"Well, unless either of you two can fly, it seems we're going by water."

"Haku said we should look for a boat," Lilly said with a proud smile, always happy to contribute to the adventure.

"Haku is a smart little dragon," Elio said, looking at Lilly.

"Wait, can't dragons fly?" he said, suddenly confused. "Get your lazy smoky ass out here and flap us to the other side," Elio said as Tama poked Lilly's hoodie antagonistically.

"Too far," she said flatly. "Haku can't go that far, even with only me on his back."

"Why not?" Ren asked curiously as he pulled Tama back slowly by his middle tail.

"It would kill me," she said coldly. "He won't do it because of the risk to me." Elio, Tama, and Ren all shared a look.

"Guess it's time to find a boat, then," Elio said with a smile as he reached into his pocket and summoned Gur. "Time to get some fresh air, big guy," he said, giving the gigantic bear a soft tussle under its neck. Gur let out what sounded almost like a cat's purr.

"Only a short walk back to the shore; with any luck, we can find something reliable-looking that floats, and we can head to the other side." He scooped Tama and led the way.

"Let's hope our boat lasts longer than our wheels; otherwise, we may end up drowning before we reach the other side," Tama quipped.

"Can I ride him?" Lilly asked, tugging at Elio's sleeve and pointing at Gur.

"That's up to him," he said, looking at the enormous bear. "What do you think there, big guy? Wanna play pony for a little?" Gur scooped his nose under Lilly and threw her up into the air. With some guidance from Haku, she landed safely atop her steed.

"He's so soft and cuddly!" she said, running her fingers through his fur.

"Softest bear I've ever pet—that's for damn sure," Elio said with a smile as the four of them followed Ren down the road. When they reached the start of the bridge, Tama broke the silence of the walk.

"Did you see that?" he said as Ren came to an abrupt stop.

"What's up?" Elio asked as he reached Ren's side.

"Tama thinks he saw something."

"Not thinks—did," he said, insulted. "I swear I saw something move over there. How did you not? There it is again." Tama motioned. A young boy ran from behind an abandoned car when a gunshot rang out. Elio dropped to the ground with a pained shout. Gur let out a terrifying roar, bucking the unprepared Lilly off as they dashed forward. A puff of smoke shaped like a cloud caught Lilly midair before she hit the ground. Gur stood at attention in front of Elio's body, which now lay still on the ground.

"Hands in the air!" a male voice echoed from behind a car at the end of the bridge. The young boy was behind him, and another man was pointing a gun at him. "I will drop another one of you bastards in ten seconds if you don't listen."

"Try it!" Lilly said as smoke swirled around her.

"Do as they say," Elio said faintly from where he lay. "We don't know how many of them there are, or what they want."

"Three!"

"Just comply. We will figure something out," Ren said quietly.

"Two!" Lilly sighed.

"Fine…" she said disappointedly as she dropped to her knees

and Haku faded back into her hoodie. Ren followed suit, his hands held in the air, while Tama lay submissively on the ground. Gur disappeared back into his case as three masked figures advanced up the bridge.

"Lights out!" one said with a swift kick to Ren's face, and everything went black.

Ren's head felt heavy as he opened his eyes. Surveying his new surroundings, Ren found himself in what looked like a jail cell.

"Finally awake," Elio said from the other side of the cell. His right hand was handcuffed to a metal bar along the wall. Ren looked up to see his hand cuffed similarly.

"What happened?" he asked, wiping his face with his free left hand. His mouth was sore and sensitive to the touch as he looked down at his hand to see blood. Taking another look around, he asked, "Where are we?"

"Hell if I know. Bastards ambushed us." He let out a groan of restrained pain. His hanging arm was bandaged poorly, but still red with fresh blood. "What's with everyone shooting me in the same damn arm? Is there a target I am missing?"

"I thought you were dead back there. Are you okay?"

"I mean, no. I got shot again, and we are being held prisoner by who the hell even knows." He let out another groan, this one combined with pain and frustration. "They took the girl—Tama and Gur, too," he said, defeated. "Soon after we arrived, they dragged her out. I made her promise to keep Haku hidden, no matter what."

"Why? Haku could take out a small army just by himself."

"Maybe. But at what cost? If they didn't just put a bullet in her head, the fight to get away may just kill her all the same. There is just too much we don't know about Haku and their true impact on her."

"Throw her in the cell; brat's not going anywhere in her condition," a voice said as a door at the end of the hall opened. Two men dragged an unconscious Lilly by her hair down the hall. The boy from the bridge was in tow with a leash that connected to a collar around his neck.

"What are you two looking at? You wanna keep your eyes? Then keep them off me," one man barked as the cell door swung open. The pair threw Lilly into the cell before slamming the door shut again.

"Can't believe that little bitch bit me," the other man said while opening another cell door opposite them, giving the young boy a kick in the back before he fell on his leash and choked. The man let go of the leash. "Whoops." He chuckled as the boy fell face-forward onto the dirt floor of the cell. The boy was still and unmoving as the door to the cell slammed shut.

"The boss was right. Everyone in Wonderland really is no better than a wild animal."

"The boss will set them on the right path. She always does." The door closed, and they were gone.

"Lilly?" Ren said to the lifeless body that lay in the center of the cell, just out of reach of either of them.

"Come on, girl, you're tougher than that. Get up," Elio said as his voice cracked with emotion and increased concern.

She let out a gasp, but remained still on the floor.

"I did as you asked. No matter how much they hit me or yelled. They don't know about Haku." She raised her head slightly off the cold ground before losing all strength and passing back out. Elio let out a sigh of relief and fell back against the wall. Ren's eyes were heavy, and he drifted back to sleep.

"Good girl. You both get some rest now." The cell fell eerily quiet.

Ren woke up again, alerted by Elio, who was whispering at him from across the room. He must have drifted back to sleep.

"Wake up, they're coming," he said as Ren blinked his eyes rapidly and shuffled up into a proper sitting position.

"How long was I out?"

"A couple of hours, I'd guess." Ren looked over to see Lilly perched up against the third wall facing the cell door. Her face was a mess of black and blue, and blood leaked from various scratches and cuts.

"You okay?" Ren asked her, only to receive a silent nod back. A woman, accompanied by the two men from earlier, stood at the door of the cell.

"Allow me to introduce myself. My name is Bellerose, and welcome to my humble home here in Wonderland."

CHAPTER THIRTEEN
Jailbreak

"What do you want with us?" Elio asked, unimpressed by her entrance.

"Want?" She laughed. "I don't want anything from you. After all, what do those with nothing have to give?" In her right hand was a black-wrapped whip, and glowing next to her was a small dragon with a blue flame at the tip of its tail. It stood on all fours at about knee height and had two compressed wings atop its back that glowed an equally bright blue to the tail. Ren looked over at Lilly. Was that what lurked under her hoodie?

"It's quite the opposite, my dear. I only wish to give to those in Wonderland, not take."

"Oh? And what is it you wish to give us exactly?" Elio said defiantly.

"Salvation," she said with a calming, almost motherly smile. "Do you know why you are here? Here, in what that damned madman calls Wonderland?" Elio and Ren passed each other intrigued glances before Ren answered her question with curiosity.

"To play his game?" Ren replied, unsure.

"That's what he would have you believe. What he would have everyone here in this nightmarish, end-of-the-world dystopia of madness he has created believe. He claims to have the keys to unlimited wealth; that he holds the locks to your dreams, and reaching him is the key." She paused, pacing back and forth as she tapped the whip against the bars of the cell door.

"What if I told you it was all a lie? If I told you that everyone who has gone to meet the madman never returned—what would you think?" The room went quiet as the question hung in the air.

"That it's a trap," Ren said plainly, answering again.

"Exactly! Like everything else in the world, both before Wonderland and now. They sell us a light at the end of the tunnel; a dream that all the hard work and time sacrificed is worth it in the end. Yet, like the madman and his little game, it's all just a façade. There is nothing at the end of the tunnel but death. So, I ask you this: Why chase something that you already have access to?" Ren was growing tired of her and her questions and snapped at the mysterious woman.

"Where is Tama? Give us back our souls and let us go." Her eyes glowed blue as the flames of her dragon burned brighter.

"I ask the questions around here!" she barked furiously before taking a soft, deep breath. "Children interrupt, and I have no time to waste on children." She turned to leave, glaring back at the cell. "Maybe a week with no food will put you in your place." She turned around to see the young boy curled up in the corner. "Back again so soon? Get the brat some water and a loaf of bread," she said to the men that escorted her.

"Yes, ma'am!" they said synchronously before she disappeared elegantly down the hall, her minions following.

"Well, she is an unpleasant bitch," Elio said, turning to Ren.

"That's putting it lightly," Ren said, slouching back against the wall.

"Guess we better get comfy. We won't get very far with our only chance for escape still asleep," Elio said as they both glanced over at Lilly, who sat slumped over and sound asleep. The cell went quiet. Each of them was sore and tired from the ambush and felt even more drained from a lack of any food or water. A few minutes passed when one man from before returned. He slid a dog bowl of water and a small loaf of bread under the gate across the hall where the boy sat tucked away in the dark corner of his cell. The man then returned to where he had come from, and everything fell quiet again.

"I had that dream again," Elio said out of nowhere. "She is tough, that's for sure." He was staring at Lilly as she slept. "Bastards beat her so bad even her nightmares are out cold."

"Why her and not us?" Ren asked, letting out a yawn. "Why only torture her?"

"Haku. Or rather, the lack of Haku. Everyone in this hellhole comes with a soul. So, when a young girl appears without one, they wanna know why and where it is."

"That is why she is so impressive. At any point, Haku could have come out and protected her, and I bet my life that they wanted to more than anything. But that girl… she took it all for us. To get back here and help us escape." Ren looked over at her. She was sleeping peacefully, perhaps for the first time in a while.

"Tomorrow, once we are all awake and well-rested, we are busting out of here." Elio shimmied down as much as he could while still being attached to the wall, his bloody arm limp as he closed his eyes. "Get some rest. Something tells me that tomorrow is gonna get wild."

Elio closed his eyes and drifted back to sleep. Ren's eyes grew heavy, and soon he, too, was fast asleep.

"YOU TOOK THEM FROM ME!" Elio screamed out from a deep sleep, alerting both Ren and Lilly from their peaceful slumber.

"You okay?" Ren asked from across the cell, blinking his eyes rapidly to speed up the wake-up process as he reassessed his surroundings. The cell had grown cold, the air bitter with the northeastern chill of winter. Traveling so far up the East Coast, they had left the warmer temperatures of the south far behind.

"Yeah… I'm good." Elio glanced around. A thin window that sat inserted above Lilly showed the outside world still sat in darkness. A small trim of white, fluffy snow sat along the lower border and was only slightly visible. "Winter is coming," Elio said dramatically with a grin.

"I think it's already here," Ren said, oblivious.

"Never mind," Elio said, shaking his head.

"I hate the cold," Lilly said, upset and shivering, speaking for the first time since they had thrown her back into the cell.

"How are you feeling?" Ren asked. Elio also turned his attention to her response.

"Still sleepy, but Haku and I are feeling better overall." She looked around, finally coherent enough to take in her new surroundings. "Where are we?"

"Some sort of basement cell, from what I can tell," Elio said. "Doesn't matter, though. I think it's about time we get the hell out of here." He looked over at Ren, who seemed distracted by something. "What's up with you, kid? You feel alright?" Ren looked down at the ground.

"What if it is a trap?"

"What are you going on about?" Elio said as Lilly made her way over to him.

"The woman yesterday—she said that no one has ever come back from seeing the madman. That it's all just a ploy to get those of us still clinging to the hope of a better tomorrow to show up to death's door with our invitation in hand."

"What about it? You just wanna turn back now? After we wandered halfway up the East Coast? And then what? Just stay here in this cell and wait for that bitch to come back here and kill us?"

"No! Obviously not. I am… I just wonder if we really should play the game. I mean, what's the point if death is all that's waiting for us?"

"Lazy and stupid," Elio said as smoke slowly flowed out of Lilly's right sleeve. The smoke seeped into the keyhole of the handcuffs, then, with a quiet squeak, Elio's arm was freed. It dropped to the ground with a tired thud. Elio lifted his sore, bloody arm and gave it a soft rub and inspection as he tore off another strip of his undershirt and wrapped the bullet wound. Lilly crossed the room to Ren to repeat the trick.

"No matter what it is we do in life, the result is always the same: that being death. We are all working to the same end, but that's not what matters." He paused as he tied off the shirt knot and stood up. "I will say it again. It's the journey there that makes life special. The bonds we form. The lessons we learn, and the impact we have on those around us and those that come after. That is what matters." Ren's wrist dropped free of the cuffs, warmed with a gentle touch from his other hand as he stood up to match Elio.

"You're right. Let's see this through to the end," Ren said, looking at his two companions. "Together."

"Together!" they both said in response.

"Lilly, if you would do the honor," Elio said as they all turned to the cell door. Ren and Elio stood ready and determined as Lilly stepped forward from the center.

"Alright, Haku, do your thing," she said as a smoky tail appeared behind her, flowing from the large hoodie. Out of each sleeve formed large dragon claws. As she reached forward, a loud scream rang out from the small hole at the back of the cell.

"It's the Collector!" a voice yelled.

"Everyone, prepare yourselves!"

"The Collector? How did he catch up so fast?" Elio said, startled.

"I mean..." Ren paused. "We did kind of just sleep for an entire day."

"Well, now is as good a time as ever, I guess. While he is searching for us, we can escape in the chaos." He turned back to Lilly, half smoke dragon, half little girl. "You two ready?"

"Always!" she said with a terrifying echo emanating from deep within the hoodie—the voice of a dragon. Lilly reached forward and tore the cell door off the sliding hinges before tossing it aside like nothing more than an empty packet of jerky.

"We need to find Tama and Gur," Ren said. "Lilly, lead the way. We will be close behind." A loud explosion rang out from above where they were.

"We better hurry," Elio said, stepping out of the cell. "This place isn't going to stay standing much longer." Ren stepped out of the cell and froze.

"What's up, Ren?" Elio asked.

"The boy."

"Yeah, what about him?" he snapped, irritated. Lilly turned around quietly and ripped the cell door from its hinges, gently setting it down to the side.

"Be careful, okay," Ren said into the open cell.

"Ren, we need to go!"

"Yeah…" Ren said, turning after him hesitantly. Lilly rushed down the hallway while Ren searched the various rooms on the right and Elio on the left until they reached the end of the hall. A circular flight of stairs rounded up to the floor above. After ascending quickly, they found the exit. Lilly punched down the door and sent it flying through the guard on the other side. Warm blood splattered out from between the door and the wall opposite where it no longer hung.

"The prisoners are escaping!" a guard shouted from the left of where they now stood. Lilly dashed right and tore through another posted guard. Split into three bloody, separate pieces as they splattered against the wall.

"Where the hell are our souls?" Elio barked at the man to the left. Lilly turned back and locked eyes with the terrified man, who dropped his gun to the ground and pointed in their direction.

"Next door on the right."

"Atta boy," Elio said with a grin as they all turned toward the door. Lilly ripped it forward and back up as Ren and Elio rushed inside.

The man at the end of the hallway reached for his discarded weapon and, in the blink of an eye, Lilly hurled the door down the hall and severed the man in half.

"Tama!" yelled Ren as he entered the room. Tama sat trapped in an odd electric case. To his right sat Gur's case and the two bunny soul cases that belonged to Elio.

"Took you long enough," Tama said. "I was wondering if you two were planning on a rescue or not."

"Good to see you too, Tama," Ren said. "How do you get out of this damned thing?" Elio crossed the room and scooped up Gur and the bunnies.

"We don't have time for this shit," Elio said, picking up the end of the table Tama sat on and rolling the electric case—Tama included—off the table. The odd electric prison shattered like static glass as it hit the floor.

"Ow!" Tama said as the static of the shattered cage made his fur stand up in the air. "But thank you. So, what now?" Ren looked down at him and picked him up.

"The Collector is here and is causing chaos outside. So, we are using our enemy to our advantage—an ally in parting, you could say."

"Where is the girl?" Tama asked before seeing the smoke dragon, girl hybrid standing guard outside the doorway. "Never mind." With the group now all back together, Elio took charge of the situation.

"Alright, Lilly, lead the way. Tama, you are on ranged attacks. Cover her well. Everyone good?" he asked as an armed man rounded the corner from another door to the left of the room. Tama quickly pierced him with a shard of ice, a trick he had pulled from Gur. It ripped through the man with the impact of a point-blank bullet, leaving a hole in his chest with a red, icy flash.

"That answers that. Let's go," Ren said as they all followed Lilly down the hall with Elio at the rear. Two more armed men awaited them around the last corner. Lilly slashed through one and tore the other in two as she roared with pent-up ferocity.

"Is she okay?" Tama asked, both impressed and slightly scared as they followed closely behind Lilly, her hoodie now soaked in a deep red hue.

"I don't think Lilly has been okay for a very long time," Ren said softly as Lilly lunged across the room in a smoky blur. Her right hand uppercut another guard. The force of the hit was so hard he flew up into the ceiling, and blood rained down all over as the body fell back to the ground.

"Lilly! To the exit," Elio yelled and pointed at a pair of glass doors to her left with a large table tipped in front of it. Four guards sat posted in a fashion to defend against the chaos outside. A bloody, sick grin spread across Lilly's face as she licked her lips with glee at her unknowing prey. She picked up the limp body next to her and dashed over to the four posted guards as they turned to see the commotion and its source behind them. Lilly cleaved all four of them with the remains of the dead body before beating them to death in a bloody blur so thick the smoke that swirled shifted to a bright red.

"LILLY!" Ren barked as she raised the body's only remaining limb into the air, pausing at Ren's voice. Ren placed his left hand on her sopping wet shoulder, the blood still warm. She turned to him; their gazes locked. The little girl chasing Tama around for pets was unrecognizable in all the blood. Her eyes were no longer pure with curiosity and innocence; instead, ravaged by hatred and rage. "That's enough, Lilly. Let's go." His stomach turned at the messy blend of what had been five human bodies only minutes ago. Elio pushed the door open.

"Come on!" he yelled, motioning them toward the door. The smoke swirled around Lilly slowly as it cleaned itself and her. The smoke returned to its hazy gray, while it also restored her hoodie to its previous shades of purple. It was as if she had gone through a car wash, with everything that had happened being scrubbed away as if it had never happened. Haku returned to rest inside.

"That's a neat trick," Tama said in shock as they followed Elio outside.

"Where to next?" Ren asked Elio, who froze in place.

"What's up?" Ren asked as he reached his side to see what had locked him in place. The air was thick with the smell of blood and smoke. Dozens of buildings burned in front of them, and the ground was littered with corpses. At least one hundred bodies lay limp in a sea of blood—man, woman, and child alike in their fates.

"Did the Collector do this?" Ren asked.

"No doubt," Lilly responded coldly.

"It doesn't matter who or what did it. We should get out of here before whatever it was comes back around," Elio said.

"And… where are all the souls?" Ren then realized that they had not seen another soul since arriving here. Only the woman from the day prior had a soul.

"Good question. No way the Collector got them all that fast."

"I don't like it here," Lilly said with a tremble in her voice, back to her usual self.

"Me either," Ren said as they stepped off the small porch and retreated, none of them daring to look back—moving forward with more questions and leaving behind more bloodshed.

CHAPTER FOURTEEN
Lyonel

"What do you mean, you're lost?" Ren asked Elio.

"Yeah, Ren. I know exactly where those bastards locked up for the past two days. Lucky for us, they were even handing maps out at the exit. The hell do you even mean? Obviously, I am lost. I have no idea how I got here to begin with," Elio snapped.

"I get it. Chill, man," Ren said. Tama held tight while riding along in his arms as they walked.

"I'm sorry…" Elio replied as it fell quiet while they wandered along the empty road. "That was… That was a lot."

"It's okay, I know," Ren said as Lilly skipped about as if nothing had even happened. Haku was missing, presumably sleeping as usual. "You okay, Lilly? You really carried us back there."

"Me? Yeah, I am fine. Why?"

"Oh, I mean… You were just awesome, that's all. The way you cleared the path for us was honestly as terrifying as it was helpful."

"I did?" she said, confused.

"Ren, I don't think she knows," Elio said. "That thing back there, I don't think it was her. Well, at least not in the normal sense. I am not sure how, or why, or even what. But whatever that was, it wasn't our Lilly. Perhaps it was a peek at the monster that haunts her sleep. A monster that only Haku seems aware of. Almost like a soul within a soul. Whatever it is, I am just glad she is on our side."

"Yeah…" Ren said, staring at Lilly as she skipped about, blissfully unaware of the carnage she had left behind.

"I know what you're thinking, and it's not worth worrying about right now. We have more important things to deal with."

"A store!" Lilly exclaimed, interrupting, pointing down the dirt road they had been traveling down since they fled only an hour ago. "There is a store up ahead," she said with her arms out and spinning around excitedly.

"Maybe we can find a map," Elio said, looking up to see the bridge to nowhere off in the near distance, with the sun peeking out from behind it. "Well, I will be damned. I can see where we started before the ambush. Just straight ahead on this road, and we will be back at the bridge."

"Then we just need to find a boat, and we will be well on our way again," Ren said optimistically.

"Maybe we can find a car at the store. I really hate all this walking," Lilly said with a pouty face.

"Sorry, Lilly, but I think we are going to have to stay on foot for this one, at least until we reach the other side. With the Collector so close and looking for us, traveling light and by foot is the better option."

"Aww," she said, disappointed. "Can I at least ride Gur?" she asked with revived hope. Elio laughed.

"I am sure we can arrange that," he said as Gur appeared from its small case in a flash of light.

"Yay! Teddy Bear!" she yelled excitedly as she rushed over to Gur. "May I ride you?" she asked the enormous bear bashfully. Gur nodded, and Haku gently placed her atop the massive bear as they came upon the store.

"Tama and I will dip inside and see if there is anything useful left."

"Jerky!" Lilly yelled to them from her loyal steed as they disappeared into the small gas station. Tama hopped down from Ren's arms and scampered down the aisle toward the back of the store. Ren followed close behind.

"Place seems relatively untouched overall," Tama said.

"Probably because it's out in the middle of nowhere. You would have to be lost like we are to end up here."

"True," Tama said as a small display rack tipped over at the end of the row. "Was that you?" Tama asked, looking at Ren still close behind.

"Not me," he said, motioning for Tama to round the corner while Ren slowly backed up to the opposite end.

"Gotcha!" Tama yelled. His target, unable to hear him, let out a terrified scream and turned the other way, only to bounce off Ren and land on his butt. "It's a kid," Tama said in surprise.

"I won't go back! You can tell that mean lady I don't want to be her pet anymore." He broke down and cried. Elio and Lilly rushed in from outside. Gur was nowhere to be seen.

"You two okay? We heard a scream and…" Elio stopped mid-sentence. "Oh, another kid." Lilly wandered over, excited to see someone her own age for once. Ren looked down to see a red circle around the boy's neck.

"I think this is the same boy—the one from the cell across from us."

"Hi, I am Lilly," she said, kneeling. "What's your name?" He looked down at the floor, scared and unwilling to make eye contact. "It's okay. We won't hurt you," she said in a calm voice, gently lifting his head up from the chin. "What's your name?"

"Lyonel," he said shakily, his eyes flowing with tears. Ren and Tama wandered over to Elio. "Wait, you are the ones that opened the cell." He started to tear up again. "Thank you." Lilly helped him up.

"Wanna help me find some jerky?" she asked. Lyonel nodded as she took his hand. "We are gonna go look for jerky, be right back!" she said to Elio and Ren before rushing off down an aisle, the boy in tow.

"He seems a little younger than Lilly," Elio said. "If I had to guess, no older than ten."

"Poor kid. It couldn't have been easy for him, seeing all that back there."

"Something tells me that back there is nothing compared to what that poor boy has lived through," Elio said, his tone drenched in sadness, or maybe guilt at leaving him behind. Lilly and the boy rushed back over.

"Jerky! We hit the jerky jackpot," she yelled, the boy carrying at least a dozen bags with him. Dropping it in front of Tama, she said, "Be right back with more!"

"One second, Lilly. I have a couple of questions for Lyonel—real quick. The jerky isn't going anywhere," Elio said.

"Fine," she said with a pouty face.

"It was you the other day, near the bridge, right?" Lyonel nodded his head. "What was it you were doing there?"

"I ran away." Elio looked at Ren and continued.

"From the lady?" Lyonel nodded again.

"Yeah… from Master. I didn't want to be her pet anymore. Her stupid, spoiled dragon always takes the best food."

"Pet?" Ren said, confused, to which the boy nodded again. Elio continued his questions.

"How old were you when it all happened?"

"Happened? What do you mean?" Lyonel asked, visibly confused by the question. Ren and Tama were intrigued by his response. Ren clarified the question.

"When the world ended, how old were you?"

"Uh… I don't know. It's always been like this, as far back as I can remember. Master always said I was a miracle in a lost Wonderland."

"Wait a second… You were born here? Inside the walls?" Elio said in disbelief.

"Mhm, mhm." He nodded again. "That's what my mom and pa told me."

"And where are your ma and pa now?" Elio asked.

"Dead. Master killed them. Their punishment for bringing a child into Wonderland without permission." Another shared glance between Ren and Elio.

"How old are you?" Ren asked as Elio backed slowly away to hide his confusion.

"I am eight and a half."

"That's enough questions," Lilly interjected impatiently. "We need to get more jerky," she said, grabbing Lyonel's hand and dashing back off in the direction they had come from previously.

"That… That's not possible," Elio said as Ren turned to him. "I was there, here. I watched it happen just over a year ago."

"Maybe the kid is misremembering? Who knows? They could have lied to him his entire life."

"Lilly woke up here. You woke up here. Why do I only remember it happening?" Elio paused. "Do I remember it happening? And the nightmares—why, all of a sudden, do they haunt me when I close my eyes?" He turned to face Ren. "Ren, I don't know what's real anymore."

"I know, Elio." Ren placed his hand on Elio's shoulder. "We will figure it out. We will get the answers from the Madman, even if we have to beat them out of him."

"Yeah…"

"But till then, we need to get your arm cleaned and bandaged. Grab a snack—jerky, I guess—and get going again to the White House," a sentence Ren never thought he would say.

"What do we do about the kid? We can't just leave him here. Not to mention, Lilly seems to have taken a liking to him."

"I guess we just ask if he would like to join us and go from there," replied Ren.

"That's fine and all. But we can't guarantee his safety. Honestly, if he is with us, he is at even more risk."

"That's why it's his choice to make, not ours. Let's be real here: he doesn't have much of a chance either way…"

"True, I suppose." Elio paused, wandering over to a nearby souvenir clothing rack. He took off his long trench coat.

"Can you grab a couple bottles of water and check to see if you can find a first aid kit?" The previous wrap from their jailbreak was sopping wet. The dried blood now refreshed and dripped along his arm.

"Yeah, I will be right back," he said, disappearing toward the fridge section to get the water, Tama close behind. The sound of ripping fabric behind him as Elio prepared for the supplies.

"That looked pretty bad," Ren said to Tama as he opened the fridge door and grabbed a couple of chilled waters. The temperatures outside chilled them perfectly, even in the powerless store.

"It does, but looks are often deceiving. The bullet went clean through, so as long as we get it cleaned and wrapped, he should be okay—though probably sore for a while. Best case, we can find a needle and thread." The fridge door closed behind Ren. With water in hand, they wandered through a couple of aisles until they finally found a couple of first aid kits.

"One for the road, I guess," Ren said, tucking the water into his back pocket and stacking the kits up in his arms. "Let's get back to Elio," Ren said, heading back toward the front of the store. Lilly and Lyonel had both returned as well. A mountain of at least fifty different flavors of jerky piled nearly as high as Lyonel stood.

"Lucky day," Ren said sarcastically. "All the jerky in the world, two waters, and a couple of first aid kits. How could the end of the world get any better?"

"It could end again," Elio said with a pained grin as he poured the water over the exposed wound. "Lilly, Lyonel, can you two do me a favor and go look for some thread and a needle? The wrap isn't gonna hold up very long, and we will need to seal the wound up before we head back out."

"On it!" Lilly said, disappearing back into the depths of the store, dragging Lyonel along for good measure.

"I don't think the kid is lying about being born here," Elio said while they waited for the kids to return.

"Oh? Why is that?"

"His soul—or rather, lack of one."

"I'm intrigued," Tama said to Ren.

"What about it?"

"Well, even if my memories are skewed somehow, the how should still be accurate, right? And if that's the case, then he would not have been around to be split."

"I guess that makes sense. But the confusing part is, how did something happen to you only a year ago when he is almost nine now?"

"I wish I knew... To be honest, I don't know what to believe anymore. And thanks to you, those goddamn walls off in the distance only make me question things even more. If the world ended, then who built the walls? Where did they come from? And why are they here?"

"The outsiders built them," Lyonel said as they returned, Lilly with thread in hand, needle included.

"The outsiders?" Ren asked, confused. "Who are they?"

"No one knows," Lyonel said. "Everyone back home always spoke of weird happenings and such—talk always just passed off as rumors."

"Like what, exactly?" Elio said, handing the thread and needle to Ren.

"I don't wanna do that."

"I don't recall asking you if you wanted to. Just like I don't remember asking to be shot twice. Yet here I am."

"Fine," Ren said begrudgingly, kneeling over and threading the needle.

"Sorry, Lyonel—please continue," Elio said as Ren pierced his skin with the needle. Elio winced as Lyonel continued.

"Odd blinking lights, strange shadows, the occasional humming in the air. That kind of stuff."

"Great, more questions for the Madman. Ow!" he snapped, glaring at Ren. "Do you have to be so goddamn rough?"

"Sorry, I am kind of new to this whole playing doctor shit."

"Yeah, yeah. Just finish it up already. We need to get moving." He turned to Lilly's collection of jerky. "Eat what you can. We are not taking all of that with us—only what we can comfortably carry.

Comfortably," he repeated with emphasis.

"Lilly, can you hand me those scissors over there?" Ren asked, pointing with his elbow as a needle and thread occupied both his hands.

"Sure," she said, passing a sad glance at her jackpot of jerky and sulking back and forth with the scissors in hand before passing them to Ren.

"Thank you," he said with a smile. "I am sure we can figure out a way to bring along most of your jerky. BUT no more," he said, tying off the thread and cutting the extra.

"Really!" she said excitedly while Elio rolled his eyes, even at the thought.

"Why don't you and Lyonel go see if you can find a way of carrying as much of it as we can?"

"Okay! Come on, Lyonel, let's go!"

"What are you doing…" Elio said as Ren pulled out a roll of tan bandages from the small first aid kit.

"What? It makes her happy and is an easy win. We don't know how many more easy wins we may get. Where we are going, we may never get another win at all."

"Fair," he said. "It's the little wins we often lose sight of as the war looms."

"All set. Obviously, take it easy." Elio met him with an unimpressed scoff before flinching in pain as he slipped back into his trench coat. "You know what I mean."

"Will this work?" Lilly said, pushing an empty stroller through the store. A small onesie sat in the child's place, its soul now wandering through the end of the world alone.

"I suppose it does," Elio said with an uncomfortable look as Lilly casually discarded the onesie and began swiftly loading up the stroller with her stash of dehydrated meats. As she went to fill the bottom slot of the stroller, Elio interjected. "Let's save that spot for some extra bottles of water." Then he turned to Ren as he finished the remaining water used to clean his wound. "Place like this must have personalized security. Ren, check under the counter for anything that goes bang. I will check the back room. Lilly, can you and Lyonel gather up some more bottles of water? A dozen bottles should be good. The rest of the space, you can cram as much jerky as you want."

"OKAY!" she said, dashing away toward the cooler doors. Lyonel chased after her of his own volition.

"I will be right back," Elio said, heading off toward the back of the store.

"You sure…" Ren said before quickly being shut down.

"Don't worry. I have no intention of blowing my brains out. If that was how I was meant to go out, the damned safety wouldn't have been on." He grinned before turning and disappearing down the hall.

"He really has a way with words," Tama said slowly, wandering over to the counter and hopping up. Ren circled around the side.

"That's one way of putting it, I suppose."

"You know, it was only a few days ago we met Elio in a gas

station not too unlike this one."

"True," Ren said, looking around.

"Time sure flies when you're running for your life. Hey, you see anything down there? Also, I wonder if Lilly still has that pistol," Tama said curiously. "Like, where does Haku even go under that hoodie?" Ren leaned over and pulled a long-barreled shotgun out from under the counter.

"I assume this will go bang," Ren said sarcastically, setting it on the counter and kneeling back down to look for any ammo to go with it.

"Nothing," he said, standing back up to see Elio wandering back from the hallway.

"Guessing there is a shotgun lurking around here somewhere," he said, before seeing his assumption on the counter. "Oh, you already found it." He dropped a green-and-black box down next to it. He lifted the dark green lid to reveal twenty-eight little red shells, with the last two slots empty. "I reckon if we have to use all these, we are probably already dead."

"That's all you find back there?"

"Yeah, not much else of value in the end of the world."

"Ready!" Lilly said, pushing the stroller over to them, a dozen waters buried under the heap of various red and black packets.

"Well, I think we have lingered long enough already. Let's get out of here," Elio said, making his way over to the entrance. All the others followed—everyone except for Lyonel. Noticing this, Tama nudged Ren and motioned toward the lone boy still standing in the center of the store.

"You coming, Lyonel?" Ren asked, taking a pause. The others stopped in the entranceway to wait. Lyonel was shaking, his voice trembling as he responded.

"I can't... He is out there. He is watching."

"You mean the Collector, right?" Ren said, to which Lyonel nodded his head.

"He killed all those people. He will kill me, too. No one is safe—not even all of you."

"That's true," Ren said flatly. "To be honest, coming with us will be dangerous." He paused for a second. "But if we hide from the fear of what bad may happen, we miss out on what good could happen. So, let's see what we can, together." Lilly stepped past Ren and slowly walked over to Lyonel, reaching her hand forward. Lyonel raised his gaze from the floor to hers; their eyes locked. Elio, Tama, and Ren stood proudly behind her.

"Together," she said with a powerful smile. Lyonel wiped away his tears and nodded as he took her hand.

"Together." The two joined the others as they stepped back out into the Madman's Wonderland together.

CHAPTER FIFTEEN
The Guardian of Hell

The stroller squeaked as it rattled down the unmaintained, middle-of-nowhere road. Abandoned cars sat parked along the edges of the desolate street, now overtaken by unfettered nature. Lilly pushed it happily along, periodically swapping with Haku, who took over while she snacked on her precious cargo.

"Will that work?" Lilly said excitedly, her mouth still full of salty meat. They had finally reached the water that separated them from their destination—the ultimate resting place of their RV. Lilly was pointing at a small overturned wooden boat that sat along the edge of the massive body of water.

"I don't see why not," Elio said. "As long as it floats and can still do so with all of us in it, we should be able to row across."

"Row?" Lilly said. "I think Haku and I can handle that," she said with a playful smile.

As they reached the boat, Elio gave it a thorough once-over while the others watched.

"Should be good. Well, good enough, anyway. Grab the other

end, would you, Ren?" he said, bending over and motioning at the opposite end.

"Yeah!" Ren said, setting Tama down and lifting the opposite side. The pair slowly carried the boat over to the water and flipped it as it made its splashing return to its natural habitat upon the deep blue river.

"Alright. Everyone, get in," Elio said as he wandered over to grab the two paddles that had been tucked comfortably under the hollow side of the boat. Lilly smirked as he wandered over to them all sitting and waiting in the boat.

"I already told you. We won't need those," she said as Elio hopped into the small boat. Ren was on the far end of where he sat now, with Lilly and Lyonel sitting in the small seat in the middle.

"Okay, and how exactly do you plan to get this boat to the other side without these?" he said, tossing a paddle towards Ren before dipping his into the water.

"Like this," she said with a grin. Smoke funneled from her hoodie and formed a twister above the boat, swinging towards Ren and forming into a fan blade. The fan spun faster and faster as the boat slid forward atop the water. "Hold on, everyone!" she said with glee as the boat sped up and then blasted off across the water. It skipped like a stone as Ren, Tama, Lyonel, and Elio gripped the side of the boat for dear life as they made their way across the vast, glistening blue that consumed their RV. Their paddles drifted along in the ripples left behind.

"How do we stop?" Elio asked as the shoreline rapidly came into view.

"Stop?" Lilly asked, confused, as if the thought had never even occurred to her.

"Brace for impact, everyone!" Elio yelled. The smoky fan slowed to a halt before reversing, the boat slowing, but it was already too late. The boat blasted onto the shore and ran aground before coming to a stop.

"That… was… AWESOME!" Lilly yelled as she jumped out of the boat. The rest of the small group were more apprehensive and appreciative of being back on solid ground.

"I will be damned. We made it to the other side," Tama said in disbelief.

"Can we do that again?" Lilly asked excitedly, tugging on Elio's sleeve, each tug reminding him of the bullet hole in his arm.

"No!" everyone responded simultaneously at the thought of ever doing that again.

"Well now, what?" Ren asked as they slowly approached the road, leaving the bridge.

"I guess we follow the road here until we reach the White House." Elio pointed to a sign clearly directing them to their destination.

"Seems easy enough," Lilly said, stepping forward onto the road, pulling Lyonel along.

"Nothing here is ever as easy as it seems," Ren said as he and Tama followed suit. Elio walked close behind, with Gur walking along his side.

Outside of the slightly worn road that crumbled and cracked as they walked along, the sights of the local area were almost fully intact—almost protected from the event that had ravaged everything else at the end of the world. The buildings that ran along the road looked well maintained, not dusty or damaged at all.

"This is weird," Elio said, looking around as they walked. "Why is it all so clean? Cleaner almost than most cities before the end of the world."

"It feels almost as if we are on a set of some play or movie," Ren said. "I keep waiting for the song and dance to begin."

"I don't like it at all," Elio said. Lilly and Lyonel held each other's hands as they dashed curiously from side to side of the road, taking in all the sights like two seasonal tourists up in the summer.

"Me either. Something feels off about it."

"True." They paused and watched as Lilly and Lyonel found a small swing set.

"Can we swing for a few minutes?" Lilly begged as the pair scampered over to Elio and Ren for approval. Lyonel smiled along at the idea. Ren and Elio looked at each other and then back at them.

"Sure. But only for a few minutes, okay? Who knows what is lurking on this side of the bridge?" Elio said, turning towards a white wooden bench that faced the small play area in the yard. "My arm hurts. Let's sit while they play."

"Sounds good to me." Ren took the handle of the jerky-loaded stroller and pushed it over to the back of the bench. They sat down and watched as Lilly and Lyonel swung while Haku pushed them gently into the air. Tama sat in the middle of the bench, with Gur to the left of Elio.

"You know, Ren? It's times like this that actually give me hope

—that they, and those like them, can still fix what's left of this world. Topple the sick games at play and put this mess of a puzzle back together." They sat in silence and watched as Lilly and Lyonel played together—two kids just being kids in a world that had taken their chance at a proper childhood away.

Elio nudged Ren awake. "Hey, time to get going," he said before raising his voice and motioning over to Lilly and Lyonel. "All right, you two, time to get moving again."

"Already?" Lilly said, disappointed, as she hopped from her swing, and they chased each other over to the bench where Elio and Ren sat.

"Already? It's been well over an hour. More than enough play time for you, too. This one here even fell asleep."

"I'm sorry. Didn't mean to."

"It's alright," Elio interjected. "You obviously needed a little top-off."

"Thanks," Ren said, getting up, Tama sliding off his lap to the ground as Ren let out a long stretch.

"Lyonel and I were talking, and when we win, we wanna get a castle and live together eating jerky for the rest of our lives."

"Yeah," Lyonel affirmed.

"That's fun," Elio said with a smile. "Room for one more in that jerky-loaded castle?"

"Maybe. That depends if you bring your own jerky," Lilly said as Ren laughed.

"I am sure I can work something out with my jerky guy," Elio winked.

"You see that?" Ren said, pointing forward. "Everyone, stay close."

"Lilly, Lyonel, get over here," Elio said firmly. The pair followed his instructions and quickly got behind him. "What did you see, Ren? Is it the Collector again?"

"Not sure. It was large, though, and it didn't want to be seen." A massive ball of fire then flew from ahead of them.

"Look out!" Elio yelled as he dove in front of Lilly and Lyonel, grabbing them in each arm and ducking forward to shield them. Ren dashed to the opposite side as Tama followed and threw a protective dome of fire over Ren and himself. The massive ball of fire exploded in the center of the road; the heat melted the pavement both at and around its impact. As they all gathered their senses, a massive figure wandered slowly down the road, led by a much smaller, more humanlike form. The large shape became clear as the smoke and heat slowly dissipated from the surrounding air. Walking towards them was a massive three-headed dog, none other than the guardian of the gates of hell itself: Cerberus.

A feminine laugh echoed from the creature's direction. Standing in front of Cerberus was a scantily clad woman. What little of her was clothed was done so in a dark red leather that left little to the imagination. Long black hair flowed elegantly over her soft, mature body.

"Well well, look what the cat went and dragged in," the woman said in a sultry voice. Her attention was drawn to Ren. "Oh, and who might you be, cutie?" She licked her lips. "Care for a taste?"

she said with a wink.

"I really hope I don't have to tell you it's a trap," Elio said, rolling his eyes. "Now is not the time to let your dick do the thinking." Ren was already lost in her lusty appearance, and Tama batted him with his right paw, knocking him back to reality.

"Yeah. Obviously," he said, glancing the other way to see Lilly and Lyonel laughing at him. "Shut up, you two."

"The boy is not on the tasting menu, lady. What do you want?"

"Me? I want the only thing that matters in life: pleasure." She touched herself gently. Her hands caressed her body from her neck and over her plump breasts, all the way down the curves that led her fingertips to her soft, peeking panties. Ever the loyal husband, Elio stood firm in his love for his lost wife.

"Go sit on a washer, you horny housewife. There are children around, so why don't you run on home and throw on some damned clothes?" She went silent, frozen in the moment as if captured by a photograph, before breaking down into a dramatic sob and dropping to her knees.

"What the hell, Elio? You made her cry," Ren snapped. Tama rolled his eyes at Ren's clueless and boyish immaturity.

"Whose side are you on?" Elio clapped back. With her guilt trip unsuccessful, the woman stood up and wiped the fake tears from her face.

"Look at that. A man that's held true love in his arms." She licked her lips again. "What happened? Did she leave you?" The woman walked slowly towards Elio. Her body flowed like a gorgeous stream shimmering in the warm sun. "She sneak around with the mailman? Or maybe she ran away with her boss?"

"She died," Elio answered flatly, unamused by her words.

"Oh? A tragedy." She walked and spoke with the confidence of a woman who'd never been told no, untouchable as her three-headed guardian stood watch patiently. "Nothing makes me drip like a man that can't be attained. His heart, always and forever, another's." She leaned forward and passionately locked lips with Elio. A kiss of frustration and pent-up passion unlocked through the soft touch of her tongue as it swirled around in his mouth. Lilly, Lyonel, Tama, and even Gur stood in shocked silence as they watched Elio melt at her sexual touch.

Filled with confusing jealousy, Ren marched forward and pushed the woman off Elio, placing himself between him and her. Elio's eyes opened to disappointment.

"What the fuck, Ren!" he said before Ren clapped Elio upside his head. Elio slowly turned back to Ren, a tear in his eye, though not from the slap.

"Thank you," he said as a gunshot rang out from behind them. Lyonel dropped to the ground; his hand hung limp in Lilly's hand. He was dead. Lilly cried out.

"Lyonel!" Elio and Ren yelled together. As another gunshot rang out, Elio turned to see a small pistol in the woman's hand. Ren grabbed his stomach and dropped to his knees, pulling his hands back to reveal a massive amount of warm blood oozing from within. Lilly screamed as another bullet flew at her, caught by Haku with grace. The woman backed up slowly towards her loyal guardian.

"You little shit! How dare you lay your perverse hands on me!" Another bullet flew towards Ren. This one was also intercepted by the now-alert Haku.

"Haku! Can you fix Ren?" Elio asked. Lilly composed herself. Tears dripped from her face as she let go of Lyonel's motionless hand and rushed to Ren's side so Haku could work his magic.

"We need a couple minutes!" Lilly yelled to Elio; her voice was shaky as she watched Lyonel slowly being swallowed up by his own blood.

"A couple minutes. I can do a couple of minutes," Elio said, glancing over to Gur. "You ready, big guy?" Gur nodded as another shot rang out. Elio glanced over at Lyonel and pulled out from under his large trench coat the shotgun they had picked up from the gas station. "All right, bitch—you wanna fuck? Let's fuck." He cocked the shotgun and blasted the scattershot toward the fleeing woman, who fired off another shot in her retreat.

With the distance between her and Cerberus cleared, the massive dog kneeled as she climbed atop its back. Once standing, the head in the middle launched a fireball from deep within its throat. Elio mounted Gur and, while rushing at the Cerberus, let out another blast of the shotgun in its direction. The bullets fell short as Gur wound up on its hind legs and smacked the ball of fire to the left. It obliterated a nearby building on contact in an enormous explosion.

The left head fired off a shard of ice as a ball of electricity flew from the depths of the gigantic dog's right head. Elio finished reloading his shotgun just in time to blast the ball of ice out of the air, while Gur bashed the sparky orb to the opposite side of the fire.

Another building decimated upon contact.

"Why won't you die!" the woman yelled. "Kill him!" she said, hitting Cerberus's back with the gun and kicking her long heels into its side. "Useless dog. I will do it myself," she finished as she aimed the gun at Elio and pulled the trigger back-to-back. The bullets both flew directly at their target.

"Well, Gur, it's been a good ride, buddy, but I am off to see my wife again." He closed his eyes and waited for the sweet release of death. His wife's beautiful blue eyes were all he could see when he heard a voice to his right.

"Not yet, old man!" Ren yelled from atop the back of a large, familiar creature. Lilly perched in front of a massive, smoky illusion of a dragon. Tama proudly rode at the nape like a captain at the helm of a pirate ship. In the air, directly in front of Elio's face, was a pillowy cloud of smoke that contained two bullets, each unfazed from the collision with the puff. Elio looked down and muttered under his breath. "Guess it wasn't time, dear. I will see you soon. Take good care of Clara while I finish things up here." Before letting out a deep sigh and turning to his comrades.

"You good?" he said to Ren as they continued their advance on the woman.

"I am. Haku is a way better doctor than I ever could be," he said with a sarcastic grin. "You should have had him stitch you up back there."

"I will keep that in mind. Alright, enough stalling. Let's finish this," Elio said, turning forward. The cloud dropped the two bullets and disappeared. Before the bullets hit the ground, Tama and Ren jumped from atop Haku, who dashed in the blink of an eye to the side of the massive three-headed dog. Haku's tail shifted into a long blade and cut through all three heads as Haku spun through the air. Gur lunged forward as Elio took aim and pulled the trigger directly at the woman.

The woman fell to the ground as the Cerberus slowly faded away. The soft clang of two bullets rang out as they bounced on the pavement next to Tama and Ren. It was over. They had won.

Elio hopped off Gur. While Haku disappeared back into the warm comfort of Lilly's hoodie, Ren rushed over with Tama in his arms. They stood circled around the body of their lost ally.

"Not even nine years old," Elio said. "He deserved better than this. A childhood, a family, a chance at life." Ren and Tama stood in silence while Lilly sobbed at the loss of her friend.

"Can we…" She took a brief pause and wiped her tears as she leaned forward and gently closed his eyelids. "Can we bury him?" Elio choked back the lump in his throat.

"Of course," he said, placing his hand on her shoulder. "He deserves at least that." Elio leaned forward and picked up Lyonel's warm body, making their way over to a small yard of a nearby house. Gur quickly went to work scooping out dirt to make a small, deep enough hole to place the body. Once done, Elio kneeled over and placed Lyonel in the small hole, folding his arms over his chest. Elio stepped out of the hole and slowly backed up as Lilly stepped forward.

"I hope you find your parents out there. As my friend, I will miss you." She wiped her face with her sleeve and turned away from the hole and sobbed. Elio took a step forward and cleared his throat.

"As children, we fear the monsters under our beds, the creatures that watch us sleep from the depths of our closets." He wiped a tear from his blood-soaked face. "However, as we grow older, we realize the creatures we hid under our blankets from as children were only hiding from what we would become. Lyonel will never have to face this reality, though he lived through things no child should ever have to suffer through. He still held tight to that childlike naivety we all once had. No child deserves to watch his own parents die. No child deserves to be born into a world that's already come to its conclusion." He paused. "Lyonel was a good kid, and he deserved better." Elio took a step backward and turned to Ren. "What's done is done. Say your piece, and let's get moving. Who knows what other wackos are wandering around here?"

Ren looked down at the peaceful-looking boy. If Ren didn't know about the bullet hole in his heart that lay below his folded arms, he would think he was only sleeping. Three words were all he could muster before turning away to let Gur put him to rest.

"I am sorry," he said as the mound of dirt that sat next to the hole washed over him and returned Lyonel to his parents.

CHAPTER SIXTEEN
A Brief Reprieve

Emotions were heavy as they wandered slowly down the meticulously maintained road. The sun was now high in the sky, and they could see in the distance their long-awaited destination: the White House.

"We should be there in about an hour," Elio said, pointing in the building's direction.

"I can't believe it; we actually made it," Ren said to no one in particular. Lilly kicked at the ground while she walked along. She had been unusually quiet since they had put Lyonel to rest only an hour earlier.

"You okay, Lilly?" Ren asked, only to be met with an indiscernible shrug. "Okay—just know we are here for you." To which Tama said, "Tell her she can pet me. I will even let her carry me if she would like."

"You wanna pet," he rolled his eyes, "or even carry Tama?" Lilly looked up from the ground and nodded. Tama jumped from Ren's arms to hers gracefully and was immediately snuggled tightly as

Lilly cried into his soft, glowing fur while Haku pushed the stroller along behind her.

"See, a little Tama goes a long way," Tama said begrudgingly, being smothered with sadness and affection.

"Tama really likes that, Lilly. You feel a little better?" She nodded while wiping her tears off Tama and sniffling.

"Yeah… a little."

"It's okay to be sad. Even though his time with us was limited and cut short, we all miss him. However, I know he is in a better place now, and I am sure he is watching over us even now as we near the end of our adventure."

"Really?" she asked, before following the question up with another sniffle.

"Really, really," Ren said with a kind smile. Tama peeked out to catch his breath and nodded to her in agreement.

"The only reliable part of life is that it will come to an end. Yet even that is unreliable in how or when," Elio said dryly. "It's been a long day. I think we should find a place to rest for the night." The large white building was now clearly discernible from where they stood. A large gate surrounded the bright green yard. "Tomorrow, each of us will have to make our final decision: to proceed or turn back. What we have to turn back to—well, I don't know."

Lilly pointed at a small yellow house, pristinely maintained like every other building they had seen on this side of the bridge—the only damage caused by them and left behind.

"What about that one?" The house was across the street from a small convenience store. Ren noted that the large sign that displayed the gas prices was lit, as was a small orange neon light that read "open" on the door.

"That store seems to have power," Ren said, while Elio turned from the house he was already heading toward.

"That's interesting," Elio said, intrigued. Lilly rushed by him to the house and gave the door a knock. Tama landed on the second step as she impatiently turned the knob and disappeared inside.

"I wonder if everything on this side of the bridge has power?" Ren added, following them up the steps.

"Water! The house has running water!" Lilly yelled from inside.

"I guess that answers that," Ren said. As he approached the door, he saw a small piece of paper tacked to the right of it.

"What's that?" Elio asked curiously. Ren read the note aloud.

"Congratulations on making it this far. Please enjoy a brief reprieve with all the amenities one could want. A warm shower, delicious food, and a relaxing night's rest—all well-earned, of course. See you tomorrow. The Madman."

"How kind of him," Elio said sarcastically.

"All that for only a week of living hell. What a deal," Ren said dismissively.

"Well, let's get settled in, I guess." Elio glanced down at the stroller; its reserves were nearly depleted, with only a couple packets of jerky left. "Why don't you and Tama go check out the store and grab some more food and water? Maybe something other than dehydrated meat, if possible."

"Sure," he said, turning toward the store, Tama prancing along at his side.

"Ren!" Elio yelled. Ren turned around to catch the shotgun flying in his direction. "Just in case." Ren nodded before going his separate way toward the store, the door to the house closing behind Elio.

The little bell above the door rang as Ren pushed the clear glass door open and stepped into the store. Like everything outside, the inside was pristine. Every shelf was well stocked with anything and everything you would expect from a typical gas station. The lights above hummed with the buzz of cheap fluorescent lighting, and the drinks in the cooler were cold even to sight.

"Hello there. How may I help you today?" an unfamiliar voice asked from behind the counter to the right of the store. Ren quickly cocked the shotgun and pointed it in the voice's direction.

"Whoa there, buddy—no need for such hostility," the man said with his hands in the air.

"Yeah, tell that to the dead kid buried down the road from here." Ren kept his weapon locked on the man and slowly circled around to the front of the counter. Tama perched atop his shoulder with two small balls of flame in the surrounding air.

"But you are here now, which means you have dealt with the last threat on your treacherous trip here—the last test of the many. Please enjoy your brief reprieve before heading off to the final stage of the games."

"Games?" Ren became overcome with rage unlike anything he had felt before. "You pieces of shit and your fucking games." He stepped forward and thrust the barrel of the gun into the clerk's face. "An innocent kid is dead. Is that just another part of the so-called game you bastards keep spouting on about?"

"I suppose it would be," he responded casually, with an uncomfortable calm. Ren lowered the gun slightly. The reaction caught him off guard. Ren's curiosity overtook his anger, and the man continued. Tama kept his guard up, however, remaining ready for anything.

"Let's not dwell too much on that, though. After all, tomorrow is the big day. You and your little gang have caused quite a stir, and everyone is on the edge of their seats to see what will happen once the games' finale starts. But that's enough about that. How may I help you?"

"Wait a second—back up." Ren raised the gun back up into the air. "What do you mean, games' finale?"

"I am so sorry, but I cannot answer that question. You will just have to wait and see." He leaned over the counter and placed his finger on the tip of the gun, slowly motioning it to the ground. "Now, let's get this hostility out of the way." Ren followed the direction of the man, his voice calm and confident as he de-escalated the situation with Ren, who lowered the gun completely. "You can have the pick of the store—anything you want."

"I don't like this," Tama said.

"Oh, aren't you just the cutest little fella? What exactly is it you are not a fan of?"

"Wait, you can hear him?" Ren said, confused. The strange man let out a casual chuckle.

"Of course, though I suppose you would find that strange." He paused. "Well, as I was saying, tomorrow is the big day. You and your friends have made it farther than most, and it's been quite some time since anyone bothered to even come all this way. As a reward for all your hard work, the meal of your choice will be prepared for each of you. Please gather your party's requests and come back within the hour. Once placed, I will get your requests gathered up and delivered to the restaurant next to the store. See you soon," he said with a smile.

Ren and Tama shared a glance before heading over to the cooler. Ren grabbed three properly chilled waters before picking up a couple packets of jerky for Lilly and two small bags of powdered donuts to mix things up for Elio before he returned to the counter.

"It's on the house," the man said with another smile and wink. As Ren and Tama made their way over to the door: "See you soon!" he said with a wave as the door closed gently behind them.

"What the hell is going on?" Tama asked Ren as they crossed the road back to the house.

"Not sure, but whatever I want to eat sounds pretty damn good right now." Ren turned the knob to the house and stepped inside. They could hear music coming from another room, so Ren and Tama followed the tunes into a large living room. Elio was lying on the long couch, tucked against the wall. The source of the music: a small radio that sat on a small coffee table in the center of the room.

"What do you want for dinner?" Ren asked Elio casually while placing the shotgun in the empty umbrella stand next to the door, not bothering to elaborate at all on the question as he set the snacks down next to the small radio. "Like, if you could have anything, what would it be?"

"I would kill for a duck à l'orange. A favorite of mine ever since culinary school." He paused. "Why do I remember something like that?" he wondered aloud before pivoting back to Ren's question. "Why do you ask?"

"I mean, to be honest, I don't think you would believe me if I told you. Where is Lilly? I need her order as well."

"She is taking a bath; I have never seen her so happy. It was almost like she had never seen running water—nonetheless water that's warm."

"Where is that?"

"Down the hall, second door on the right."

"I am glad she is doing alright. It can't be easy just pushing forward with everything that's happened today."

"She is tough. Something tells me this isn't the first time she has lost someone since waking up here in Wonderland."

"Let's make it the last," Ren said as a tear formed in the well of his eye.

"Yeah. Together till the end."

"Together," Ren said, turning down the hall. "Oh, we have dinner in a couple of hours at the restaurant across the road." Lilly came out of the bathroom, steam flowing all around her, disguising her unwrapped body.

"Go get a towel, Lilly," Ren said, turning away.

"Oh, yeah," she said, disappearing back into the room,

returning more modestly in a long, light blue towel.

"If you could have anything for dinner, what would it be?" he asked as she dried her hair with another towel. This was the first time that Ren had seen Lilly not wearing her hoodie. He wondered where Haku was.

"A Happy Meal! With twenty nuggets and sweet and sour sauce. Oh! And strawberry milkshake—the biggest one I can have."

"I don't know if that's possible."

"You said anything!" she said, disappointed.

"You did say anything," Elio said, leaning over the back of the couch, eighties rock playing in the background.

"Alright," Ren said with a sigh. "I will let him know."

"Let who know?" Elio asked while Lilly disappeared upstairs excitedly to get dressed.

"You hear that, Haku? We get McDonald's for dinner!" Ren rolled his eyes and turned to answer Elio.

"The guy at the store. He said we earned a brief reprieve before tomorrow. That, and a bunch of other crazy stuff. Not that he would elaborate on any of it."

"Not a threat?"

"No—the opposite, in fact. Said we can have anything we want from the store, and said that we had earned the meal of our dreams—just to let him know within the hour, and that he would see it done."

"Guy sounds just as crazy as everyone else we have met. But if he isn't a threat and is offering us free food, I say why not? What's the worst that could happen? We get poisoned the day before we probably die." He chuckled. "You asked all of us, but I am curious, Ren. What do you want?"

Ren hadn't thought of that. What would he want? He had never been a fan of food, really, that he could remember. As a poor kid, he never got to try anything all that special. He thought back to when he first met Elio, the meal he had made them.

"I think a simple filet mignon would be good, though. I can't imagine the chef could outdo the best chef I know," Ren said with a smile, picking up the shotgun as he stepped out of the house. "Just in case," he said, grinning as he closed the door behind him.

"Don't you think this is all a bit weird?" Tama asked Ren as they made their way back to the store.

"I mean, yeah. But I think Elio is right. What's the worst that could really happen? We have all kinda come to an agreement that something is not right—the walls, the strange dreams, and the flashbacks—not to mention the fact no one seems to know when everything landed the world in its current state. It seems we are only a good meal and a night's rest away from any potential answers to these questions. So, why bother searching for additional problems now?" The bell above the door echoed through the store as Ren pushed it open.

"I suppose you are right."

"Back so fast? Delightful," the man said from behind the counter. "So, what do our spectacular guests want for dinner this fine evening? Let's start with Elio."

"Elio would like…" Ren paused, realizing that he had

mentioned none of their names previously. "Duck à l'orange. How did you know his name?"

"Tsk, tsk—you know I can't tell you that," he said dismissively as he wrote something down on a small piece of paper. Ren assumed it was Elio's food order. "Great, and what about Lilly?" Tama and Ren shared a concerned glance, both curious how the odd man knew their names.

"A Happy Meal. With a side of twenty McNuggets and the largest strawberry milkshake you can order. Oh, and a few sweet and sour sauces for the nuggets."

"Of course, of course. What else would a twelve-year-old want?" Ren raised his eyebrow at that. How did he know her age as well? Just who was this strange clerk? His pen stopped moving and went crooked in his hand. "And for you?" he said, looking at Ren.

"Wait, you can do that?" he said in shock. There was no way. It wasn't as if he could just go to McDonald's and buy a Happy Meal, right?

"No need to fret about the logistics. Have no fear: Lilly shall have her Happy Meal."

"But that's not possible," Ren said in disbelief.

"Anything is possible when the façade of perception is no longer the reality," he said with a grin. "Now, about your order. What would you like?" Ren was growing irritated with the riddles and realized that he would never get a straight answer out of the man.

"A filet mignon. I will let the chef decide the sides."

"Wonderful! I will get this order in ASAP. Dinner will be at six." The man glanced over at a clock hung on the wall to the left of the counter. "That's about an hour from now. We look forward to seeing you next door. Additionally, each of you will find a spectacular array of clothing in your rooms across the street. Please come dressed in a comfortable, yet proper, fashion."

"Thanks…" Ren said, passing another uncomfortable glance to Tama, who stood at attention near the door.

"See you soon!" the man said excitedly as he opened a hidden door behind the counter and disappeared behind it.

"That guy really weirds me out," Tama said while walking along with Ren, who loaded up a small basket with more jerky, water, and an assortment of other snacks.

"I agree. He knows too much and says a lot, but what he says rings hollow and only leaves more questions than answers." They left the store and returned to the others, opening the door to see Lilly in a bright yellow dress, with a deep purple bag hung around her arm—most likely containing a sleeping Haku within.

"Dinner is at six," Ren said, setting the basket of goodies down on the table. Only one bag of donuts remained from his previous store run. "Looks like you are ready. Where is Elio?"

"He just finished in the shower and is getting dressed upstairs." Lilly spun around in her fancy dress. "I feel like a princess!" she said with childlike glee, not uncommon for her.

"You certainly look like one, too," he said with a smile, glad to see her back to her happy self. "I will follow suit then and get cleaned up a bit as well. Let Elio know dinner is at six when he comes down."

"Okay!" she said, with another excited twirl while ripping into a packet of freshly delivered jerky.

The door closed behind Ren before he quickly removed his clothing and slipped into the shower. The water was instantly warm, most likely from the previous users. He took a deep breath as the water flowed over his body. Various shades of red and brown washed away with the stress of the past few days. So much had happened, and all so fast—and now he was taking a warm shower and heading to dinner at a restaurant, a turn in events he did not see coming when he woke up in a jail cell the night prior.

Then his thoughts flashed to Lyonel. What would he have wanted as his last meal? Surely, he deserved better than a packet of jerky.

There was a loud knock at the door.

"Not to cut it short in there—trust me—but dinner is in fifteen minutes," Elio said, cracking the door slightly.

"Okay!" he yelled back. Reality kicked in as he turned the water off. The soft, lingering drips of water grew cold as they slid down his body. He grabbed a large white towel and quickly dried off before opening the door. Standing at the end of the hall, next to a spinning Lilly, was Elio, dressed in a long black suit. He was clean-shaven and even had his hair slicked back.

"You clean up well," Ren said.

"Thanks," Elio said, almost embarrassed at the compliment. "Your room's the second on the right. I think Tama's already there."

"Awesome. Be right down," he said, dashing up the stairs to his room. Once inside, he looked around to see Tama curled up on a massive king-size bed, with more pillows than anyone could ever possibly use. Directly across from the door was a window, and to the left of the room was a sliding door that opened into a massive closet.

As he stepped into the room, he saw clothes laid out on his bed next to the sleeping Tama: a suit nearly identical to what Elio had been wearing, only altered to be his size. Quickly getting dressed, he finished up with a tussle of his hair to give it that just-woke-up look and poked Tama.

"Time to head out," he said as Tama let out a long stretch.

"Do I have to?" Tama whined. "I was so comfy. What about my brief reprieve?"

"Yes. You have to," Ren said as he scooped him up and proceeded downstairs.

"Not too bad-looking yourself," Elio said with a snarky grin. "Everyone ready?"

"Oi!" Lilly said with another spin. Ren wondered if Haku could throw up, and if so, how many more spins it would take.

"Yes," Ren said with a smile, while Tama let out an uninterested yawn.

"Off to dinner, then," Elio said, opening the door as they all stepped outside. Ren turned back and stepped inside.

"Oh, I almost forgot."

"Not tonight," Elio said in a comforting tone. "Whatever happens next, happens. Let's just enjoy the time we still have."

"Okay," Ren said, glancing apprehensively at Tama before closing the door. The shotgun was still inside as Ren closed the door and returned to the group as they all made their way across the road together. Next to the store was a sign that read "Now Open" and, in big letters above the restaurant door, read the word Eden.

CHAPTER SEVENTEEN

Reservations at Eden

Elio opened the restaurant door, and they stepped into a large open space. A large black piano sat in the far-right corner of the room, and in the very center of the room was a single large wooden table with three chairs placed around it. Standing at a small podium next to the entrance was the same man from the store.

"Hello, party of three?" he asked, glaring at Tama while scooping up three menus from a small slot in his podium. "Right this way, please," he motioned for them to follow him. When they reached the table, he pulled out Lilly's chair, and she hopped up and gently slid forward while Elio and Ren seated themselves. "We have a spectacular variety of beverages this evening," the man said as he placed a copy of the beverage menu in front of each of them. Ren, sitting in the middle, noted that Lilly had a different menu, one that had no alcoholic beverages on it. However, even though Ren was not of legal age either, they did not filter his menu down to exclude alcohol. While sliding a much smaller chair up next to the table for Tama, the man leaned in and whispered in Ren's left ear.

"I won't tell if you don't."

"Whiskey—the bottle can linger at the table," Elio said, handing the menu back to the man.

"Knows what he wants, this one," the man said with a chuckle. "And you, deary?" he said, turning to Lilly. "Or is the biggest strawberry milkshake ever made enough for you?" he said with a wink.

"Really!" she said with glee.

"Really, really," he replied, as Lilly composed herself and sat up proper in her seat as she replied.

"That will do delightfully, kind sir," finishing up with a giggle as she kicked her feet back and forth under the table.

"Wonderful. How about you?" he said, looking at Ren from the other side of the table.

"A strawberry lemonade would be delightful," he said with a smile.

"Great!" the man said with a peppy smile. "I will go gather those up and be back in a jiffy with your meals." He then turned away from the table and disappeared behind a deep red curtain that hung along the left side of the room.

"He certainly is odd," Elio said once he was out of earshot.

"I like him!" Lilly said.

"He is the same man from the store. He took the orders and said a bunch of other weird stuff."

"Anything of note?" Elio asked, but before Ren could answer, the man came out with two massive silver discs, one on each hand.

Almost like a magician, he dropped a small table from his right wrist that plopped open, where he delicately set a covered silver disc. In his opposite hand were the drinks.

"The world's largest milkshake, trademark pending," he said with a chuckle as he set a massive glass loaded to the brim with a creamy red, whipped topping nearly a foot high above the massive glass. A large bendy straw poked out through the cloud of fluffy white, on which a small red cherry sat at the top.

"That's for me? Like, all of it?" she said in utter disbelief, childlike confusion and amazement in her gaze upon the milkshake of her dreams.

"That it is, deary. All for you. That is, unless you would like to share, in which case I can provide additional glasses." Lilly looked at Ren and Elio, then back at the shake. After a brief pause, she turned back to the man.

"No additional glasses will be needed," Lilly said with a devilish grin. The man chuckled as he set a medium glass down on the table and filled it halfway with whiskey. He then set down a small metal ice bucket in the center of the table and placed the bottle of whiskey next to it.

"For you, sir, we have a Macallan Sherry Oak, aged for twenty-five years. A fabulous choice from our chef, if I dare say so myself." Elio picked up the glass and took a small sip before swirling the vast array of various hints and aromas around his mouth. Satisfied with his appraisal, he finished the rest of the glass in one swift go.

"That's a damn fine whiskey."

"I am glad it is to your liking. Last, we have your humble

strawberry lemonade."

"Thank you," Ren said, ignoring the obvious shade at his completely average beverage compared to what now surrounded him at the table.

"Now for the main course." He lifted the lid atop the other large disc, revealing a duck à l'orange, a filet mignon, and a Happy Meal, which sat next to a small white box of twenty McNuggets—five small green-and-white packets to its side. The man placed each dish on the table and stepped back. "Is there anything else I can get for you?"

"Even managed the damn Happy Meal," Elio said in disbelief. "I think we are all set for now. Thank you."

"My pleasure. I will check back in shortly." He took a bow and then disappeared behind the curtain again.

"He is still odd," Elio said as he cut into his meal.

"I still like him!" Lilly said excitedly, tearing into her Happy Meal, pulling out a small yellow toy: a mouse with little red cheeks and a lightning bolt for a tail. She pretended to make it hop along the table while she ate a nugget followed by a french fry from inside the box. Elio took a bite and noticed Ren hadn't started eating yet, his attention focused on his untouched meal in front of him.

"What's up, Ren? Something wrong?"

"No… the opposite, actually." He paused.

"It's exactly the same," Tama interjected.

"How? How did they know?" Ren said in disbelief.

"What are you—" Elio started as he looked down at Ren's

meal and went silent. Lilly, curious about what had made her fellow diners so distracted, finished chewing a chicken nugget.

"What's going on with you three? Even kitty looks confused," she chimed in before taking a long slurp from her milkshake.

"You see it, don't you?" Ren asked Elio.

"I do." Ren's meal was identical to the plate that Elio had prepared for him only a few days prior—the first meal that he had since he had awoken in Wonderland.

"I didn't ask for a side." He paused. "I left it up to the chef. I also never specified how to cook the meat."

"Maybe it's all just a coincidence. Steak and potatoes are a classic pair."

"A coincidence that it's plated identically?" Ren cut into the plump piece of meat, a perfect cook, a perfect match to the one Elio had prepared only a few days earlier for him. "The cook is identical. Is that also just a coincidence?"

"Could be…" Elio said, growing less sure in his stance. "How does it taste?" Ren cut off a sliver of the filet and placed it in his mouth.

"It's the same. If I didn't know where you were all afternoon, I would swear you cooked this." He took a bite of the mashed potatoes. "That meal you made that night was the best thing I had ever had the honor of eating—a meal I will never forget. This meal is undoubtedly identical in every way." Lilly had lost interest in whatever it was they were going on about and had returned to her McDonald's, dipping a nugget into a mound of golden sauce.

"How is everything?" said the quirky man as he stepped out

from behind the curtain.

"It's great!" Lilly said, happily sipping away again at her milkshake.

"Glad to hear that, dear. What about you two? How is everything?"

"My meal is perfect," Ren said.

"Delightful!"

"Too perfect. I actually had this exact meal only a few days ago."

"Oh, what a spectacular coincidence," he replied flawlessly, dodging the assumption in the air. "And how is your duck? A nice pairing with your beverage, I hope."

"Excellent. Thank you," Elio said as the man poured a fresh glass of whiskey.

"Wonderful! Wonderful, so glad to hear it. Now, I know that dinner was prepared special and with a request for each of you. However, dessert is more of a surprise, and it should be ready shortly."

"Dessert!" Lilly said excitedly, her excessive meal and shake not even slowing her down.

"Oh, if it's as good as dinner, I am looking forward to it," Elio said, taking a sip from his freshly refilled glass.

"I certainly hope it doesn't disappoint." He bowed. "Please enjoy the rest of your meal, and I will return shortly." And just like that, he disappeared once again behind the ominous curtain. Elio glanced back over at Ren.

"That man really can dodge a question." He noticed Ren hadn't eaten any more of his food. "Look, don't worry about it. We already knew some weird stuff is up, but food is food—and good food like this," he motioned at the table before pivoting his motion to exclude Lilly's meal, "it doesn't come every day in Wonderland." He finished his glass and poured another. "Enjoy what you can when you can, because you never know when things will end."

"I guess, but…"

"No buts. Tomorrow, we get our answers, or we die trying. So, why worry about it now? Eat up." He took another swig of his drink and turned his attention back to his meal.

"I suppose…" Ren said apprehensively.

"He is not wrong," Tama interjected. "Our questions and their answers are tomorrow's problem. Tonight, we need to gain our strength and prepare to earn them, no matter what we encounter." Ren cut off another piece of the filet and slid it through the creamy mashed potatoes, looking at it as he held the fork in front of him.

"If you don't eat it, I will," Elio said with a grin. The bottle of whiskey now sat half empty.

"I think you have had enough," Ren said with a sassy smile as he took a bite and started in on the rest of his meal. Once Ren took his last bite, the man stepped out from behind the curtain, carrying on his left hand another disc, though this one was much smaller than the previous two.

"Everyone ready for dessert?"

"Yeah!" Lilly blurted out, mid-suck from her straw.

"I suppose there is a bit of extra space," Elio said as he

shuffled up in his seat.

"I see your appetite has changed for the better. Glad to see you enjoyed your meal," the man said, looking at Ren. Tama glanced between them as they locked eyes.

"It was just as good as the last time I had it," Ren said with a mischievous grin.

"I bet it was," the man said, matching Ren's energy. "Tada!" he said, pivoting his tone and body language in the blink of an eye. "For dessert, we have the world-renowned Wonderland tiramisu." He set one glass dish down in front of each of them.

"Tirama-what-now?" Lilly said, confused as she examined the odd blend of items in the glass.

"My apologies—allow me to explain the dish. The Wonderland tiramisu is a spectacular blend of espresso-soaked ladyfingers, a lightly sweetened whipped cream, and a rich mascarpone mix, all topped with a delightful touch of cocoa powder sprinkled on top."

"I don't know what half of that stuff is." Lilly took her spoon and quickly scooped up a bite and swallowed it without hesitation. "But that's the best damn thing I have ever tasted."

Elio and Ren followed suit, each taking a bite.

"I agree. That is quite spectacular," Elio said, watching as Lilly's disappeared in the blink of an eye.

"Very good," Ren said, taking a second bite.

"So glad you like it. Special nights like these are so rare these days. Few make it this far."

"What do you—" Elio started to ask the man as he disappeared once again. "Speedy bastard," Elio mumbled under his breath before taking another bite.

"Lilly was right. That was damn good," Ren said, taking his last bite.

"Do you think I could have another?" Lilly said, licking her dish.

"I think that's enough sugar for one night. Not to mention, I am pretty sure a proper tiramisu contains alcohol. So, yeah."

"No worries there. Our chefs customized the young lady's dish with almond extract—same delightful flavor without that pesky buzz," he added while stepping out from behind the curtain. "And with that, your meal has concluded, and such has our evening together. It has been a pleasure meeting all of you, and I wish you each the best of luck tomorrow."

"Yeah, about tomorrow. What exactly is happening?" Elio asked, hoping to get something from the man as everyone stood up and made their way to the exit.

"The finale. Just make your way to the White House in the morning and do your best."

"That didn't really—" Elio started as the door closed, the man on the other side. "He really has a gift." Ren chuckled.

"It certainly would seem that way. You were right, though; he says a lot that doesn't mean much—at least not to us."

"I like him," Lilly said for the third time that evening. As they crossed the road back to the house, Lilly's yellow toy mouse flew in front of them, guided by a playful Haku cloud, while Lilly chased it about.

"That was a pretty good meal, I must say," Elio said, satisfied and a little drunk. "Been a while since someone else cooked me a meal I was so impressed with."

"That dessert was something special too," Ren said. "Though my entrée still sits a bit weird for me."

"Well, with any luck, this game of theirs will end with some answers." They stepped inside. Lilly entered first, spinning around as she had been earlier and saying, "Haku and I are tired. Night!" She dashed up the stairs and out of sight.

"Can't imagine how she sleeps tonight after all that sugar and espresso, but she has the right idea." Elio turned to Ren, who was carrying Tama in his arms. "I'm gonna turn in for the night as well. I suggest you do the same. Who knows what kind of hell we will step into tomorrow?"

"Yeah, right behind you," Ren said as Elio disappeared upstairs. Once his door latched shut, Ren opened the door behind him and stepped back outside.

"Where are we going?" Tama asked.

"To see about getting some answers," he said as they made their way across the street and back to the store. The bright orange neon sign was still lit. Ren pushed the door open, and the bell hanging above rang just as it had before.

"Still hungry?" a familiar voice asked from behind the counter. It was the same man as before.

"You could say that. I was hoping you may be a bit more helpful with some lingering questions I have."

"Always happy to help. Ask away."

"The walls, off in the distance. They seem to surround what the madman calls Wonderland. What is their purpose, and how did they come to be?" The man's eyebrow raised, intrigued by the directness of the questions.

"The very function of a wall is to contain or exclude. Who is to say which is truly the correct answer in this case?" He paused, thinking over the second question a bit more cautiously. "Time. As with most things, they came to be with time." As expected, it was not much of an actual answer.

"What is on the other side of the walls?" The man's body language shifted slightly, growing more defensive.

"A greener grass perhaps, though I would wonder if that's true for everyone." So, there is something on the other side, Ren thought to himself. Finally, he was getting somewhere. "Oh my, look at the time. I need to get closed up for the night. So, if you wouldn't mind wrapping up so that I can lock the door for the evening."

"Sure thing," Ren said, grabbing a few more packets of jerky and a couple of extra bottles of water before heading over to the door. The man tried to hide a sigh of relief as Ren paused and turned around. "One last question—that is, if you don't mind." Concern washed over the man as he turned to Ren. The man was visibly uncomfortable for the first time since they had interacted.

"Of course."

"What time does McDonald's close?" The man was speechless. A smile sprinted across his impressed face.

"Good luck tomorrow, Ren." As the lights went dark in the

store for only a second, and upon return, the man was gone. Ren looked over at the empty counter.

"You see that?" Tama asked, directing Ren's attention to the clock above. It was no longer ticking along as it was earlier. Instead, it was stuck—the small hand on the two, and the large hand on the twelve.

"Let's go. It's been a day." Ren smiled and closed the door behind him. The duo returned to the house, and just to be safe—and not wake anyone—he plopped down on the couch. Tama landed on the back of the couch before making his way down onto Ren, curling up as they both promptly drifted off to sleep.

CHAPTER EIGHTEEN
The Wonderland Games

His eyes still heavy, Ren awoke to the sound and smell of something cooking in the other room. Tama let out a long stretch as he unfurled from where he had slept, curled up all night atop Ren's back.

"Aw, good, you're finally awake. I thought I would have to wake your lazy ass up. Go get dressed; food is almost done," Elio said from the doorway as Ren slowly sat up and gave his eyes a quick rub.

"Sure," Ren replied as Elio disappeared back to the kitchen. Ren made his way upstairs to get ready for the day. Tama curled back up in the warm spot left behind on the couch. Opening the folding closet doors in his room, Ren selected his choice of outfit from the wide array of options, all of which matched his preferred style. Satisfied with his choices, he slipped into a pair of dark blue jeans and a pair of ankle-high socks. Topped off with a black T-shirt, covered up with a black-and-blue plaid button-up, with the top two left undone.

"Looking good," Tama said, entering the room, as he had

been unable to fall back asleep. He let out a long stretch as Ren finished up with a rough tussle of his hair in his usual fashion. "Now let's get some food."

"Yeah, I am starving. However, last night's meal will be hard to beat. Especially that dessert. It only got better the more I ate. The worst part of it all is knowing I will never taste anything like it again."

"I agree. It was quite good."

"Wait—you can taste what I eat?" Ren asked, slipping on the pair of shoes he had been wearing since he woke up. It was strange; they felt like an odd connection to the Ren he was before he had lost his memory.

"Yeah, though I never really thought about it. Since I only see food as energy, I rarely bother to indulge in the taste side of things."

"Well, let's go get our taste on, then," Ren said as they stepped out of the room.

"That sentence feels weird when you say it," Tama sassed as they made their way downstairs to join the others.

"Hope you're hungry," Elio said as Ren and Tama entered the large kitchen space.

"Very. Also, this place is massive," Ren said, looking around curiously while taking in the space. He had been in and out the day prior, his mind just as busy. He hadn't stopped to take it all in.

"This house is my dream home. Instant hot water, a full bar, and the most equipped kitchen I have ever seen inside a residential property." Ren sat down at the bar seating that rounded the fully exposed kitchen and separated the dining room. Lilly sat in the next seat over, with Tama to Ren's right.

"That looks delicious," Ren said as Elio placed a massive plate of food down in front of Tama and Ren.

"Would Haku like to join us for breakfast?" Elio asked before preparing Lilly's plate.

"He's still sleeping."

"Okay," Elio responded, setting a full plate in front of her and then turning around to grab a plate for himself alongside a platter of bacon, sausages, and toast. The plate in front of each of them contained three sunny-side-up eggs and a side of grated hash browns cooked to golden perfection.

"Where did this all come from?"

"Funny you ask, since I don't actually know. When I came downstairs this morning, there was a knock at the door. However, when I opened the door, there was no one there—only a small wooden crate alone on the stoop. Upon further inspection, it contained everything you now see in front of you."

"Our friendly store clerk, server, and presumably also our chef last night," Ren said, taking a bite.

"Most likely," Elio said as he watched Lilly tear into her plate. Haku, who was conveniently now awake, handed, with smoky hands, toast, bacon, and a couple of sausage links to Lilly, who scarfed it all down in a spectacular blitz. "Find out anything interesting last night?" Elio said, turning his attention to Ren while snagging a couple of bacon strips before they were all snapped up by a ravenous Lilly and her smoky companion. Ren was a bit surprised by the question. He had assumed that he had slipped out successfully.

"Nothing concrete. Our host of many skills is very good at

avoiding direct answers."

"Well, good try anyway."

"However, as non-concrete as his answers were, I am almost one hundred percent sure that there is still a world on the other side of the walls. A fully functioning world."

"If that's true, then the real question changes to: what is the purpose of everything inside the wall?"

"Yeah," Ren said, taking another bite.

"Well, we should get our answers soon, or we will die trying." The room went quiet. Nothing but the sound of food disappearing filled the kitchen. With the platter and all plates empty, Elio raised his head and broke the silence of the meal.

"Before we head out, I wanted to thank you both." He paused. "I had given up on fighting, attached to a lingering thread of a life I was unwilling to cut. Throughout our trip here, you have witnessed me at my lowest, and though the gun didn't kill me, it was you two that saved me. No matter what happens today, just know that I am grateful that I met both of you, and these past few days have reinvigorated my will to live. So, let's go get our answers. So that tomorrow, we can share another meal together for those we have lost along the way."

"Lyonel," Lilly said with a quiver on her lip. The room fell quiet again, all eyes turning away from one another. Ren cleared his throat as he wiped a tear from his cheek.

"On that rooftop only a few days ago, I promised my life to you, Elio." Elio raised his head and turned to Ren. "I know now that promise was a lie. As I sit here now, I want nothing more than to live on. To keep going for Lyonel and all of those that came before. For you all here with me now." Ren cried. "I was already dead to this world when I woke up, so promising you something I never felt I had on that roof was easy." Ren's face was red and wet as he turned to face his companions. "You two didn't just save me; you revived me. So, thank both of you, for everything." Elio smiled and turned to Lilly, giving her a chance to say any last words. However, she was silent. Haku snagged what remained on the table as she gobbled down every bite.

"All right, enough of the soppy shit. We have a game to play," Elio said, turning to Ren.

"Together!" Ren said confidently, with a smile.

"Together!" Lilly and Elio said at once as they stood up and made their way over to the door. Elio turned the knob as Lilly extended her arms with Haku's smoky grasp and embraced Elio and Ren. Tears flowed from her eyes as she held them tight. Haku quickly faded away as Lilly stood back quietly and wiped her tears.

"Thank you," Lilly said. Elio and Ren smiled as she dashed past them, embarrassed, down the stoop. Ren, Elio, and Tama followed her as they finally set out to their long-awaited destination: the White House. It was only a short walk down the street to the massive white building. Just as impressive as it was before the end of the world. It had, like everything else on this side of the bridge, been meticulously well maintained. A moment in history perfectly captured through the end of the world.

"Either of you ever been here before?" Elio asked as they walked along the sidewalk that bordered the tall gates to the entrance.

Lilly shook her head.

"No, at least not that I can remember. You?" Ren asked Elio as they turned left and began their walk down the path to the building.

"Once, many years ago. If the memory can be trusted, that is. I actually met my wife on the same trip that took me here. Nearly twenty-two long years ago. I think I was too young to even care about the amount of history this place once had and the impact of this very building. Her unmatched beauty was all that I had on my mind once I had laid my eyes on her. Nothing else mattered in the world."

"I bet she was super pretty," Lilly said. Elio let out a chuckle.

"That she was." A fond smile spread across his face as he stepped forward, the others close behind as they finally reached the massive white doors.

"Ready?" Ren said, with his hand on the knob and looking at the others. Lilly, Tama, and Elio confirmed with a confident, synchronous nod. Ren took a deep breath and turned the knob. All four of them stepped forward into a dark room. The only light faded as the door slowly closed behind them.

"Hello?" Ren said into the darkness, taking another step forward. Tama's glowing tails lit the way for the others. Suddenly, the room flashed with a blinding light. Each of them covered their eyes as a familiar voice echoed from ahead.

"Hello, ladies and gentlemen! Welcome to the stunning finale of the twentieth season of the Wonderland Games! I am your deranged host, the curator of chaos, the ender of worlds, the Madman!" As the blinding light wore off, Ren saw dozens of robotic drones flying around the room, each equipped with a large black camera that, together, caught every angle and corner of the room. On the other side of the room was a small stage about six inches off the ground, atop which stood three podiums. The names Elio, Ren, and Lilly were written on them from left to right from where they now stood in the room.

"Now, the moment you have all been waiting for, our guests of honor have arrived. First, we have Elio." A small creature nudged Elio apart from the others. It was a soul. However, there were at least a dozen that all looked the same. A small ghost-like soul, its eyes glowing through the sheet that was draped over it. A unique color emanated from underneath where it floated gracefully in the air. It guided Elio over to the stage and up to the podium with his name.

"The heartbroken heartthrob. There isn't a soccer mom sitting at home that hasn't pictured this man on her pillow. I mean, in their dreams." Fake applause rang out from the audience that sat posted along the left of the extensive set. Cardboard cutouts of all ages in the place of a real audience. As Elio took his place behind the podium, they continued. Another nearly identical soul prompted Lilly towards the stage.

"Wonderland's own daughter, the hidden dragon, Lilly! The youngest ever to reach the podium here in Wonderland and the most adorable as well, if I dare say so myself." Lilly excitedly skipped along to her podium. No additional prodding needed, even playing it up for the cameras and cardboard viewers as she smiled and waved. Another soul nudged Ren, as he was the only one remaining now. Tama hopped up into his arms as they started forward toward the last empty podium in the middle.

"Last but not least, we have the kid that started it all. Since he woke up only a few days ago, Wonderland has and will never be the same. Clueless, he gathered those before to not only take down a couple of Wonderland's most prominent and vicious alumni, but also he landed a shot on the collector himself. All while they blasted their way across the East Coast to stand before you now. Ren and his ever-present soul named Tama." Ren reached his podium and the crowd falsely erupted with applause, much louder than his two companions' prior. Overwhelmed in the moment, he took a play from Lilly and threw out a wave before Tama hopped forward to sit on the podium. Ren stood in anticipation with the others as they waited to see what would happen next. Talking into a nearby camera, the Madman continued while Elio and Ren shared an odd glance. Elio nodded and pulled out the hidden shotgun that he had tucked under his coat and pointed it at the Madman.

"Enough of the fucking games. We want some goddamn answers, you piece of shit." Without breaking character, the man laughed and continued.

"Enough games? But we are only getting started." He smiled while motioning for Elio to look around. Every single camera in the room now pointed at him, all of them guiding a red dot that trailed back to a firearm. "Now, now. Everyone has been patiently waiting for today."

"I don't give a rat's ass about everyone else. Last time I checked, the world ended, and there isn't an everyone out there to even watch your warped little show here." The man kept his composure as Elio cocked the shotgun. Now only a few feet away, he grinned irritably at Elio.

"Audience or not, the show must go on." The dots were no longer focused on Elio. They had all now taken aim behind him at Lilly and Ren. "I would really hate for the games to end early. You wouldn't want to disappoint all the adoring fans back home now, would you?" A synchronous click came from all the machines in the air. The man reached forward and gently pushed the readied shotgun to the right and down to the ground. His expression returned to its previous playful look. "So, let's give them a good show, alright?" he said with a clap. Two of the ghost-like souls were now on each side of Elio as he handed the shotgun to the man.

"You win. I will play your goddamn game." The man let out an uncomfortable laugh as he pushed the weapon back to Elio.

"It wouldn't be much of a game if you gave me that right now," he said with a wink. The two souls on either side escorted Elio back to his podium, weapon in hand. Each of them scampered off the stage while Elio tucked the shotgun back away under his coat. "Now, with all that out of the way, let's get started." He threw his hands up into the air as confetti blasted out from behind where all three of them stood. The sound of fireworks rang out from speakers that sat scattered around the stage.

"For those of you new at home, allow me to explain how it all works. The games comprise three rounds. However, this year, for the first time, we have three contestants all playing for the highly sought-after prize. So, we have had to mix things up a bit, primarily with our first game." From above the stage, slightly behind where the three of them stood, a flashing sign slowly lowered from the ceiling.

"All or Nothing!" he announced as the fake crowd erupted with excitement. A poppy jingle played from the speakers. "In the past, our first game here was a series of questions where missing even one would cost you the round, immediately triggering the next. However, with three contestants, we have adjusted things a little." The man paused as the fake crowd applauded again.

"Following the tradition of the game, implied within its name, the answers will be all or nothing. Only this time, it's truly all or nothing. Ten questions from left to right; however, just as before, one wrong answer will launch all the contestants into round two. That's right! The fate of your allies is on the line with each question." After another pause for the crowd, the man quickly pushed through and continued.

"But remember, if they successfully answer all ten questions correctly, they get to skip round two. Victory claimed, and all the contestants will move on directly to the final round." Another pre-recorded applause. Ren and Elio shared a glance. Tama broke his silence.

"Calling it now. It's rigged," Ren quietly responded while making sure not to look down.

"Probably, but if this isn't all a ploy and there is a real audience watching out there…" He glanced at the various cameras floating around the room. "Then it can't look to be unfair, right?"

"Maybe… But what about Lilly?"

"What about her?" he asked before the man continued.

"Alright, enough of the boring details. It's time to play, ALL OR NOTHING!" he energetically announced while turning to face the three contestants. The small fleet of robotic cameras buzzed about as they adjusted above to maintain the full scope of the room.

"Question number one goes to Elio. Are you ready?" Elio shrugged.

"I guess so."

"Correct! The obvious answer, since you don't really have any other option now. Ren!" He quickly turned to Ren and shot out the next question. "Where are we right now?"

"The White House," he said, expecting it to be a trick question.

"Correct again! Question number three!" he said, pivoting over to Lilly. "Where in America is the White House located?" Lilly paused, thinking over the question. Ren realized what Tama had meant. Elio and Ren nervously watched her until she finally responded.

"Washington, D.C." Ren let out a sigh of relief.

"That's three for three! Things are really heating up now!" Another canned applause echoed throughout the studio. The Madman turned to a nearby camera. "We will be right back after these paid messages."

CHAPTER NINETEEN
The Games Begin

Once the cameras dropped, the man walked over to the stage. "That was great! Elio, my man, pulling that shotgun on me right out the gate." He shook his entire body like a wet dog. "Fuck me, was that exciting? The ratings have never been higher. For a second there, I thought you may even pull the trigger." He laughed as he wandered back over to where he had been prior. A bright red number was now visible on each of the camera bots, ticking quickly down to zero. A loud buzz triggered the man back into his performance. He looked dead into the camera hovering in front of him, and the show continued.

"A huge thank you to all our wonderful sponsors, and with that, back to the game. Before we continue, how about some background on our contestants here? Let's start with Elio, the heartbroken heartthrob. Since awakening around a year ago, he had a blatant disdain for the proposition posed, opting not to take part in the Wonderland games, though he would prove quite the combatant. Accompanied by his soul Gur, they have taken down an array of very dangerous players when forced."

"Given up on an actual future here in Wonderland until the day that started it all. One normal morning of scavenging supplies, Elio and Gur stumbled upon a sleeping Ren and a pretending Tama. Ren's lucky day, as Elio begrudgingly warned him about being out in the open, letting him keep his life and even circling back to defend him only moments later. Wonderland's own hidden hero." The faux crowd erupted into cheers and applause.

"Our duo, now together, Ren, would soon receive his call—his invitation to take part in the game. It was also at this time that Elio's motivation to play the game was ignited." The man looked ahead at a small screen, most likely his feed of what roughly to say and keep the show rolling. "Blah blah blah. Oh, and then, in a dark alley, a young girl offered to help them. Apprehensive, Elio would follow Ren as he chased after her. The very same young girl that would take Wonderland's heart—none other than Lilly. Accompanied by perhaps the most powerful soul ever seen in Wonderland, Haku. Lilly quickly dealt with the current threat and crowd favorite, the ruthless and bloodthirsty Luka and his soul Basher. From there, these unassuming three would form the team that you all see here today." There was more canned applause; the man continued as it rang out.

"With everyone now caught up, let's get on with the next question. This one comes from those of you watching at home. Elio, what is Lilly's favorite snack? Wow! That's a lowball from the audience." Elio looked over at Lilly, who was literally eating the answer, as she waited excitedly for her next question.

"Jerky," he said, returning his attention back to the man.

"Correct again! Four for four. Ren! How about some math?"

"Sure."

"Correct! Lilly—" Ren's heart sank as panic kicked in. It had happened so fast he hadn't thought about it. Would it have even mattered? The question's answer was all the same, right? Or if he had responded no, would he still be correct, but the next question wouldn't be math?

"What is twelve times twelve?" Elio and Ren both locked their gazes on Lilly as she fired off the answer with no delay.

"One hundred and forty-four."

"Correct! That's six for six!" Lilly jumped up and down behind her podium in celebration.

"Yay!" she exclaimed. The man turned to a nearby camera.

"And with that, we will turn it back to our sponsors. When we return, the final four questions of ALL OR NOTHING!" The cameras all went idle as they had before. A timer ticked down from two minutes on their small displays.

"You care to explain what's going on here?" Elio snapped at the man as he took a casual sip from a bottle of water. "You are obviously just messing with us. These questions are incoherent."

"We are playing a game. You win, you get the greatest prize of your miserable lives. You lose… well, that depends when you lose, I suppose. But you don't wanna be a loser, do you? Also, don't be rude—my questions are always on point." He grinned as the time passed sixty seconds, Ren chiming up.

"The audience—the people presumably watching. They are on the other side of the wall, aren't they? They're real." Elio turned to

Ren in surprise. "Admit it! I am right." The man smiled; his eyes were impressive.

"Charade or façade—you'll just have to win the game to find out." He skipped to his spot excitedly as the last few seconds ticked away. "I am starting to see why you have so many fans."

"Fans?" Ren said, confused, as the buzzer fired off and the man started talking into a robot again.

"Welcome back to the Wonderlands Games. I know personally the suspense is killing me, so let's get on with it! We are six questions in, and so far, our contestants have nailed each question without fail. A flawless performance. Which is good because in this game, it's ALL OR NOTHING!" he yelled as he turned away from the camera, circling to the side as he turned to Elio.

"Question seven. Elio, did you know the answer to the last question?" Elio rolled his eyes. Another stupid question designed to mess with them.

"Yes."

"Correct! Who doesn't love math after all? Right, Ren?"

"Uh, yeah."

"Correct again!" He turned quickly to Lilly. "Lilly, we have another viewer question just for you. Can we see Haku?" The man spun to face a camera, all three of them watching from behind him. "A simple question with no incorrect answer, but will she comply?" He turned back to the stage, the camera following his gaze. Lilly's mouth moved, most likely asking her secretive companion their thoughts about making an appearance.

"Sure," she said, looking at the man. She lifted her right sleeve as a small stream of smoke slowly fumed out from within. It flowed slightly up to the podium, where it took the form of a small, winged dragon. Haku looked around the room slowly, as if they were scanning for any hidden threats. Satisfied, Haku playfully breathed a small flame of purple fire and flew into the air. He did a quick spin and a loop before diving back into the opposing sleeve. The false crowd erupted unlike anything heard so far.

"Not only was she correct, but she was correct in style," he said, motioning his arms in the air to the fake crowd, amping up the audience of cardboard cutouts. "And now for the last question." The room went quiet, and ominous music filled the room. "This one is for all the marbles. Get this one correct, and the three of you will be on the fast track to round three. Elio, what time does the local McDonald's close?" Elio grinned confidently as Ren turned to him, his stomach flipping over on itself. This was his question from last night. How did he know? Tama sighed.

"Told you they would rig it," he said as they waited for Elio's answer—a much shorter wait than anyone could have expected.

"That's easy. It's a trick question." In that moment, Ren and Tama both knew they had lost. "The world is over, and with it, so is McDonald's. You can't close something that's not open." The room went quiet again, and the music faded in anticipation.

"I am sorry, but that is not correct." A loud buzzer echoed through the room. A sinister grin crawled across the Madman's face. "See you in the next round." He winked, and before any of them could react, the floor below them dropped, and with it, so did they. Each of them deposited into a small tube. Tama hopped in after Ren from where he sat on the podium.

"What an exciting turn of events as, once again, the game All or Nothing claims its victims as it continues its undefeated streak. While our contestants make their way to the next round, a brief word from our sponsors. Thank you for watching, and we will be right back."

Exiting the tube, Elio, Ren, and Lilly all dropped into a large open space. Massive walls surrounded them, forming a circle. Tama popped out last and landed right in Ren's arms as the three of them took in the spectacle of the impressive room.

"Crazy bastard. He converted who only knows what was down here into a damn coliseum. Who the hell paid for all this?"

"Aww, we were so close, too," Lilly said, disappointed.

"Yeah, well, how would I have known that the bastard would cheat? Lying piece of shit."

"They didn't cheat," Ren said. "The local McDonald's closes at two a.m."

"And how the hell would you know that?" Elio sassed, embarrassed.

"Last night, when I snuck out to go back to the store, I asked the store clerk a bunch of questions."

"Yeah, yeah, I know that. You said that he didn't say anything useful."

"Until just then, he hadn't. However, the last question I asked him had to do with McDonald's. Since he had successfully gotten Lilly a Happy Meal, I asked him what time McDonald's closed. This allowed me to confirm my suspicions that there is more going on outside of these walls, outside of Wonderland."

"Okay, but there is no way he answered you, right? That would be too much information."

"And you're right. He didn't answer me. Actually, it was this question that caused his retreat. After the lights went out, Tama and I were alone in the store. The clock on the wall, though, had skipped forward a couple of hours and was no longer ticking away. The small hand stuck on the two, the large on the twelve."

"I will be damned. The crafty bastard actually answered you."

"Yeah, and with that, he confirmed that there is far more going on than what meets the eye. All that is even more confirmed by the Madman's little production he has going on."

"I should have pulled the trigger when I had the chance," Elio said, upset.

"I don't think that would have ended well for any of us. In fact, if he really is streaming all this to somewhere or someone, I can't imagine that whoever they are would just have let us walk out of here."

Suddenly, dozens of small balls poured out of various other pipes scattered about the room, slowly falling towards the ground as a slight hum filled the room. Each scattered apart in the air and buzzed about like a fleet of robot flies. The mob faded from easily discernible to the naked eye to nearly impossible to see. Each of the mysterious flying items dissipated into the massive stadium.

"Ladies and gentlemen! Welcome to round two!" the man announced as he descended from a large circular hole at the top of the stadium. "Our contestants walked—or rather, fell—away with nothing after a stunning, nail-biting, nine out of nine blitz in the previous round, only to lose it all in the end. It is almost as if it never even mattered." He winked at the only large flying camera drone they could see now as it slowly descended with him. He was floating atop a small circle, with only a microphone in hand, as he flew toward them.

"Hello again!" he said with a sinister grin. "Really unfortunate how that all ended. I was really rooting for you, too." He turned back to the camera. "Allow me to run through how round two works for our spectacular contestants and all our delightful first-time viewers." Ren noticed that his fancy floating board was being carried atop the backs of four of the little soul ghosts from round one. As it did a fancy trick in the air for the camera, the Madman continued.

"Round two comprises three smaller rounds, each one focusing on combat. Our contestants must overcome all three sub-rounds to continue on to the third and final round. Each round will get progressively harder as they battle their way through to the next. Round one is a cooperative effort, pitting our esteemed competitors against one of the best Wonderland has ever seen." A massive bang rang out from a large, sealed door to the north of the massive arena, at least a football field in size. "Oh, it seems they're ready!" he yelled as the door came bursting down.

"Allow me to introduce your first challenger." A small blue dragon stepped out of the smoke and rubble. Walking behind it was a child, around Lilly's age, with a similar hoodie covering his face. As the dragon grew closer, Ren noticed it moved oddly, almost like flowing water as it stepped gracefully across the stadium. Then it disappeared, and in the blink of an eye, it sent Lilly flying backwards into the wall of the stadium. "Rowdy and his slippery, supersonic soul, Slipstream!"

"Lilly!" Ren yelled as the liquid dragon appeared from thin air in front of him. A massive claw of water pooled in the air as it went to strike, only to be smacked backwards midway through by Gur.

"Bastard's fast," Elio said as he came to Ren's aid.

"I'm faster!" Lilly said as she blasted between Elio and Ren towards the boy. A claw formed of smoke emanated out of both her sleeves. Closing the distance in a flash, she swung at the boy. The dragon deflected her attack before encompassing itself in the same fashion and formed two equally sized claws of water. The two continued to trade blows almost faster than Elio or Ren could even see. Lilly landed a hit on the water-clad boy. Her strike went clear through the blue liquid. The boy smiled as his body pooled back together; his right arm coated with a flurry of water, formed a sword, and smashed into Lilly. In a puff of soggy smoke, Lilly flew backwards through the room and collided again with the massive concrete border that held them.

"Lilly!" Ren yelled, turning to Elio. "What do we do?"

"I don't know. One on one, we have no shot against that thing." The boy grinned as he turned towards them and slowly headed their way.

"Tama, any ideas?"

"How the hell would I know? Elio's right—we can't keep up with a dragon." Ren took a deep breath, his thoughts clearing in the moment. Lilly picked herself up and staggered slowly back towards them.

"I have an idea. Elio, do you remember when we met?"

"Yeah, what about it?" Elio said as a flash released Gur from his cozy home. Prepared for a fight to the death, Haku coated Lilly, and she dashed back to the threat.

"You tried to kill me with a hammer of ice. That's Gur's magic, right? Ice?"

"I mean, yeah. But I don't follow." Ren dashed off with Tama in hand. "Just be ready with that in mind!" he yelled at Elio, who glanced at a stretching Gur.

"Do you have any clue what he is going on about?" Gur nodded as he followed Ren. "Care to explain?" Elio yelled as he started after them.

"Care to elaborate for me?" Tama said as the fight grew closer. "It's just a hunch, but it's all I have. When I say now, I need you to hit the dragon with a ball or two of electricity. Elio and Gur will handle the rest."

"That's not what elaborate means," Tama snarked as they were now upon the brawling, dragon-engulfed children.

"Now!" Ren yelled. Tama jumped to attention and into the air as he launched a dozen balls of electricity at the boy, who dodged them with ease. Another dozen appeared from thin air around him and, before he could react again, they engulfed the boy. Each strike combined with the water to amplify the effect of the electrifying stun. "Elio, you're up!" Ren yelled as Gur blew by him, Elio riding atop with a massive hammer made of ice in hand.

"Yeah, yeah," he said with a grin as he smashed the icy

hammer into the stunned boy. Upon impact, the ice quickly spread and froze the boy in place. As Lilly walked over, she threaded her two smoky hands together in the air and brought them down on the icy statue, shattering the boy and his dragon into millions of tiny pieces.

"Not bad, kid," Elio said with a high five.

"Not bad yourself," Ren said, impressed his plan had actually worked as they each turned to Lilly, their hands in the air as they waited for a double high five. Lilly filled with glee as she rushed over and slapped both hands high above with a slight hop to reach.

"Another impressive show of skill from our competitors! Together, they have cleared the first combat round in record time. Who's ready for round two? I know I am!" The fake applause had followed them from the previous floor. The trio noticed the stadium had been packed with the same cardboard cutouts as before, filling the rowed bench seating high above the concrete walls. Everything then went dark, and Ren felt his body go weightless as he struggled to no end. Lilly let out a scream while he could hear Elio cursing. Their voices and struggle grew farther and farther away, and after less than a minute, the lights returned.

Ren and Tama were now alone. The others were nowhere to be seen. The pair were no longer at the center of a massive stadium. Rather, they now found themselves in a small room. A timer on the wall sat idle with two minutes left. The Madman's voice filled the room from a small speaker in the top left corner of the room.

"Round two is a solo battle to the death. Each competitor will simultaneously battle it out in a one-on-one deathmatch that will begin as soon as the timer hits zero, at which point the exit to your waiting room will open and the fight will begin. Just like in All or Nothing, all parties must survive to continue forward." His tone changed to a more sinister pitch. "Good luck." After a quick pause, he continued, "And now a word from our sponsors." The timer started as the room went quiet.

CHAPTER TWENTY
Together Till the End

Ren and Tama watched as the timer quickly ticked away.

"Guess we have no choice," Tama said, turning to Ren, who was still quiet.

"They will be fine, right?"

"I mean, Lilly will be," Tama chuckled. "Elio and Gur are a scrappy pair as well. I have no doubts they will all come through just fine. Honestly, we are the weakest pair, I think. It made me angry when you mentioned it the other day, but it is true. Gur packs quite the kit and is massive to boot, and let's be real... few compare to Haku."

"Yeah." Ren tousled Tama's furry head. "All that aside, I think you are the best." The timer was down to the last thirty seconds. Ren sighed, Tama watching as the timer continued to tick down.

"I call bias. Too bad what you think can't save us."

"It worked well enough last round," Ren sassed.

Tama sighed. "I can't argue with you there." They glanced at the timer. "Alright, fun's over; it's almost time. We have no clue what's on the other side of that door," Tama said as he readied himself. The timer hit zero, and the door zipped open.

"It's quiet… almost too quiet," Tama said, peeping out around the door. Ren scooped up the curious Tama and peeked out around the corner as well. Their room was inside another room, with an exact copy of it directly across the large open space. Its door was also open. A flash of bright red and orange shot from within the opposing room. A massive ball of fire flew directly toward where they stood. Ren dashed over to the side and rolled out of the way with Tama still tucked safely in his grasp.

Coming out of his roll, Tama tumbled free. The pair quickly got back on their feet as their opponents stepped out of the opposing room. A human silhouette, blurry like a shadow, approached them, followed by a small cat-like figure with three snow-white glowing tails swaying behind as it walked slowly in their direction. Two balls of electricity appeared in the air of the ominous black creature, quickly flying at Ren and Tama.

"They don't waste any time," Tama said as Ren scooped him back up and rushed away from the incoming attack. A colossal explosion launched them forward. It reduced the room they had started in to a fiery crater.

"That was close," Ren said, getting back to his feet, Tama now at his side.

"These two don't quit," Tama said, shaking off the dust in the air.

"Something feels off about this—eerily familiar."

"Look out!" Tama snapped, dashing to the right while Ren

dashed to the left as a massive fireball flew between them. The creature stepped through the hazy room; the stench of smoke filled the air.

"Tama, look," Ren said, pointing. Standing there between them was none other than another Tama. Behind him stood a carbon copy of Ren. Their opponents this round were none other than themselves.

"What the hell is going on?" Ren asked aloud, confused.

"Oh, you know, just another day in Wonderland," Tama said. "We can fight with fire, too." A dozen small fireballs appeared in the surrounding air before pummeling the shadowy duo. An enormous wall of fire shielded them. However, unlike Tama's shield, which absorbed the impact, it deflected Tama's barrage, sending the balls of fire back at him, peppering Tama in a barrage of explosions.

"TAMA!" Ren yelled helplessly, watching the smoke dissipate. Tama was encased in a small dome of fire.

"I'm okay," he said, giving a shake of his body as the dome faded. "That's a neat trick. Too bad it only works once." The creature turned to Tama, intrigued as Tama disappeared and reappeared next to Ren. "I've got tricks too."

"That's a new one," Ren said, impressed. "You can teleport now?" Tama chuckled.

"Seems that way." He turned to the duo. "Though it will take more than just some flashy new tricks for us to get out of this round alive," Tama said doubtfully.

"We got this!" Ren said, following his gaze with shaky confidence. Tama's impostor disappeared just as Tama had and reappeared next to them. Its body glowed red and emanated heat.

"Look out!" Tama shouted as his clone detonated itself like a small bomb. The smoke from the explosion dissipated to reveal the Tama clone standing in a small crater. Tama and Ren stood opposite each other, with a large pillar of fire between them.

"Thanks," Ren said, looking down at Tama, his fur now glowing a hazy black. "You okay, buddy?" Tama looked up at Ren; their eyes locked.

"You trust me?" Tama asked.

"Of course," Ren responded as they turned to their cloned adversaries.

"I am going to kill that impostor," Tama said confidently as he disappeared and reappeared next to Ren's clone. A dozen fireballs formed above him and flew at Tama's clone before Tama disappeared again, this time reappearing behind his clone. A dozen balls of electricity formed in the surrounding air before flying at them. Tama disappeared again as a wall of fire and electricity formed to counter each flurry of attacks. The cascading explosions sent the entire space up in a blitz of explosions and smoke, with Tama nowhere to be seen. Ren looked up to see a massive black orb slowly falling from above the pair. Tama appeared out of thin air between the two shadow clones.

"It's over," Tama said with a sassy grin. The smoke from the explosions dissipated. Above, an uncountable volume of orbs encompassing fire, electricity, and an unfamiliar black energy formed, all much smaller than the massive black orb dropping from the sky. Tama's glow grew darker; his fur shifted to a deep, bottomless black opposite the white of his clone.

"I have to thank you," Tama said as his glow shimmered with a red hue. "Without you, I would have never pushed myself to this point. I seem to have shattered my previous limits to a wacky degree." Various shields appeared around them as the duo panicked. They started throwing out anything they could to slow the impending blow. Then Tama's glow flashed brightly before taking its ultimate form: a deep, ominous glow that mirrored the deep black orb falling from above. The energy that now surrounded Tama shattered the shields from the inside. Tama glanced over at Ren, a smile on his face as the dominoes all fell into place.

"TAMA!" Ren yelled as the flurry of orbs pelted them. His best friend was still inside as the deep black orb exploded atop them like a teardrop of pure energy. The force of impact rippled out in a blinding black flash. The pressure from the explosion lifted Ren off his feet, as if the impact had deleted gravity. He flew backwards, floating through the air uncontested until the flash ended, and he promptly dropped to the ground. Ren wiped his eyes while getting back to his feet. "Tama!" he yelled as he rushed toward the impact of the explosion, only to find a massive crater. Ren slid down the curve of the large hole and rushed toward the center. There was nothing left— no shadow clones and no Tama. He cried out, "Tama!" as he dropped to his knees and tears flowed from his face. "I trusted you... You can't leave me. You can't."

"You won't get rid of me that easily." Ren turned around to see, sitting casually in the settling dust, Tama. His fur and glow had returned to normal. "I am tired." Tama tilted over as Ren scuttled in the dirt and caught him with his arms spread wide.

"Don't you ever do something like that again!" Ren said as tears streamed down his face. "Ever!"

"Yeah, yeah," Tama said while embracing Ren's aggressive smother, doing his best to hide how much he enjoyed it. "I may need a lift for a bit." Ren smiled.

"Any time, buddy. Any time."

A loud buzzer rang out from the silence of the resolved battle. The massive dome that encased their encounter opened from the top and slowly swirled down and back into the ground. Two identical domes were visible from where they stood in the middle of the vast arena from round one.

"Lilly and Elio must still be inside," Ren said, sitting down with Tama in his lap. Exhausted, Ren let out a sigh while Tama looked up to see a small parachute floating down from somewhere up above.

"Look," Tama said as Ren reached his hands out from where he sat and caught it. "A care package? Or maybe a reward for winning?" Ren set it down and lifted the flaps of the box. Inside were a couple of granola bars, some trail mix, and two bottles of water, accompanied by a note that read:

'From your biggest fan.'

"Thank you…" Ren said quietly, looking all around. "Thank you!" he repeated louder, as tears streamed down his face. Opening the water, he chugged it before opening a package of trail mix. Tama, unable to move much on his own, rested his head on Ren's lap.

"Fan?" Tama asked, feeling a bit more energized as Ren charged him back up with each bite of trail mix.

"Seems so. I have no clue what's going on. But it seems someone is watching out for us."

The dome on the right shifted as another buzzer rang out before slowly rotating into the ground. Standing there in the center was Lilly, a massive figure of gray next to her. Blurry from the distance between them, it quickly faded away. Ren stood up, displacing Tama, who Ren placed gently into the care package to rest, before he picked it up and started toward Lilly. Another loud buzzer echoed as the dome on the left swirled away into the ground.

"Lilly!" Ren yelled as he approached.

"Ren! Kitty! You win too?"

"That we did. Let's go get Elio and wait for the next round," he said with a smile. Ren looked up to see another small package float down toward Lilly. He glanced over at Elio to see another was on its way down to him as well.

"Presents!" Lilly yelled excitedly as she jumped into the air to receive her box. Elio grabbed his box and started toward them. Without pause, Lilly tore into her box. "Sky jerky!" she exclaimed, tearing into the loaded box of dehydrated meats.

"Ren! Lilly. You two made it out okay," Elio said as he approached, covered in blood.

"Glad to see you, Elio," Ren said. "You okay?" he asked, glancing at all the blood.

"Yeah, bastard of a clone didn't come equipped with a shotgun like I did," he chuckled. "Didn't think a shadow would bleed, though. Man, that bastard was plump, full of the red stuff." He opened his box and pulled out a slip of paper.

"From your biggest fan," he read aloud.

"I got one too!" Lilly said as she tossed it aside and ripped open another sleeve of jerky. Elio poured a bottle of water over his head before wiping away the blood that had drenched his face with his sleeve.

"Want some help?" Lilly said, taking another bite.

"Sure?" Elio replied, confused. As Haku flowed out of her baggy sweater and engulfed Elio in a thick gray cloud. Before Lilly even finished her current packet of jerky, Haku had returned to the comfort of her hoodie.

"Looking good," Ren said with a grin.

"That's a neat trick. I didn't know it could work on others, though."

"Yeah! Haku has gotten really good at cleaning up after me, so why not those we care about too?" Elio smiled as he watched her tear into another bag, no idea how meaningful her words were to him. They relaxed together for a moment, the most relaxed they had been since the day had started what felt like weeks ago. A reprieve abruptly cut short as the Madman returned to the skies.

"Another round goes to our spectacular contestants!" he yelled as he descended from wherever he had been hiding away. "And what a spectacular round it was at that. Let's keep the momentum going and kick off the next round." He paused as a terrible howl rang out from the south side of the arena. "The fan favorite you have all been waiting for." Another gruesome screech echoed out from behind the massive gate. A small door opened as one of the small ghost-like souls looked around, confused. "Allow me to introduce!" The door opened, one half slowly going to each side of its massive frame. "The Soul Eater!"

A massive beast lunged out of its cell. It tore its rear left paw free of the massive shackle that had bound it inside. The chain now dragged behind it as it opened its massive mouth and ate the small, frantic soul released to play the role of bait. Gone in one swift gulp, the monstrous-looking creature turned its attention to its terrified onlookers. Its form was that of a shaggy-looking dog, its fur unkempt and tangled. It stood on four rotted-looking enormous legs, each missing patches of fur and skin alike. Its long, unmaintained fur covered its eyes, its jaw exposed with bone and flesh.

The creature let out a horrendous howl as hundreds of small holes appeared on the ground. Its belly glowed with a hazy clarity; its insides were visible as the recently eaten soul floated about in a pool of green acid. Another gut-wrenching howl echoed out while acid dripped from the creature's mouth. Out of a nearby hole crawled a small puppy-like version of the disturbing creature. Its body trembled as it gave a shake of dirt and acid, its tail wagging off what little fur and flesh remained.

"He's kind of cute," Lilly said with a smile.

"No!" everyone else said together without hesitation. It startled the small undead creature, and the dog pivoted its attention to its source. It charged at them with terrifying force and lunged at the closest person, Ren—only to be smacked aside by a cloudy fist of Haku.

"Thanks," Ren said with a grateful grin.

"I don't think we are in the clear just yet," Elio said, pointing at the lingering threat only a couple hundred feet away. Hundreds of small undead puppies clawed their way out of the field of holes between them. Each one snarled and grumbled as it shook itself free from the dirt that had held it captive. A dusty gray fur covered their bodies as a peculiar purple acid dripped from their mouths. Decaying hearts lay visible in their chests, pumping it out at a startling rate. The small undead army turned to their assumed leader, each one sitting attentively as they awaited instruction. Another howl rang out, this one sadder than the last, as each of the small creatures stood up and turned their focus to them.

"Get ready, everyone," Elio said as he pulled out his shotgun, popping it open and slotting in two shells from his long coat. He kicked it closed as Gur stood by his side. In each of Gur's massive paws was an equally massive hammer of ice. Lilly became wrapped once again in smoke, her hands now massive claws, with a long gray tail now dragging across the ground. Her legs had also changed form. Massive dragon legs now lifted her an extra couple of feet into the air, where she now stood at a height on par with Gur. Ren glanced over at Tama.

"You ready to show off your new tricks?" he said with a sassy grin. Tama smiled back at him.

"We can't let those two have all the fun, now, can we?" Tama said as his fur shifted colors, his eyes now a deep red as his glow became dark and more chaotic.

"It's been fun, everyone. Let's make it out of this together," Ren said as the horde of angry undead creatures hurtled toward them.

"Family stays together, right?" Lilly said.

"Always," Ren said with a comforting smile. Lilly nodded back at him with glee.

"Don't be so dramatic, you two," Elio said with a roll of his eyes, a tear sneaking out. "See you both on the other side," he said, dashing forward into the fray. "Together!"

"Yeah! Together!" Lilly yelled excitedly, following behind him. Ren smiled and turned to Tama.

"Till the end?" Ren said with a soft smile.

"Till the end," Tama replied as they chased after the others onto the battlefield.

The sound of shotgun blasts rang out from Ren's left, while purple acid flew about the field in a torrent of smoke as Lilly tore through the dozens of ravenous undead dogs without breaking a sweat at the right. Meanwhile, Ren and Tama set their sights on the master, the massive, decaying dog slowly making its way across the field. Tama quickly dispatched any incoming dogs easily with a swirling black orb, each one quickly ripping through any attacker.

"Ready?" Ren said with an unfamiliar feeling. Was it fear? No, he knew fear well. It was excitement. His heart raced, not panicked or afraid, but excited to see what might happen next—excited to live, but no longer afraid to die. Now willing, willing to do whatever it took to protect those he would now call family: Elio and Lilly.

"No turning back now," Tama said, blasting away another lunging dog.

The massive creature let out another eerie screech, and all the smaller dogs froze in place. Their bones cracked and popped as their forms shifted. Now standing on two legs, they appeared more human, more skeletal as well, with their fur nearly gone. Purple acid circulated throughout and around their bones. Synchronously, they all leaned forward and punched the ground repeatedly. Each hit shook the entire room with cumulative force until they broke through one by one and dragged out various weapons. The skeletal army was now equipped with an array of swords, axes, bows, and even guns.

"Ren!" Elio yelled. "We will hold them back. Finish the big one!" Ren nodded as Tama slapped away an attacking creature to Ren's right with a large shadow paw—a trick he had borrowed from Haku. Tama smiled, impressed with himself.

"We can talk about that later. It's all you, buddy. Finish it," Ren said as Tama grinned and disappeared and reappeared above the massive creature. It shook its monstrous head and drooled acid down onto the battlefield. A massive spear of black formed in the air under Tama as he fell. His four paws pursed together atop it as it grew in size and speed. At the tip of the large spear was an orb of swirling black energy, which was growing. The ball of energy smashed into the head of the enormous creature, and the spear followed suit and tore through its head in an explosion of green acid. The creature's body smashed into the ground with the force of an asteroid. Each of the smaller skeletal creatures froze in place as their master now lay defeated in a puff of black dust.

Tama reappeared at Ren's side. Weak, his form returned to its normal blue with a crisp glow. The round was over. They had won.

"We did it!" Lilly yelled from off in the distance. Ren could see Elio nearby and gave a satisfied wave.

"Good job, Tama," Ren said, glancing down at him. "Who

has the best soul now?" he said with a sarcastic grin, as Tama lost his balance. He was drained to zero and could no longer hold himself up. Ren caught him and gently scooped him up into his arms.

"Yeah, yeah. I always knew I was the best. Glad you finally caught up," he let out a tired laugh.

"Shut up and rest," Ren said with a smile as they started toward Elio to find Lilly.

Another howl rang out from the corpse of the massive dog.

"How?" Ren said in shock as he turned to face the creature once again. Tama gathered what little strength he had left and flashed back to black and prepared to attack. But it didn't move. It stayed down; it stayed dead. "What is going on?" Ren asked as the skeletons crumpled to dust, each one dropping into a small pile. The acid that had flowed through their bones was now hovering above the mound of remaining skeletal dust. Slowly, the acid dripped from the air. Drop by drop, it sizzled with the dusty remains.

"Why am I suddenly so tired?" Ren asked aloud. His body felt heavy as he saw Elio drop off in the distance. "Elio?" He looked down at Tama as his eyes grew heavy. "Tama?" he said aloud as he fell to the ground, his eyes heavy. Tama's glow was the last thing he saw before it all went black.

CHAPTER TWENTY-ONE
The Final Round

Cheap fluorescent lights buzzed from above, and a young man's reflection looked back at him from the chilled glass of the cooler unit he stood in front of. Ren raised his hand, and the one looking back at him followed suit as they both tousled their hair. Sure enough, the one staring back at him was, in fact, him. There was no Tama in the reflection—no Lilly or Elio either. He was alone.

What was going on? Ren wondered to himself. Was this the next round? The last test? And if so, what was the test? He thought back to that day at the Walmart—the events that took place and how visceral they had felt then. He felt the same way now.

The bell above the door rang, and there was a commotion at the front of the store. Ren dropped the contents in his hands and turned to see the commotion when he bumped into someone. The collision was awkward and knocked them both to the ground. A gunshot went off, and a man yelled out in pain. Ren frantically slid back and grabbed the pistol, standing up while quickly pulling it on the man clutching at his leg. Blood oozed through the fingers of the baggy, black-clothed man.

It was all happening again—the same events from the crazy clown's Walmart. With a deep breath, Ren restrained himself from pulling the trigger. Instead, he kept it pointed at the man, wincing in pain on the floor only a couple of feet away. A shadow curved around the corner as Ren turned and aimed the gun in its direction, ready to end whoever or whatever rounded it. He could hear screeching tires from the parking lot. With a deep breath, his finger felt firm on the trigger as a middle-aged woman rounded the corner, shotgun in hand. She pointed it at the man crying in pain on the floor.

Overcome with relief, Ren lowered the pistol as he dropped to the floor, the gun cradled in his lap.

"Are you okay?" the woman asked, concerned, as the sound of sirens grew closer. Red and blue lights flickered from outside.

"Yeah. I'm good," Ren responded as half a dozen men in blue rushed inside. The woman set the shotgun down next to her and placed her hands behind her head. She winked at Ren to do the same. Following her lead, Ren set the pistol down to his left and placed his hands behind his head. He closed his eyes as a tear slipped down his cheek. It was then that he realized what he had done.

"A round of applause for our winner!" a familiar voice yelled.

Ren opened his eyes to find himself in the center of a large stage. A familiar stage. He stood up slowly as he lurched forward from the sound of explosions behind him. Fireworks. A small hole appeared in the stage floor, and Tama slowly rose out.

"Tama!" Ren shouted with relief. "Are you okay?"

"Yeah, what happened? When I came through, everyone was

gone, and I was back in one of those damned sparky cages."

"Reunited once again," the Madman said as he took to the stage. "Allow me to be the first to congratulate you on your successful rehabilitation and victory in today's games."

"Rehabilitation?" Ren asked, confused, before quickly being interrupted.

"As of today, you and your soul, Tama, will be free to return to Paradise. Your time served. That's not all, though!" He handed a small digital card to Ren. "That is your SID, or Soul Identification Card, which gives you unfettered access to a special VIP account that, at this time, only you have access to." Ren flipped it over in his hands; the picture of the same young man from back at the gas station stared back at him.

The announcer turned to a nearby camera and continued. "That concludes the show. For the first time in the history of the games, we have a winner!"

Ren looked around for Lilly and Elio.

"Where are my friends?" he asked the Madman, who ignored the question and continued his speech. "A tale of hope, friendship, and redemption over the course of the most exciting few days Wonderland has seen in a long time. I am your host, the Wonderland Madman, and, as always, we will see you next time."

The Madman turned to Ren and pretended to talk, patting him on the back as he guided him to the back of the stage, Tama following close behind.

"That was exhilarating," the man said as the red light to the left of the stage went dark. He let out an exaggerated stretch as he continued. "You put on quite the show, kid. See you around, or not really. I don't get to go where you're going."

"Going?" Ren asked, looking around. "Wait, what happened to Lilly and Elio?"

"Didn't make the cut, kid. Look, I am sure everything will make a bit more sense once you reach Paradise. Someone on the other side will fill you in." The man pushed a small button that blended in with the wall at the back of the stage, and a hidden door opened. The man gently, yet oddly forcefully, guided Ren inside, nudging Tama with his foot. Displeased with the prodding, Tama hopped up into Ren's arms.

"Hold on!" Ren snapped. "I am not leaving without them."

"You don't really have a choice, kiddo. Go live a good life. You earned it."

Ren went silent as the door slammed shut between them and the room shifted slightly. A feeling of force underneath them; they rose slowly. Ren slammed his fists against the door.

"Answer my fucking questions!"

"Calm down, Ren," Tama said, noting that they seemed to increase in speed.

"How can I calm down? We just left our friends back there. Who knows if they are even still alive?" Then the walls that surrounded them disappeared, and they were in a glass cylinder floating through the open air. "What the shits?" Ren said in shock as he gazed out at the vast walls that seemed to go on forever down the coast. With Tama still in his arms, Ren made his way over to the glass and looked up as four blades fanned out and spun at a furious speed.

"Ren, look," Tama said from the other side of the small glass room.

Ren turned and took a couple of steps to see what Tama was looking at.

"Wow…" Ren said in disbelief. On the other side of the wall was a massive city with buildings that went on forever. Their glass cylinder slowly lowered to a building on the other side of the massive wall, the tube going dark again. Only a small light in the right corner lit the space now.

"Well, we made it to the other side of the wall," Tama said as they descended slowly into the unknown.

"I wish we were all here, though. What happened? Why are they not here?" Ren asked aloud.

"I'm not sure. I guess they failed whatever test you passed. What happened after we got separated?"

Ren thought about each trip to the gas station—how the first time he had killed the woman rounding the corner while consumed with panic. He had killed her and the strange man he had bumped into. The man who introduced the gun to the situation to begin with. However, the second time, he held it together. He didn't kill anyone. Was that why he passed?

He turned to answer Tama when the tube came to an abrupt stop. The door flung open, and standing there to greet them was a tall, young-looking woman.

"Hello, Ren," she said, looking at him, then down at Tama. "Hello, Tama." Then back to Ren. "Allow me to be the first to welcome you both to Paradise," she said with a pleasant smile while motioning them out of the small tube.

The duo followed her welcoming guidance out of the tube and stepped into a small room.

"Let's get you all cleaned up and proper for your reintroduction into society." She paused and looked Ren up and down with a disapproving look. His clothes were tattered and stained with blood and bone dust. "Follow me," she said with a cute smile.

They made their way down a short hallway and came upon a door. A sign hung on the front of the door that read: Ren and Tama. Across the hall was another sign that read: Lilly and Haku. Ren assumed the next door over had Elio and Gur on it.

"You can get cleaned up here. We have provided clothes inside, custom-made by the best designers Paradise offers. We hope they are to your liking. I will be just outside should you need anything." She turned the doorknob and motioned them inside, promptly closing the door behind them.

"I am even more confused now than I was at the games. What the hell is going on?" Tama asked while they looked around the large room and everything it offered. A glass-encased shower sat on the room's left, opposite of which sat a large open closet.

As they explored their way deeper into the room, Ren undressed.

"I guess we just do what she says. What other choice do we have?" Ren said.

"They haven't explained a single thing yet. Are we supposed to just know what the hell is going on? We just buried Lyonel, and now we have no clue where Elio and Lilly are."

"I know, Tama!" Ren snapped as the room went quiet. "Sorry… I know. I just don't know what else to do right now."

Ren stepped into the shower and turned the small dial to hot as the steaming water instantly poured over him. He leaned forward and cried, his tears washed away with the blood as they swirled down and into the drain. Tama sat silently on the other side of the glass. Ren let out a deep sigh as he grabbed a small bar of soap and scrubbed the Wonderland off.

Minutes passed in complete silence. Clean and a bit more relaxed, Ren slid the glass door open and stepped out of the shower. He dried off as he wandered a few steps forward to see hanging in the closet one outfit. He tossed the towel to the floor and took the clothes out, and piece by piece he got dressed. It was almost a direct copy of his previous outfit that he had selected earlier that morning for the games, with only slight variations in the colors.

"Looking good," Tama said while Ren messed his hair up as always, giving it that I don't give a shit look that he wore so well—a fine contradiction to the crisp style of his clothes.

"Thanks. It feels weird, though…"

"Yeah…"

"I know it's naïve, but I keep hoping that when we turn that knob, Elio and Lilly will be on the other side."

"Yeah," Tama said as they made their way back over to the door.

Ren placed his hand on the knob and glanced down at his loyal friend.

"Thanks, Tama. You know, for always being there for me. I

just wanted to say that before we go any further."

"Don't be getting all mushy on me now," Tama said, embarrassed, turning away from Ren's words.

Ren laughed.

"Yeah. You're right. Ready?"

"Ready."

Ren turned the knob and opened the door.

"Oh my, don't you look handsome?" the woman greeted them. "I hope the clothes are to your liking." She paused and waited for an answer.

"Uh, yeah. I guess so," he said, inspecting each arm awkwardly.

"Wonderful! Then let's be on our way."

Ren paused; his attention locked on Lilly's name hanging on the door.

"Coming, dear?" she said with a prodding tone.

"Yeah," he said as he followed her, his gaze on Elio's name as they passed the next door down.

"Okay, so there are a few details to run through before our next stop. For starters," she stopped and turned to Ren, "may I see your SID card?"

"My SID card?" Ren said, confused, then remembering that the Madman had given him something. "Oh, this card?" he responded, pulling it out of his right pocket.

"Yes. That's the one." She then pulled out a card of her own and gently tapped it against his card. "I just unlocked your assets."

She smiled. "Your well-deserved reward for successfully winning the Wonderland games. I am not sure how much he told you." There was a layer of vitriol in her tone when referencing the Madman. "So, allow me to start from the beginning. That card is genetically linked to you." She glanced down at Tama. "Much like Tama here is. No one other than you can use it because of this link. Pretty much everything inside of Paradise requires the use of these cards for verification, access, and even basic purchases."

Ren inspected the card as she spoke.

"Additionally, it will grant you access to your new home, another reward for overcoming everything you have been through. To your successful rehabilitation. Oh, and on that note, there are quite a lot of people waiting to see you."

She leaned forward and pushed open a large pair of double doors.

"Me?" Ren asked as a sea of people yelled and clapped as they appeared through the opening doors.

"Allow me to once again welcome you both to Paradise!"

CHAPTER TWENTY-TWO
Welcome to Paradise

Applause rang out from the other side of the doors. The woman motioned them forward. "Your fans await." Tama and Ren shared an uncomfortable look as they stepped through the doors. There was a red carpet that ran a short distance to a long black car. The rear door was held open by an elderly man in a fancy-looking suit.

"Come along," the woman said impatiently, her previously welcoming tone fading as she stepped by them and proceeded towards the car.

Ren and Tama shared a glance and followed her down the red carpet. The walk felt uncomfortable. The surrounding people yelled their names excitedly as they followed their guide down the crisp, red path. A soul also accompanied each person, each of various sizes and glows. Massive buildings littered the skyline, and there was no shortage of flying contraptions buzzing about in the air above. They were like the ones that they had seen earlier during the Madman's games. The screams and applause all blended into an unintelligible noise. Ren did his best to avoid making eye contact with any of the onlookers as he tried to take in the views washed out by them.

About halfway down the strip, a young woman around the same age as him caught his eye. She stood out in a sea of chaos as she watched, calm and collected. She wasn't screaming; she wasn't yelling; she wasn't even smiling—just watching attentively as he and Tama approached the car. His attention focused on her as he reached the man at the door. Her lips moved as if she were talking directly to him.

The dapper-dressed old man interrupted Ren's gaze by forcefully escorting Ren into the car behind Tama. Their guide was getting in by herself on the other side.

The door slammed shut as Ren frantically fidgeted with the door to get the window to go down. As the car slowly moved, the window lowered, and Ren glanced out the window for the girl. She was gone—washed away in the sea of crazed people now chasing after the car.

"Didn't get enough along the walk?" the woman laughed. "I get that. There really is nothing like it." Ren slumped back into his seat. The window slowly slid back up.

"Like what?" he said disappointedly, glancing over at her. A small, glowing, dog-like creature sat on her lap. Its eyes locked on Tama as he matched its aggressive gaze in silence.

"Fame. The unrelenting love and affection from those beneath you." She let out a noise comparable only to an orgasm as her body gave off a quaking shiver. Her attentive soul was unaffected by the odd behavior.

"Where are we going?" Ren asked, doing his best to get off the topic.

"To your new home, of course." The car went quiet for a little while. A soothing tune played at a low level in the background as Tama sat on his lap and they watched the world pass by outside—a world that felt oddly familiar, and equally distant.

"So... is anyone going to explain what exactly is going on?" Ren asked the woman after what felt like hours had passed. She was doing her makeup in a small folding mirror. Her tiny, glowing dog feigned sleep as it kept one eye glued on Tama.

"Oh, look at that. We are here," she said, ignoring his question altogether as the car slowed to a stop. The door to Ren's left opened as the elderly man held it propped open.

"We have arrived, sir," he said as Ren got out of the car, Tama held snug in his arms.

"Welcome home!" the woman said with a strange amount of excitement as she rounded the rear of the car. "Congratulations once again on your remarkable rehabilitation." She handed Ren a small piece of paper. "That's my card. If you need anything, just call this number, kay?"

"Sure..." Ren said as she turned around and started back to the car.

"Ta-ta for now. Talk soon." She blew him a kiss as she got back into the car, this time from the side Ren had been on. The elderly man closed the door behind her and quickly made his way back to the driver's seat.

"But..." Ren said as the car started and quickly drove away.

"You didn't answer my question." He looked down at Tama, who looked back up at him. "Just you and me again."

"Seems that way," Tama said, looking forward at the massive two-story house in front of them. "Should we head in?"

"I guess. Nowhere else to go, I suppose," Ren said, making his way up the six brick steps that led up to the massive brown door. A small light-green square sat above the knob of the door. Ren poked it, confused, to no avail.

"Try that fancy card they gave you," Tama said. Ren shifted his hand to keep hold of Tama with his left while he pulled the card out of his right pocket. With a soft tap of the card, the door made a loud click. Ren placed his hand on the knob, gave it a twist, and pushed the door open.

"Success!" Tama said excitedly as Ren stepped inside, the door closing behind him.

"This is ours?" Ren said in disbelief as he took it all in. They were standing in a massive open room facing a pair of stairs that curved as they eased up to the second floor. On both the left and the right were two large open rooms, separated only by a small doorless entryway.

"Seems like a lot for one person…"

"Yeah, it's kind of overwhelming, to be honest," Ren said, still looking around. "Oh, and everything else that happened over the past few days—what was that?" Ren chuckled. "I suppose you're right."

Tama's ear twitched. "You hear that?" Tama asked.

"No? What is it?" Ren replied, glancing down at him.

"Not sure, but it's coming from that direction." Tama

motioned to the left of the room, and Ren wandered cautiously in that direction. Tama's glow shifted color to deep black, ready for whatever may be on the other side. With a quick pivot around the corner, Tama jumped from Ren's arms, prepared to strike.

Ren let out a soft laugh. "It's just a TV. They must have left it on while preparing the house for our arrival." He meandered over to the large brown couch that sat in front of it, Tama joining him on the next cushion over.

"In other news, as many of you know, the Wonderland games took place today and, in a stunning turn of events, the undefeated trio was down to only one in the final round."

"Is this a recap of what we went through today?" Ren said, grossed out. "It really is a show?" He said, confused, as the footage of their travels played on the screen—meeting Elio and Lilly, the event at the Walmart. "They were watching the entire time?"

"Look, it's Elio," Tama said as an older picture of Elio was on screen.

"Elio Demartos, age forty-three. Convicted of the murder of Edgar Swans. Mr. Swans was on trial for manslaughter for an incident while drunk driving—a car accident that left Demartos's wife of twenty-three years dead and his daughter, age nineteen, in a coma. The footage you are about to see is graphic and not recommended for young audiences." Elio was sitting in the second row of a courtroom. Suddenly, he stood up and unloaded a small handgun into the back of the man sitting in front of him.

"Didn't Elio say he had a dream like that?" Tama said as it continued.

The screen cut to a picture of Lilly, a couple of years younger, in the photo. "Lilly Patel, age twelve. Convicted for the brutal murder of her mother and father."

"That's awful," Ren said. "Lilly would never do anything like that."

"A bus driver alerted the police to the incident when Lilly attempted to go to school the following day with her clothes soaked in blood. When they searched the house, they found her father dead in her bed. He had been stabbed over a dozen times with a kitchen knife, with most of the incisions made in the genital region."

"Oh, my God," Ren said in disbelief.

"From there, it is believed that Lilly made her way down the hall to her parents' room and stabbed her mother repeatedly in the chest. During the trial, Lilly never said a word."

"It's the same too—the dream she told us about that night on the bus. That really happened. It wasn't just a dream," Ren said, his arms shaking anxiously.

"Look, Ren, it's you."

"Ren Watts, age twenty. Convicted of manslaughter. During a robbery gone wrong at a local gas station."

"Enough!" Ren yelled at the top of his lungs. His body trembled as he jolted up from his seat. "I am tired of these goddamn games! I know you're listening; I don't know who you are or what you want from me." Before he could finish, the screen flickered and flashed a bright light before turning into a salt-and-pepper spectacle. Then, a man appeared on the screen. It was none other than the Madman.

"Oh, hello there," he said to the camera, pretending he didn't realize it was on. "Congratulations on your rehabilitation. If you are watching this, it means that you have successfully returned from your sentencing to Wonderland. Now it doesn't matter what you did to get there, or even what you did to get to where you sit now. What matters is who you are now—free with a clean slate, the crimes of yesterday washed away by the deeds of today. You have undoubtedly been through a lot to get to where you now sit. True rehabilitation, tried and tested through the Wonderland games."

"Wonderland may be a fresh start for all, but not everyone is born good. So, I designed Wonderland to give a second chance to those that want it—to those willing to earn it. To those like you watching now. So, allow me to congratulate you once again on your successful rehabilitation. Enjoy the rest of your life to the fullest. The reward money and impressive home you sit in now should help facilitate your dreams come true." He paused, as if distracted by a wandering thought.

"Well, that should be about it. If you have any further questions, please use your rehabilitation resource assigned to you. You should have their card on your person by now. Please take this second opportunity to live an honest life. Freedom may be a right for all. However, where and how you spend that freedom is up to you." The Madman gave a bow as the screen went black.

"Can't say that was all that helpful," Tama said, turning to Ren. Tama could tell Ren was exhausted. In the few days since they had met, Ren looked as if he had aged ten years. The clueless immaturity he once had was gone. "Are you okay, Ren?"

"To be honest, I don't even know what okay is anymore." He paused, his eyes still locked on the black screen as if he were watching something that only he could see. "That's it? Thank you for playing our fucked-up little game. Congratulations on winning. Now here's your reward, so go be a good boy and move on. What about Lilly and Elio? Are we supposed to just leave them behind?"

"I know, Ren. Look, it's been a long day and so much has happened. But what can we do? We are out here, and they are still on the other side of the wall."

"I… I don't know what to do." Ren wiped his face. "Everything since I woke up, it led me here. Us here. But for what? A fancy house and some money. I would give it all up for them to be here on the other side with us."

"Me too." Tama looked over at Ren from his cushion on the couch. Ren had cried himself to sleep where he sat, exhausted from it all. Tama smiled softly as he crawled into Ren's lap and curled up into a ball. "Good night, Ren."

Ren jolted forward, his breath heavy as he looked around in a panic. His eyes flickered as he looked around. "Tama?" Ren asked, noting that he was alone on the couch. A loud thud rang out from the floor above. "Why are you upstairs?" Ren asked, confused, as he stood up and made his way out of the room and up the massive, rounded stairs to the second floor.

Rounding the corner, Ren looked down a long, empty hallway that seemed to go on forever. "There you are," Ren said as he saw Tama's light-blue glow fade into a room on the right. Ren rounded the corner of the room and stepped inside as the door closed behind him.

Tama was nowhere to be seen. A lone pink-framed bed sat in the otherwise empty room. A pile of blankets tucked tightly around a small, snug lump as it slept.

There was a soft tap on the door. Ren pivoted to the side as the small brass knob turned and an average-looking man stepped into the still room. The man's face was blurry, as if scratched out with various colors of crayon. He smelled as if he had been dipped in a pool of sour booze as he passed Ren and made his way closer to the bed.

"Hey there, Lilly Bell, it's time to play," he said, his speech just as sloppy as his walk across the room. The man tugged at the tightly pinned blanket, no longer as innocent as Ren had first thought. The cocoon was intended for protection, not comfort. He loosened the blankets and slipped under the covers. Ren's stomach turned as the man pushed the blankets off the bed to reveal a much younger Lilly lying under him.

"Hey! What do you think you are doing?" Ren yelled. Ignored, the man continued to press his body against Lilly. "I said stop!" Ren yelled again, to no avail. He rushed forward and swung at the man; his fist phased through him. Lilly squirmed, doing her best to delay the inevitable, as Ren stumbled back and the feeling of helplessness washed over him. What the hell was going on?

The man grinned as he revealed himself fully. Ren screamed again as Lilly's eyes flashed black and she quickly plunged a knife into the man's exposed privates—a large kitchen knife previously hidden away under her pillow. Ren watched as she repeatedly stabbed the man as he yelled out in pain. Blood splattered everywhere, drenching

Lilly as she persisted until the man went quiet and fell over in the bed. Ren was speechless, frozen in place as he watched Lilly sit quietly on the blood-soaked bed. The knife held tight in her right hand as she raised it into the air and drove it into the man's back repeatedly while she screamed out in pain. Her voice was finally free.

Her breathing was heavy as she slipped out of the bed and made her way out of the room. Ren followed closely behind, dodging the dripping blood from the knife still clutched tightly in her hand. Lilly paid him no mind as she crossed the hallway and stepped into the room opposite. Ren watched from the hall as Lilly slowly approached the bed sitting in the dark room. The blade glinted in the moonlight from the nearby window as it rose into the air above the bed. The door slammed shut as the knife dropped. Ren knew what came next and sighed with relief as he stepped back from the door.

He took a much-needed deep breath when a loud bang echoed out from down the hall. Ren caught Tama's furry glow as it disappeared into another room.

"That's enough, Tama. Let's go," Ren yelled down the hall as he chased after him.

Ren turned the corner into the room to find himself standing in a courtroom filled to the brim with people. A hooded man towards the front stood up and fired a flurry of bullets into a man only a row ahead. Ren panicked and fell backwards through the hallway and into the room opposite.

Applause rang out, drowning out the ringing from the gunshot. Ren stood up and saw Tama meander casually across the stage. A man holding a microphone patted him on the back.

"Congratulations to our big winner," the man said, circling by him. Ren looked around as Tama hopped up into his arms. "How does it feel to be our first winner?" He asked, pointing the microphone up to Ren's mouth. Two more men, identical to the Madman, stepped out from behind Lilly and Elio. Each one raised a small black pistol up behind them. "So modest. What else would we expect from our winner, am I right?" he said as the sound of applause rang out. "A well-earned prize." He leaned in to Ren's ear and whispered, "But at what cost?" as gunshots rang out.

"NO!" Ren yelled as he jerked awake.

"It's okay, Ren. You're safe," Tama comforted. Ren was dripping with sweat, wiping his brow with his right arm as it trembled.

"What happened?" Tama followed up.

"We may have won their sick game, but I won't be a part of its outcome." Ren paused, ignoring Tama's question while pulling out the card that the woman had given him. Sitting on the small coffee table in front of the TV was a small cellular phone. "You trust me?" he said, glancing over at Tama.

"Always," Tama replied with a confident nod of his head.

Ren leaned forward and picked the phone up. With a deep breath, he dialed the number on the card. It rang twice and went quiet.

"Hi?" he said, confused. He placed the phone on speaker and set it down so Tama could hear as well. "I want to make a change."

"Of course, anything for my favorite winner." The woman's voice was unfamiliar—different from the woman that had dropped them off.

"I want a new house, located as far away from other people as possible. Nothing fancy, just a basic house that won't draw too much attention. Secluded, if possible. Oh, and with a grocery store nearby. I don't want it linked to me in any way. Additionally, I need a car, at least ten years old—something that won't draw too much attention. Can you do that?"

"Sure, gimme just one second." The line went quiet for about a minute, an awkward silence in the air. "And done. Would you like a car sent to pick you up?"

"Yes, that would be great."

"Wonderful. It will be there in just a few minutes. Is there anything else I can assist you with today?"

"No, that should be all for now. Thank you kindly."

"Glad to help. Just gimme a ring if you need anything else." Ren hung up the phone.

"Moving out already? I was just getting ready to pick out new curtains for the third and fourth living rooms," Tama chuckled, and Ren cracked a smile as they made their way out of the house. The car was already in the driveway, waiting.

"She's good," Tama said, impressed.

"Scary good," Ren replied. "Together?" Ren said, looking at his best friend.

"Together," Tama responded as they hopped inside the car. "What's next?" Tama asked.

"No clue. But whatever it is, we won't forget them. We will live on for them, and we will not take part in anything this so-called 'Paradise' offers. We will not partake in their games anymore."

"Left behind, but never forgotten, we wander together even though we may be apart," Tama said.

Their friends, Wonderland, and even Paradise all faded away in the rearview—behind them, but never to be forgotten—as the sun set on their adventure.

CHAPTER TWENTY-THREE
A Fresh Start

Ren stared up at the blank wooden ceiling that awaited him every morning. He wondered what it looked like from up there while it watched him silently each night. Its wooden gaze locked on him as he tossed and turned, haunted by the events that took place nearly a year ago. Tomorrow was the day—one year since he had fought his way through Wonderland. Tama, who was sleeping peacefully at the foot of his bed, had been by his side from the beginning. There hadn't been a day, or even a moment, since they arrived in Paradise that he had not thought about Elio and Lilly—his Wonderland family that he forcefully left behind.

Ren let out a long, relaxed stretch as he sat up, leaning over and gently petting Tama awake.

"Time to get up, buddy. We have a long day ahead of us."

Tama let out an equally long stretch, his paws extended out in front, as he laid his head back down in defiance.

"Today can wait five more minutes," Tama chimed.

Ren grinned and gently picked up and tossed his pillow at

Tama. Startled, he reacted in a panic and slid off the edge of the bed. Ren burst out laughing as the pillow slowly rose from the floor, held in the air ominously, before flying back at Ren and clomping him in the face.

"Pulling out the magic card? I thought you were better than that," Ren said, picking up the pillow and slowly circling the bed for his next attack. "Gotcha!" he yelled as he pivoted around the bed's corner and hurled the pillow at an empty floor.

"I am afraid that it is you that is, in fact, gotten!" Tama yelled as the blankets from the bed floated up and into the air, covering Ren. All the pillows in the room collectively pummeled him to the ground while Tama laughed maniacally.

"I surrender!" Ren yelled, nearly out of breath. "You win—you always win," he yelled as the pillows fell to the floor. Ren untangled himself from the flurry of sheets that encased him.

"Loser makes the bed," Tama said with a grin as he pranced out of the room while Ren smiled and got started on the bed's reassembly.

"Yeah, yeah, and the winner picks breakfast," he said, finishing up and making his way out of the small bedroom and into the rest of the fully open cabin. "So, what will it be today, my furry friend?" Ren said, making his way behind the countertop bar and pulling down a skillet. He set it on the propane stove and lit the burner for a hot pan.

"I am thinking two eggs sunny-side up with a side of sizzled veggies and some steak."

"Great choice! Always know what I am in the mood for,

don't you?"

"Well, I wouldn't be a very good soul if I didn't."

Tama watched as Ren sliced up a steak into six or seven strips and tossed them into the hot pan with a small slice of butter. Then he quickly chopped up a pepper and onion and tossed all the pepper and half of the onion in on top of the sizzling strips, before giving the contents a quick flip with a flick of his wrist before making his way over to the fridge to grab a couple eggs.

Nearly a year ago, Ren had no clue how to cook. Every meal came out burned or extra burned. However, he kept at it. Cooking relaxed him. Even though he didn't really enjoy it that much, it reminded him of Elio, and that was reward enough. However, after a month of nearly inedible food three times a day, Ren figured things out, and after another couple of months, fancied himself a decent enough home cook. Now, nearly a full year later after his first blackened meal, he floated through the kitchen as if it was second nature and even looked forward to the time. He could just turn off his mind and cook.

He split the food up onto two separate plates, each one perfectly portioned, with a beautiful sunny-side up egg atop each plate, as he and Tama made their way out to the small deck that overlooked a large pond. They both sat down at the small wooden table that sat outside, a plate in front of each of them. Ren ate while they watched as a raft of ducks slowly floated across the sun-skimmed water.

"What you want to do tonight when I get back from work?" Ren asked before swapping his empty plate with Tama's full one.

"A quiet night out on the pond sounds fun. Catch us up some fresh fishies for dinner?" Ren laughed.

"Funny, I thought that was what we did last night, and the night before, and the night before that."

"What can I say? I am a creature of habit."

"No... you just have a fish addiction."

"How dare you!" Tama said playfully. "And after I let you make the bed this morning?"

They both laughed together before the table went quiet again. Ren slid his second empty plate forward.

"I hope they are doing okay."

"We could always tune in..." Tama said, knowing Ren's response.

"I won't do it. I won't engage with their game. Elio had it right from the very first time I met him. Fuck them and fuck Wonderland. I want no part in it."

The table went silent again. "Well, I suppose I should get to work," Ren said, stacking the two plates on one another. The pair of forks capped them off as he went back inside. Tama hopped down from his seat and meandered behind.

"I will have the boat prepped after a fun day of napping," Tama joked as Ren threw on his coat and chuckled.

"Nothing like a hard day's work, huh?"

"Exactly. See, you get me," Tama sassed. "Drive safe, honey." Tama winked at Ren, who glared back at him as the door slowly closed.

Ren drove away in his 2008 Subaru Legacy. An old Hybrid Theory album played in the background as he made his way to work, pulling into an empty lot of the area's small grocery store where he stocked shelves five days a week. A red Honda Civic sat running idle a few spaces over. A familiar-looking girl sat in the driver's seat asleep, but Ren couldn't remember where he had seen her before. Assuming she was just an infrequent regular at the store, he brushed off the strange feeling and headed in to start his shift.

The day went by uneventfully, just as it always did. Ren started his morning restocking the cooler with various milk products. Once all set with the cooler, he stocked various aisles and products throughout the store. It was a small store, but it saw a decent amount of traffic throughout the day—enough to require a full-time employee to keep it stocked throughout the week. After his shift wrapped up for the day at four, he clocked out, grabbed anything he needed for the next couple of days, checked out, and made his way back home. No interaction with his boss, or any other employee at the store, outside of the typical pleasantries when purchasing his personal goods.

It was a good job—peaceful, almost. Just the same routine each day, paired with a fresh set of various tunes to listen to while he worked. No one knew who he was, what he had done nearly a year ago. That was a secret shared between only him and Tama. Well, there was also his handler, who had set everything up, though he hadn't heard from her since that fateful day. Outside of kick-starting his new life, Ren had made the personal decision to take no part in the reward system of the Wonderland games. As far as he was concerned, it was blood money, and even what little he had used to get where he had made him sick. Which is why he planned to save up enough of his own money and buy the property with his own earned money. Only then could he live guilt-free.

Loading his two bags of groceries into his car, he noticed that the same red Honda was sitting in the lot, though a couple of spaces removed from where it had been earlier that morning. However, the car was not running, and it didn't appear that it had a passenger.

"Must have forgotten something," Ren said under his breath as he rounded the rear of his car and got inside, turning the key as she caught his eye. She stepped out of the store with a small bag of items in hand and made her way over to the red Honda. She had long black hair that ran down past her shoulder blades; a slender body, complemented by her tight denim jeans and plaid button-up top. Ren realized he was staring and gave his head a slight shake, backing out of his parking space. He took one last glance before pulling out of the lot and heading back home to go fishing with Tama.

Ren turned right down a tucked-away dirt road as he made his way back home. Tama watched him from the screened porch as he pulled in. Ren turned the car off and opened the door, making his way to the passenger side to get the groceries.

"Welcome back, dear," Tama said with a sarcastic grin. "Did you remember the milk and eggs?"

Ren rolled his eyes and nudged the door shut with his foot, making his way up the stoop and inside to the porch.

"Only the best of both for you, sweetie," he sassed back as he made his way inside and set the bags down on the countertop. Tama walked in behind as the contents of the various bags slowly floated up and into the air. Each item found its way to its proper place while Ren changed out of his work clothes and swapped his shoes. The fridge closed shut, and the bags were now empty and moved to the table. Tama turned to Ren with a satisfied smile.

"Fishies time?" Tama asked. Ren smiled.

"Yes, fishies time," Ren said, heading to the door. "Is the boat ready?"

"For fishies, the boat is always ready," Tama said as he scampered over to the door and dashed through Ren's legs and down the steps to the small dock that ran out into the pond. Sitting happily at the bow of the boat, Ren finally caught up. Inside the boat already sat Ren's fishing pole, tackle box, and bait. Ren stepped inside while the connecting rope untied, just as the groceries had taken care of themselves. The boat slowly drifted away from the small dock.

"You know, we could just fish from the dock," Ren said, prepping his rod while Tama steered the boat slowly into the center of the pond. "Also, you are getting pretty good at that. Soon I won't need to lift a finger here at home."

"Thanks. I don't have much else to do while I am home alone all day. Also, it's not the same from the dock. Something about just disconnecting from everything and pushing the boat away as we drift unhindered by the world—it just feels right. It feels almost needed."

"Okay, we can use the boat," Ren smiled as he gave a quick flip of his baited rod. The bobber hit with a ripple as a squirmy worm sank down below, weighted by a small lightweight ball. The boat went quiet as a slight warm sprinkle danced atop the water.

"Hey, Ren," Tama paused. "You ever think about them..."

Ren looked down at the water, his focus locked onto the pitter-patter of the rain.

"Yeah... There isn't a second that goes by they are not there, lingering on my mind—like a cloud looming above me." He looked up at the sky, the soft droplets blurring the newly forming tears as they dripped from their wells. "Like the clouds above, only they are filled to the brim with guilt. Guilt that I am out here while they are still in there."

"It's still all a blur to me. It happened so fast. One second, we were fighting together, and the next we were on the other side of the wall—Elio and Lilly left behind."

Ren felt a tug on the pole and gave it a quick flick to set the hook deep inside their prey. The line grew tight as Ren slowly reeled in the frantic fish below.

"It's a big boy!" Ren said excitedly, distracted from the conversation and now fully focused on the hook.

"Big fishies are the best fishies!" Tama said while his tails wagged, his paws firmly planted on the rim of the boat as he watched Ren with anticipation.

"We got him!" Ren said as the fish slowly rose out of the water. A large foot-and-a-half-long grayish-blue fish now flopped about in the boat. "This may be our biggest catch yet."

"Fishies gonna be fished!" Tama said, licking his chops as he watched it flop freely in the boat before it slowly lifted into the air and fell with a splash into a large white cooler in the middle of the boat while Ren prepped his hook for another catch. The bobber returned to its favorite place, floating freely atop the water. After about an hour, there were now four fish swimming about in the cooler.

"Should we head back?" Tama peeked over the rim of their captured prey, his head swirling around as he watched the fish swim in circles.

"Yeah." The boat slowly spun in the water; the bow now pointed toward the well-lit cabin that overlooked the glistening pond. The moon watched through the clearing sky above.

"No matter where in the world we are, when we look up to the sky, we all see the same moon. Maybe someday we can see it together again, atop a peaceful pond just like this one, and look back to the many moons we shared before—together or apart."

"That would be nice, though hopefully that pond is on this side of the wall," Tama joked.

"I agree. I never want to see the other side of that damned wall again. Never. I just hope that they can say the same someday."

"Yeah." The boat gently nudged against the dock. The rope uncoiled where it lay and slowly tied itself to the boat. Tama hopped gracefully to the wood and scampered towards the house with the large white fish cooler floating close behind.

"I have the fishies!" Tama yelled along the way while Ren rolled his eyes as he wobbled his way back to the dock and followed behind him.

Ren quickly cooked up dinner, and the pair spent the night playing a card game called Wielder Wars. Ren had bought a starter pack out of curiosity during his first week of work, and by the end of the night he and Tama were hooked. Now, they spent most of their free time and money collecting various cards.

"No fair!" Tama snapped as Ren won his third game in a row. "You cheated."

"Oh, did I now. Did you ever think that maybe I was just better than you?" Ren sassed, playfully sticking his tongue out from the other side of the table.

"Yeah, I am sure it has nothing to do with you having first pick of the cards," Tama sassed back.

"And on that note, I think it's time for bed," Ren said, grinning as he stood up from the table.

"Oh, is it now? What a delightful coincidence," Tama said as he followed Ren down the hall to the bedroom.

"You can have the first draft of the next batch of cards. How does that sound?" he said, dressing down for bed and brushing his teeth.

"Pretty good, actually," Tama said, satisfied. "How could I argue with such a smooth victory?"

"Oh, I am sure you will find a way," Ren snarked between spitting and rinsing.

"Oh, is it going to be like that?" Tama said, hopping up onto the bed while Ren slipped under the covers and gave his pillow a quick fluff.

"Never," Ren said, turning off the light. Tama's glowing tails formed shadows along the walls that danced in the darkness as he purred softly. "Hey, Tama," Ren said quietly.

"Yeah, Ren?"

"Tomorrow will be one year. Time sure has flown by."

"That it has. I look forward to many more years to come."

"Yeah… Me too," Ren said as they both drifted to sleep.

CHAPTER TWENTY-FOUR
Haunted

When Ren opened his eyes, he was lying in a field. The moon leered from the starry sky above. He sat up slowly and looked around. His heart dropped from his chest.

"TAMA!" he screamed out in agonizing pain. His eyes locked on his furry friend, who lay in a pile of warm blood. Ren rushed over to Tama, stumbling and unable to get his balance. He dragged his weakened body through the bloody mud until he reached him. Ren scooped him up as tears streamed down his face. The world around him was hot and surrounded by a bright hue of oranges and reds that faded into a thick gray. Elio was a couple of feet away, his body mangled and missing an arm. Lilly was to his left, or rather, what little remained of her tattered body.

Slowly, various glows blurred with the flames that burned all around. The glow grew brighter and brighter as it encased him and left nowhere to retreat to. A mysterious human silhouette made its way through the sea of souls and now loomed over him and his dead friends. The figure's right arm hung limp. He stood in silence as he raised his left arm, equipped with a massive sword that he held without pause in the air. A sick, crisp white grin revealed sharp teeth as the sword came swiftly down on Ren.

"TAMA!" Ren yelled as he lurched up from his bed. Tama, startled awake, slipped off the bed, quickly hopping back up to check in on the source of the commotion.

"Ren, it's okay. I am right here," he said calmly. Tama had gotten used to these things, first in Wonderland while traveling with Lilly and far more consistently with Ren, since they had settled down after the games. "The same one?" Tama said as he made his way to Ren's lap.

"Yeah, he was there. You…" Ren paused; his body trembled as his breathing eased.

"It wasn't real. You're safe. You're good. He can't get you on this side of the gate." Ren's guilt had taken the form of the mysterious person who had followed them as they traveled through Wonderland. Though, without even knowing it, the collector had captured a piece of Ren's wandering soul.

"I know. I am good now," Ren said, shifting back under his covers. Tama curled up next to him. "Thanks, Tama."

"Always, Ren. Always," he said as they drifted back to sleep.

A bright beam of light shone through a small gap in the thick curtains that hung over the window along the right of the room. It caught Ren in the eye and seemed to pursue him as he sleepily tried to avoid its attack, to no avail. With a defeated stretch, Ren sat up, Tama still sound asleep next to him.

Ren grinned, seeing an opportunity to get one up on Tama.

Today was the day Tama would make the bed. Ren slowly removed his pillow from its case. With his trap now in hand, Ren scooped Tama up inside and barraged his captive with the loose pillow. He laughed exaggeratedly as he took solace in his long-awaited victory, even if he had stooped rather low to achieve it. Satisfied, Ren pulled back his improvised pillow weapon to look at the loser that lay beneath. The pillowcase was empty. Tama was gone.

"You about done?" Tama said from behind Ren as dread washed over him. Ren slowly turned to see Tama standing on the wooden headboard of the bed, with a pillow floating on each side. "That was quite the show you put on. However, now it's my turn." Tama grinned with the smirk of the devil. "Any last words?"

"Yeah, actually." Ren gripped the pillow lingering in his right hand.

"Oh?" Tama said, his head tilting in curiosity.

"Catch!" Ren yelled as he hurled the pillow at Tama. The pillow was easily deflected as Ren scattered out of the room. The bed sheet untucked and pursued him, before soon returning, Ren encased inside, the top tied like a bow.

"Maybe tomorrow," Tama said as he exacted his revenge on Ren, who was laughing in his well-tried defeat.

"You win, Tama. You win," he said as the sheet dropped to the bed. The blankets floated down around Ren as Tama hopped down victorious.

"I think a classic sausage-and-egg breakfast sandwich with a side of hashed potatoes sounds pretty good today," he said as he meandered out of the room, and Ren began his bed-making in shame.

Ren wrapped up the bed-making and got dressed and ready for the day. Then, he made his way out to where Tama sat and prepped the meal. He chopped up a green bell pepper along with the other half of the onion from the day prior, before cubing a russet potato. On a small plate sat a large white egg and a round sausage patty next to a cinnamon raisin bagel. With his two pans heated, Ren scooped up the potatoes and tossed them in the skillet with a little oil, flicking the contents around with a wooden spoon to coat and heat the potatoes evenly. Next, he dropped each half of the bagel on the other skillet, the sausage patty next to it, before spraying a space with canned oil and cracking the egg to a satisfying sizzle.

"I really must say, it's quite fascinating to watch you," Tama said, impressed, as Ren floated so elegantly around the small kitchen space just behind the bar seating.

"I am glad you enjoy the show," he said, grinning at the compliment while he added his bell pepper and onions to the potatoes and gave them a stir, flipping the bagel and sausage over on the other pan. A small slice of peppered cheese found its way out of the fridge and was floating elegantly towards the counter.

"Thank you!" Ren said happily, taking the cheese and flipping the egg over, gently placing it atop the gooey yellow goodness. He gathered all the sandwich bits together and set the bagel down on a plate, slipped the sausage on next, followed by the cheesy egg goodness, all topped off with the second half of the bagel. Ren cut it down the center, and the egg oozed throughout the empty spaces of the sandwich. He then placed one half on another plate before adding the potatoes to each; the crisp greens and whites glistened with their starch counterparts on each plate.

"Now that's a sandwich," Tama said as his tail wagged with excitement. Ren picked up the plates as they both made their way outside to eat.

"So, what's the plan for tonight?" Ren asked as he sat down and placed one plate in front of him and Tama.

"That's easy. Obviously, we need more fishies," he said with a happy tail wag as Ren ate. "Maybe we can even get a two-footer tonight. I bet there are all kinds of the big bastards just swimming around in there, waiting to be caught." Ren laughed.

"You know what? I bet you are right," he said, finishing his plate and swapping the dishes.

"And it's our job to find them. To prove to the world that they are real."

"It's a hard job, a thankless job," Ren said as he took another bite, the gooey yellow of the eggs dripping down the sandwich.

"That it is. But who else will do it if not us?" Tama said with a smile.

"So true," Ren said, wiping his face and standing up from the table, with the plates stacked on one another and in hand. "But the world must wait. I gotta get to work, and those shelves won't stock themselves," he said, heading inside.

"That's fine. I am not sure the world is ready yet, anyway."

"That may be the case right now, but some day, they will be, and when that day comes, we will be ready."

"Oi, oi!" Tama said excitedly as Ren laced up his shoes and

headed outside to the car.

"I will be back at the usual time. Stay out of trouble."

"Pshh, I don't even know what trouble is," he sassed as the door to the car closed and Ren backed up, and disappeared down the dirt road to work. After a short drive with Meteora cranked, he reached the parking lot and slowly spun the dial as he pulled in next to a familiar red Honda. The same Honda from the day prior. Ren turned the key, the hum of the engine dying down as he stared at the empty car. He grabbed the handle and stepped out of the car, his eyes glued on the Honda as he made his way into the store. He spent the morning restocking the cooler before purchasing a small packet of jerky and heading outside to take a quick break.

"She really loved this stuff," Ren said quietly to himself as he tore into a piece and took in the fresh air. Sitting in the same spot was the red Honda. Ren's boss came outside and stood next to him.

"Hey, Ren, you mind cleaning up a spill on aisle three? Some kiddo bumped a pickle jar, and the entire store's gonna know it." He laughed.

"Yeah. Hey, real quick, though. Has anyone new started?"

"Nope, you were the last one I hired, and that was nearly a year ago. Best damned choice I made in a while, too. Finding good workers these days isn't easy, what with that glory hole Paradise rotting all the young minds of this generation. Everyone would rather let them damned robots do everything for 'em. I tell you, back in my younger days…" Ren tuned out the man's story, his focus locked on the strange Honda. Why was it still here?

"Ren?" the man said, poking him. "You never listen to my

stories."

"I am so sorry, sir. I will get right to work on cleaning up the pickles."

"Aisle three," he said again as Ren dashed off towards the janitor's closet. Distracted by the lingering scent of pickles in the air, and a busy day of deliveries, Ren's day flew by, and before he knew it, he was checking out with some fresh veggies and other items for the next couple of days. After all, he never knew what Tama would want for breakfast after he inevitably won the morning battle. As he stepped out of the store, his eye caught a quick blur from inside the red Honda, yet upon deeper inspection, there appeared to be nothing and no one inside.

Must be my mind playing tricks on me, he thought to himself as he placed his bag of groceries in the passenger seat and got into the car. Backing out, he noticed the Honda start in his rearview as he turned right and made his way back home. His eyes locked on the rearview as he drove along while Breaking the Habit played softly in the background, as he watched the red Honda behind him. He flicked his turn signal and slowed down before pulling in onto the dirt road that would lead him home. He stopped his car a few feet in and waited and watched for the red Honda. After only a few seconds, it pulled up along the side of the road. Ren quickly jumped out of his car and rushed over to the red Honda, only to find that when he reached the running vehicle, there was no one behind the wheel. The car was completely empty.

"What the fuck?" he said in disbelief as the gas pedal slammed to the floorboard and the car launched out of the driveway and down the road. Ren threw his hands up into the air and yelled after the car. "What do you want from me?!" He watched the red Honda disappear down the road. Frazzled, Ren got back into his car and made his way back to the house, back to Tama. Ren pulled in more abruptly than usual, and Tama could immediately tell something had happened.

"You okay?" he asked as Ren got out of the car and grabbed the groceries.

"Yeah, I think so. There was this red Honda today and yesterday at work." He made his way inside, and Tama unloaded the bag, its contents floating through the room to their respective locations. "It followed me home today."

"That's strange," Tama said as the last cabinet closed. Ren folded the empty bag on the table.

"That's not even the strangest part. They stopped in the driveway."

"They did what?" Tama said, growing concerned.

"Yeah, so I jumped out of my car and rushed theirs. But when I looked inside, it was empty."

"Wait, what?"

"Yeah, but then the car jolted down the road."

"That's new."

"Sure is. I think I scared them off, though. Just in case, though, let's lock up tonight."

"Does this mean no fishies tonight?" Tama said, looking down at the ground, disappointed. Ren smiled and kneeled down to Tama, giving him a gentle pat on the head.

"Of course not. We have a world to prove wrong, after all. I feel a two-footer staring at me as we speak."

"Really!" Tama said excitedly, perking up and dashing over to the door to the porch. "Well, let's get going then. The moon waits for no one."

"I'm coming, I'm coming," Ren said, standing up as they both made their way outside and down to the dock. It wasn't long before they had pushed back out onto the pond and a bobber hit the water with a satisfying plop.

"One year…" Ren said ominously, breaking the silence.

"I know. It still feels just like yesterday we met. Or, I guess, re-met. I am still fuzzy on the details." Ren chuckled.

"Yeah, I remember you tried to burn me. You were a feisty little fella."

"What do you mean, were? I will cook your ass right here and now," he bluffed.

"Careful now, you don't wanna scare away your precious fishies," Ren snarked, much to Tama's dismay.

"You win… for now," he said playfully back at him.

"Got one!" Ren said as he reeled in the third fish of the night, pulling it out of the water and dropping it into the boat to flop about. "Another small boy," he said as the fish rose into the air and dropped into the white bucket to join its friends. "Alright, one more, then we will head back for the night."

"Okay, the next one is the one. I can feel it," Tama said as the bobber landed with a soft splash.

"Do you ever wonder if we made the right choice?" Ren said as they waited for the next fish to bite.

"What do you mean?"

"That day, in the large house. After everything happened and we learned how Lilly and Elio ended up in Wonderland. Did we make the right choice when we threw that life away? Our life in Paradise?"

"I mean, are you happy?" Tama asked bluntly.

"I think so. I guess I don't really know how to define what happiness is. We have a great life, a simple life with little care in the world. Is that what happiness is? Is it settling down with a family…" He paused. Family? Did he want a family? What did a future like that even look like for him after what he had seen, after knowing what humans are truly capable of when they are detached from the rules that bind a society together?

"I am happy," Tama said, interrupting Ren's train of thought. "Just me and you. That's all I need." Ren smiled.

"Thanks, Tama," he said, looking out at the glowing pond as it glistened under the moonlight. "What about the fishies, though?" Ren said with a sarcastic grin.

"No need to bring them into this. Just enjoy the moment," Tama said as Ren felt the line grow firm.

"This is it!" he said excitedly. "Bugger's a struggler," Ren said, jerking the rod to wedge the hook in deeper.

"Don't let him get away!" Tama snapped with glee as he went to the side of the boat to watch. Ren slowly reeled in the catch as the line swerved left to right in the water as it grew closer and closer to the boat.

"I got him!" Ren said as he pulled the massive fish up and over the side of the boat. Ren and Tama watched as the largest catch they had ever seen was now in their boat.

"He is even bigger than I ever imagined! Two and a half, even three feet!" Tama hopped about the boat happily.

"I will be damned," Ren said, pulling a tape measure from inside the tackle box and doing his best to run it the length of the fish.

"So, what's the number?" Tama said in anticipation.

"Thirty-two… no wait, thirty-three inches, give or take."

"That smashes our old record out of the water, no pun intended."

"That it does," Ren said with a satisfied grin. "He won't even fit in the cooler."

"Take that, world!" Tama yelled out over the water. Ren burst out laughing.

"Yeah! Fuck you, world!" he yelled out after as they laughed together while drifting slowly atop the water. "I am."

"You are what, Ren?"

"Happy. I am happy," he said as they shared a smile under the moonlight. "Alright, let's get these bad boys cooked up then." When Ren heard a splash, their big catch of the night swam furiously away. Tama watched as it disappeared under the glistening water.

"Why did you do that?" Ren asked, confused.

"Because next time we catch him, he will be even bigger," Tama said with a smile.

"Yeah, next time," Ren said as they drifted back towards the dock. Heading inside, Tama set the cooler of fresh fishies down next to the counter for Ren to cook when there was a knock at the door. Sharing a glance, Ren wandered over to the front window and peeked around the drapes to see parked outside, sitting directly next to his Subaru, was a red Honda.

CHAPTER TWENTY-FIVE
A Knock on the Door Back to Hell

There was another knock at the door.

"It's the red Honda," Ren whispered to Tama, who was on the opposite side of the door, his glow becoming darker as he prepared for a fight. Another knock followed, accompanied by a female voice.

"Hello? I just wanted to apologize about earlier. I…" She paused. "Please open up."

Tama stayed prepared as Ren nodded and placed his hand on the knob. The door slowly swung open to reveal an empty porch.

"Really… this stunt again?"

"Oh, sorry. Chi is a bit shy." A voice came from directly in front of Ren.

"Chi?" Ren said, confused, as the gorgeous girl from the day prior appeared out of thin air in front of him.

"Hi, uh. I'm Clara, and I need your help."

"My help?" Ren said as a small dog with a soft lavender glow appeared next to her side. It growled at Tama, who glared back as a ball of black energy formed in the air.

"Stop it, Chi!" Clara snapped. "We are their guests." Ren nodded to Tama to lower his aggressive stance. Tama's glow quickly reverted to its original soft blue hue. The ball of black dissipated as well. Ren turned back to Clara and was immediately lost in her emerald eyes.

"Would you like to come in?"

"May I come in?"

They spoke over each other, followed by an awkward pause as both Tama and Chi rolled their eyes before quickly glaring back at one another.

"Of course. We were just about to get dinner started. May I interest you in a fresh fish?" An offer that left Tama very displeased.

"Yeah… that sounds nice." Chi glared at her. "I mean, I wouldn't want to impose."

"It's fine. There is plenty to go around."

"No… no there isn't." Tama hissed at Ren. However, Ren was already a lost cause. The last time he had been this close to another woman, she had nearly killed him. Clara slipped out of her shoes and tucked them next to the door before she stepped into the room. Ren did his best not to stare as he closed the door behind her. She wore a red-and-black plaid button-up that her long black hair hung over as it swayed down to her knee-high skirt. Tama cleared his throat impatiently to get Ren back to dinner.

"The fishies won't cook themselves." Ren gave his head a subtle shake and made his way around Clara and over to the kitchen.

Clara wandered over to the bar and took a seat as she looked around the room with intrigue. Tama had already claimed his usual seat, which left only one other option for her to sit. Her soul, Chi, shrank in size to better fit in her lap. While Tama filleted and prepped the fish like a wizard with his intangible magic, Ren sliced up a pair of zucchini and summer squash to pair with the plain white rice that would accompany it, the water now at a boil.

"Nice place you have here." She paused and waited for introductions, as Ren had not yet introduced himself.

"Oh, yeah. I am Ren, and this here is Tama." She smiled at his awkwardness.

"I know. I was just playing. You may not know this, but you two are kind of famous." Tama raised an eyebrow, intrigued.

"Oh? And why is that?" Ren asked, playing dumb as he dropped the zucchini and squash into a steam-ready pot and poured the rice into the boiling water, setting a lid on each.

"As if you don't know. Everyone across Paradise was watching. One year ago was the conclusion of the greatest season of the Wonderland Games ever—the three-player spectacular where only one winner and their lucky little soul returned to Paradise. However, when it was all said and done, he just disappeared without a trace, with only one public appearance recorded since they returned to this side of the wall."

"Interesting," Ren said casually. Ren had gotten very good over the past year at avoiding the topic of the Wonderland Games. He would occasionally hear it discussed at work while attending to his shelves, or while out hunting for the latest release of Wielder Wars cards. One time, while perusing a card shop, a young man around his own age had identified him. However, Ren managed to sneak away before being approached, at the cost of a rare card he was about to buy. After that, he always wore a hat and avoided lingering any longer than needed in a store. Ren flipped the fish as it sizzled; its sides were all finished and waiting for the main course.

"Yeah, it was interesting." She smiled. "I was there that day, you know." Ren glanced over to Tama. If that was true, then she knew undoubtedly that they were who she thought they were. Ren pushed the issue, not ready to concede the façade just yet.

"Oh? That must have been cool. I bet it was quite the spectacle." She rolled her eyes, growing bored with the whole charade.

"As you both know, it was. So, why did you two give it all up? A perfect, all-expenses-paid life in Paradise." Ren caved. She knew.

"All right, you got us. However, before I answer your question, answer mine."

"I'm listening," she said, accepting the terms.

"How did you find us?" he asked. "No one has ever actually bothered to look for us. So, I guess I would pose two questions, the second being: Why did you find us?" He plated up the food, separating it evenly between four plates—one for each of them and their souls. The plate intended for Chi confused Clara as she ignored it and took a warm bite.

"This is delicious!" she said, shocked at how good it was, quickly taking another bite before answering. "Okay, so the how is far more complicated than the why. I have wanted to find you—rather, to speak to you—since the day you won the games. However, because of the security on the red carpet that day, I couldn't. I could only mouth my words through the sea of pictures and screaming fans."

"Help me," Ren interrupted, much to her and Tama's surprise. Ren had forgotten all about it until right now, and so he never thought to tell Tama. He knew she looked familiar, and this confirmed it. She was there that day, and in a sea of random faces, hers was the only one that still held a place in his memories.

"That's right. I wasn't sure if you even saw me."

"It was all so much that by the time we arrived at the house, everything had blurred together. I am sorry."

"Details. I don't like to get attached to those," she said with a smile, pivoting back to her answer. "I showed up at your house the next day, but no matter how many times I knocked on the door, there was no response. I assumed at the time you were asleep—tired from the events of the games—and so I waited, and I waited, until I fell asleep, alone on the brick stoop of the house." She watched as Ren finished his meal, traded plates with Tama, and started in on the other. She continued.

"I woke up to the sound of rain dancing atop the streets. A sneaky drip from the roof had left my cheek wet. Slowly standing up, I noted the house was unlit and appeared to be empty. Tired and confused, I checked my phone to see a press release provided by your assigned caretaker. It stated you had opted out of the game's winnings for the time being and had vacated Paradise with only enough to get started."

"That was nice of her," Ren said, impressed at how honest and transparent she had been with the entire ordeal.

"Defeated at the news, I went back to my mundane life as a server at a local high-end bar. That was until a couple of days later, when I saw my father re-dropped in Wonderland."

"Your father?" Ren said, confused, passing a glance to Tama. Clara blushed.

"Yeah, Elio is my dad."

The room went quiet while both Ren and Clara finished their meals. Ren noted the untouched plate next to Clara. He broke the silence.

"You gonna eat that?" Ren asked, motioning toward the plate next to her.

"Can I?" she said, still confused by the plate.

"Yeah, sorry. I guess it's kind of odd to an outsider, huh?" he said as Clara reached for the plate and ate it.

"Tama and I are the same, and so when we eat together, I simulate a proper meal the best I can. So, each of us gets a proper portion, and I merely eat it in his stead." Clara glanced at Tama, then at Chi, and back to Ren.

"That's so cute, but I guess it makes sense, since it's just been you two for the past year."

"So, back to your story," Ren said, pivoting the conversation again, leaving out that he had picked the habit up from her father.

"Oh, yeah. Realizing I still needed your help, I did some digging and found that only a short list of properties had been sold that day. From there, all I had to do was track them each down. That handler you got is brilliant, using an alias to purchase the property. Seems unlimited funds can do just about anything." Ren thought it was even more impressive how fast she had done it. Clara did not know this, but she had handled everything in only a brief phone call. This was even more impressive the more Ren learned just how far she had gone for him.

"After around a dozen misses, I finally found you a couple of days ago while catching a quick nap in my car on my way to your house—to here. I couldn't believe it. There you were. After months of failed searching, I had found you."

"So, you did. But why didn't you just introduce yourself then?"

"Well, Chi is super shy. So, every time I tried, she hid, taking me with her. The same thing happened earlier today at the end of your road. I tried then, but Chi freaked out. I was so frustrated I just gunned it down the road. She promised she wouldn't do it again, so I came here, and after a brief argument with her in the car, I came and knocked on the door." She turned to Chi, who was pretending not to notice. "However, as you saw, she did not hold to her end of the agreement." Ren smiled at Chi.

"Shy? Or overprotective, I wonder?" he said passively to Chi. "I don't understand how that all relates to Elio—to your father?"

"That's where the question comes. The why I wanted to speak to you." She paused. "Sorry, I have spent the last year thinking about how to ask you this." She went quiet.

"It's okay. You can ask me anything. I owe Elio my life, so it's the least I can do."

"Well, I was kinda hoping you would say that."

"Uh oh," Tama said, growing concerned.

"Will you help me get him back? Will you help me save my father from Wonderland?"

CHAPTER TWENTY-SIX
Of Dreams and Nightmares

Tama let out an uncomfortable laugh.

"She's funny." With his eyes locked with hers, Ren replied to Tama.

"I don't think she's joking."

"What? She must be," he said, confused. "There is no sane fucking person alive who would voluntarily return to that place." Ren glanced at Tama, then back to Clara, who sat and watched as they debated, only able to hear one side of the conversation—probably for the best.

"You're serious, aren't you?"

"I am. Will you two please come to Wonderland with me and help save my dad?" The room went quiet. What the hell was he supposed to do—just blindly agree in that moment? He turned to Tama. It was his choice as well. It was not only up to him to decide.

"I..." Ren started as she interrupted.

"No need to answer right now. Obviously." She rolled her eyes at even the thought of an answer being given so quickly. "Why don't you two sleep on it? I can come back tomorrow night." She stood up and made her way over to the door. She slipped her shoes on and placed her hand on the knob. "You can cook me dinner again," she said with a smile and a flirty wink before departing outside, Chi close behind. Ren wandered over to the window and watched as she paused at the bottom of the steps to the small porch and took a deep breath before heading to her car and disappearing down the driveway and into the night.

"Yeah, she's crazy," Tama chimed.

"I want to help her," Ren said flatly.

"Wait, what?" Tama snapped as Ren returned to the other side of the bar. Tama playfully hissed at Ren. "Stay away! You have caught her crazy," he said, swatting at the air. Ren rolled his eyes while taking the dishes from the counter and placing them in the sink. The dishes began washing themselves casually as Ren stepped away.

"She is not crazy." He paused, realizing she might be a little crazy to think about what she was suggesting. "She… she just wants her dad back."

"That's fine and all, but I fail to see what that has to do with us. It's not our problem."

"You're right, it's not." Ren paused again as the last dish hung in the air, a crisp blue towel giving it a proper dry. "But…" Ren's voice grew heavy. A thickness filled his throat as if the words he wanted to say would choke him where he stood. "This guilt."

"No amount of guilt is worth throwing away your life. Our life." The room went eerily quiet.

"Maybe it's not," Ren said, breaking the silence.

"We have no responsibility to them, or their families on the outside. They made their bed, and it's time to sleep in it—even if it's in Wonderland." Tama was done with the conversation and pivoted the night away from any further discussion on the matter. "Then it's settled. Now, let's play a couple rounds of Wielder Wars before bed." Tama hopped down from the bar and made his way to the living room area of the small cabin. Ren meandered behind him.

"Tama," Ren said as he watched Tama magic the cards out onto the small coffee table that sat between their two chairs. Ignoring Ren, Tama continued.

"I think I have a real shot at winning tonight. I obsessively dream-decked last night and think I came up with a solid counter."

"Tama…" Ren said again, this time slightly louder.

"Although you do still have one card, I can't figure out how to play around. Kind of cheap, if you ask me, that you even still use it."

"TAMA!" Ren yelled as the cards that had floated through the air fell to the table. "I can't do it anymore. I can't just keep going knowing that they are still in there. We owe them both our lives. We wouldn't even be here to have this conversation if it wasn't for them." He paused, lowering his tone. "Look, I love our life. I love everything about it—the road trips for cards, the morning battles to make the bed and choose breakfast, and…" He paused, choking up at the thought of never floating out atop the pond with Tama again.

"I know, Ren," Tama said, caving to Ren and his overflowing emotions.

"Tama, I won't give any of that up. Not forever… I won't. But I think I have to do this." Tama sighed.

"I better not catch the crazy."

"Does that mean you are with me?"

"Of course. I was never not with you," Tama said with a smile. "I still don't like it, though. In fact, I think this is the dumbest thing we have or ever will do. But we stick together. No matter what."

"No matter what," Ren said with a smile. He gave Tama a soft pet, which was reciprocated with a nuzzle, before then continuing.

"I have a condition, though."

"Oh, what's that?"

"Lilly—we don't leave without her, either."

"Of course. I already knew that."

"You do, but Clara needs to agree as well. Let's be real. She is only in this for Elio—her father."

"No arguments here. I don't think Elio would leave without Lilly, anyway."

"Then I guess that's that, then. If she agrees to that condition, it looks like we are heading back to Wonderland."

"Seems that way," Ren said as the room went quiet again. Ren made his way over to his seat and sat down. "Now, about that card game."

"Yeah," Tama replied softly as they distracted themselves with a couple rounds of Wielder Wars. Ren continued to take the wins before the pair turned in for the night.

Ren felt a warm liquid tap on his face. Blinking his way awake, he wiped the strange liquid from his face. It was deep, thin red. Confused, he looked up at the source of the odd drip and caught another splash on the face. Startled but curious, he wiped it away and slipped out of bed. He wasn't sure where he was, or where Tama had gone off to, either. The room was empty, with cracks along the exposed sheetrock walls and some bare shelves covered with thick white dust.

Ren made his way over to the only door in the room—the only way to the outside world, as there were no windows present in the room. He placed his hand on the brass knob and, with a turn, stepped outside into a narrow hallway. To the right was a blank white wall, and to his left was a set of stairs that only went up. His hand felt wet as he looked down to see it covered in the strange red liquid. His heart skipped as the door slammed shut behind him. The knob was tight and unyielding to his touch. With going back not an option, and more questions, he made his way up the stairs to the next floor. He wiped his bloody hand on the bottom of his white shirt.

Once at the top of the stairs, he found another narrow hallway. A familiar glow flickered through the threshold of the only door on the floor.

"Tama?" Ren said aloud as he proceeded toward the door and stepped inside. Tama sat with his paws pursed together over a body—the source of the blood that seeped through to the room below. Tama silently motioned his head toward the still body. Ren stepped closer to see who it was Tama wanted to show him, his stomach turning as he realized who it was. Lilly lay with her chest exposed, her heart missing—a vacant hole where it once pumped.

Tama disappeared and reappeared next to the door before

fading through it to the other side. Ren felt another drip on his head. Tears ran down Ren's face as he turned to chase after Tama. He dashed back out into the hall and turned to see the steps he had taken to get here were gone, a wall in their place. Tama's glow faintly lit the steps now at the other end.

"Tama? Answer me, damn it!" Ren snapped as he rushed down the hall and up the stairs after him. He reached the top and glimpsed Tama as he once again faded through a door. The hallway was the same as the two prior, and Ren quickly dashed to the door and flung it open. This time, the body Tama sat over was easily identifiable from where he stood. It was Elio.

"I hope it was worth it—the price paid for your guilt," Tama said as he disappeared once again into the hallway behind Ren and meandered up the stairs. Ren dropped to his knees and sobbed in the doorway.

"I'm sorry… I shouldn't have left you behind. I should have fought and stayed."

"Tick tock," Tama said from atop the stairs. "Apologies do the dead no good."

"Stop this, Tama!" Ren barked, his throat hoarse as he wiped the tears from his face and chased after him to the next floor. "What do you want from me?" Ren yelled as Tama once again entered a room on the left of the hallway. He had noticed it, but the walls became more claustrophobic with each floor. "Tama!" he yelled again as he rushed to the door and flung it open. His lungs deflated; he couldn't breathe.

The room was quiet as Ren stepped deeper inside. Tama sat

in the center of the room and was staring at a blank wall, his back to Ren.

"Enough games, Tama. What the hell is going on?" Ren said as he ambled closer. Tama sat silently, with no response. "This isn't funny," Ren said as he rounded the motionless Tama. A hole in his chest. Ren exhaled the last little breath he had as he dropped to the floor and kicked his heels back against the bloody floor till he couldn't kick any further. Tama's cold, dead eyes watched as Ren sobbed. The room grew icy cold as Tama spoke.

"The consequence of action is often paid by those left behind." Tama's body fell over limp as it laughed a familiar laugh Ren hadn't heard in over a year. The Madman. Ren screamed out in agonizing pain as he stood up and rushed out of the room, turning the corner immediately. He dashed up the stairs. This time, he found himself in a room, a door on the opposite side. In the center of the room was a faceless human figure. The Collector.

"Will you pay the same price as those lost? Or will you live on with the guilt of their sacrifice? The choice is yours, as all choices in life are… or are they? Though, perhaps the illusion of choice is enough." The door at the end of the hall opened; its hinges creaked as it revealed more stairs on the other side.

"What's the point? I already lost them—everyone I cared about," Ren said with a lump in his throat as the Collector chuckled ominously.

"What's the point of anything we do? In the end, we are all the same—our legacy left to those we leave behind." Ren paused. His blood-riddled hands were shaky as he turned his gaze from the

Collector to the door. "What will be your legacy, and who will carry it for you when your soul no longer wanders this world?"

Ren closed his eyes and took a deep breath as he stepped forward—one step, then another—until he stood next to the Collector. Trembling, Ren turned to him. His face was a series of scribbled scratches from an unsharpened pencil. The strokes of lead phased in and out as if they were being erased as the pencil touched the pad.

"My legacy is my own," Ren said with confidence as he pushed forward to the other side of the room and proceeded up the dark steps. As the door slowly closed behind him, he heard the Collector speak once more. His voice was sad, almost broken.

"The road to paradise starts in hell." The door latched shut. His last words hung in the air as Ren turned towards the light at the top of the steps. With a heavy breath, he climbed.

Once at the top, he stepped out into the blinding light. He found himself outside, standing on an open rooftop. The door behind him slammed shut. A table sat in the center of the rooftop with no chairs surrounding it. Curious, Ren stepped forward to the table where a small pistol sat atop a piece of paper. He slid the gun aside and read the paper aloud.

Dear Ren,

"If you are reading this, then the time has come to make a choice. A choice you may have already made but are not yet convinced is the correct way forward. I hope this letter will help ease your mind.

"Attached to this letter is a gun. A fascinating weapon, a gun is. Used to protect or to kill, to hunt and to defend. A simple tool with many uses. However, how it is used is left up to the freedoms of those that wield it."

Ren picked up the gun and inspected it with deep fascination before returning it to the table.

"How would you use it? To protect those you care about, or avenge them when they are gone? Turn it on others as an act of revenge, or on yourself for the guilt of inaction?"

Ren froze. The words shook him to the very core as his hand uncontrollably reached for the gun, gripped tight in his bloody hand. His pointer finger trembled on the trigger as his arm slowly rose into the air. The gun pressed firmly against his temple as he read the last sentence.

"The choice is yours… or is it?"

Ren screamed as he opened his eyes. The sound of a gunshot rang throughout his head as he scoured his surroundings to find himself sitting up in his bed. The sun peeked through the curtains that hung over the window. Tama watched him, concerned.

"You okay? That one seemed worse than the others."

"Yeah… I am okay," Ren said, falling backwards with a fluffy plop back into his pillows. "Hey, Tama."

"Yeah, Ren?"

"Do you think dreams can come true? Not like those we set for ourselves in life, but like the ones we live through while we sleep."

"Pretty sure that's not how they work. But… I guess anything's possible. Why?"

"Because if dreams can become reality, then what's stopping the nightmares?" Tama smiled as he stood up and made his way onto Ren's chest, where he stared down at him.

"That's easy. It's the dreams." Two pillows rose behind Tama. "As long as we keep dreaming and pushing forward together, the nightmares can't win. You know, like the power of friendship or some shit." A sinister grin spread across Tama's face. "Too bad for you, though, because your worst nightmare is right here!" he yelled as he pelted Ren with the pillows.

"Not today, kitty cat!" Ren yelled as he flung both his arms up and around Tama, each covered with blankets, as he trapped Tama underneath and tied them together at the top. "I win!" Ren shouted victoriously as he dashed out of bed. "I'm thinking waffles today—topped with berries, syrup, and why not, whipped topping too." Tama laughed as he squirmed his way out of the mess of blankets.

"Look at that—dreams can come true," Tama snarked as the bed made itself and Ren made his way to start breakfast. For the first time in nearly a year, he got to choose. The nightmare of the night prior was just a memory now, just as Wonderland had been for the last year. However, Wonderland would soon no longer be a memory, as they intended to return—back to the nightmare again. The only way out was to play their game again, and this time, they were all leaving together.

The story continues in "Wandering Souls: Return to Wonderland."

www.ingramcontent.com/pod-product-compliance
Lightning Source LLC
LaVergne TN
LVHW010155070526
838199LV00062B/4372